MW01231565

# THE
# *Asheville*
# CHRISTMAS
# TRADITION

CAROLINA CHRISTMAS ✳ BOOK FOUR

## HOPE HOLLOWAY
### AND
## CECELIA SCOTT

Hope Holloway and Cecelia Scott

Carolina Christmas Book 4

The Asheville Christmas Tradition

Copyright © 2024 Hope Holloway

This novel is a work of fiction. Any references to historical events, real people, or real locales are used fictitiously. Other names, characters, places, and incidents are the product of the author's imagination, and any resemblance to actual events or locales or persons, living or dead, is coincidental. All rights to reproduction of this work are reserved. No part of this publication may be reproduced, stored in or introduced into a retrieval system, or transmitted, in any form, or by any means (electronic, mechanical, photocopying, recording, or otherwise) without prior written permission from the copyright owner. Thank you for respecting the copyright. For permission or information on foreign, audio, or other rights, contact the author, hopehollowayauthor@gmail.com.

# The Carolina Christmas Series

A special note to readers...

As this book went to press, life in western North Carolina changed forever. The flooding from Hurricane Helene cut a swath through Asheville and all the surrounding towns and villages, ending lives, destroying businesses, demolishing homes, and breaking so many hearts—including ours. We love the area (Cece lived there for several years and her in-laws live in Asheville) and we ache for those who have been affected by this tragedy.

In an effort to help, we have committed to donate a portion of the proceeds from the entire Carolina Christmas series to Samaritan's Purse, an organization based in Boone, NC, that has been on the ground helping people from the moment the rain ended. Please know that your purchase of any book in this series, in digital, paperback, audio or Kindle Unlimited, will add to our donation and help a family in need. Our goal is to raise $10,000 before the end of 2024 and continue those donations until North Carolina is strong, beautiful, and safe again.

In the meantime, when you read about the rolling hills, the good-hearted people, the stunning architecture at Biltmore House, and the precious streets of Asheville on these pages, remember how it was, not how it is. And know that with your help, North Carolina will be breathtaking again.

Love, Hope and Cece.

# Chapter One

## Noelle

"It's time for my favorite tradition!" Aunt Elizabeth—now simply called Bitsy by the family—stood at the head of the long farmhouse table, bringing the chatter, clatter, and platter-passing of an eighteen-person gathering to a sudden silence. "The Gratitude Attitude of Thanksgiving Dinner!"

"Brace yourself, Jace." Noelle leaned a little closer to her husband. "This one requires a live performance."

From the kids table, Noelle's stepdaughter sat up with interest. "What's the Gratitude Attitude?"

"One of Bitsy's favorite traditions, Cassie," Noelle told the little girl she'd grown to love with every cell in her body. "And this one is sacred."

Bitsy smiled at them, then her gaze moved over the many faces of friends and family, all spread around two large tables that filled the dining room and spilled into the living room of a sprawling Blue Ridge Mountain cabin.

"All traditions are sacred," Uncle Sonny told Cassie.

"And for my wife"—he beamed at Bitsy—"they're usually a lot of fun, too."

"Exactly," Bitsy said. "But no silly jokes. This tradition is serious."

"How do you play this game, Aunt Bitsy?" Sawyer, Noelle's rambunctious seven-year-old nephew, asked.

"You don't play anything," Bitsy said. "You stand up and share the one thing—or two or even three, if you've been blessed beyond measure—that you are most grateful for this year."

"Fun!" Sawyer announced, his soft chocolate curls bouncing as he shot to his feet. "Can I start?"

"Yes, you can start." Bitsy laughed, sliding back into her seat. "Anyone can stand when they're ready, but no one can duck out."

"You mean 'turkey' out, Aunt Bitsy," Sawyer joked, getting a cascade of giggles from the kids' table. "Okay. I am most thankful for—"

"You can't say bears, video games, or something dumb," Bradley, one of his two older brothers, muttered. "You heard Uncle Sonny. It's sacred."

Sawyer held up two hands, shooting a side-eye that said he could do serious if he had to.

"I'm grateful for...Jackie." He pointed to his eleven-month-old baby sister, currently dipping her finger in a small mound of sweet potatoes on her high chair tray. "'Cause she made me not the youngest anymore. And Mom finally has a girl in our family."

"Aww." Noelle's sister, Eve, pressed her hands to her

cheeks as her eyes crinkled with a smile directed to her boy. "That's sweet, honey."

"That's soft, Soy Sauce," James scoffed at his brother, but stood and cleared his throat with the air of firstborn leadership, despite the fact that he was only twelve. "I'll go next. I'm thankful for..." He shifted his gaze to his father, David, who held a spoon in front of Jackie even though she obviously preferred the finger-in-potatoes method. "Dad not being a neurosurgeon anymore because now he's my soccer coach and we went all the way to the county finals this year! Woohoo!"

That got a big reaction from the crowd, as David and Eve shared a happy look over the baby between them.

"Leaving neurosurgery was a risk," David said, using his napkin to dab at some food on Jackie's rosy cheeks. "But my gratitude goes to my wonderful wife, who persuaded me to leave a sixty-hour-a-week job and take over a family practice. I have never been happier or—" Jackie swatted his arm and a drop of potatoes splattered on him. "Or more covered in puréed vegetables."

"I'll go next!" Cassie stood as the laughter died down. As always, she commanded all the attention in the room. She may only be eight, but Noelle's stepdaughter was a presence, fearless and spunky, and she loved any chance to perform. "I'm thankful for my goat, Sprinkles, of course, and my new stepmommy..." She smiled at Noelle. "I love you, Miss Noelle."

Touched, Noelle blew her a kiss, tamping down the tendril of disappointment that Cassie simply couldn't, or wouldn't, call her Mommy. The "step" part was always there, and she still addressed her as "Miss Noelle," as she had since the day they met last Christmas.

After a few requests, Noelle stopped asking, and Jace assured her it would have to happen naturally.

They'd only been married for six months, so they agreed it was a big change to ask a child, even if she didn't remember her mother, who'd died when Cassie was a toddler.

A few others chimed in to share their gratitude lists, all of them managing to mention something fun and sweet.

To a person, they revealed an important fact about this blended family—that the love was genuine. Also, it was clear they'd made the most out of this past year when the triplet Chambers sisters moved to live near each other in Asheville, North Carolina.

As Noelle listened, she couldn't help releasing a soft sigh of satisfaction and sharing a look with Eve and Angie, who had to be thinking the same thing.

A year ago, they'd had Thanksgiving dinner at Eve's home in Charlotte, just the sisters and Eve's family. That night, they'd received a cryptic email from their beloved Aunt Elizabeth asking them to spend December at the Asheville family cabin, where they hadn't been for twenty-five years.

During that one month, while living together and helping their aunt prepare to marry Sonny MacPherson, the lives, hearts, and homes of all three of the sisters had changed. And all for the better.

Moving around the table, Sonny's daughter, Caroline, stated the obvious—that she was grateful for Tyler, her now six-month baby boy, and Joshua, her nine-year-old son. Her husband, Nate, agreed, and added that he was also happy that Red Bridge Farm, the gorgeous homestead owned by Sonny and Bitsy, was thriving under his management.

Next to Caro, her sister, Hannah, a bubbly brunette with a kind heart and an easy laugh, gave a wistful smile to her boyfriend, Keith.

"I'm grateful for..." She hesitated, clearly not sure what she wanted to say or if she should say it. "This man right here," she finished, reaching toward Keith, who looked a little uncomfortable with the attention. "Nearly eleven years of..."

Noelle held her breath, waiting for Hannah to finish. The two women had gotten so close in the past year, and Noelle knew her friend struggled with Keith's unwillingness to make a lifetime commitment after eleven years of...*dating*.

"Happiness," Hannah finally said, leaning closer to her boyfriend. "How about you, Keith?"

"Oh, well." The burly redhead brushed self-consciously at his beard. "I'm just a good ol' boy grateful for my truck and a good huntin' season."

Everyone gave a polite laugh, but Noelle's heart cracked a little when she saw Hannah's bright smile waver. A quick glance around the table confirmed that others noticed, too.

"Triplets next," Bitsy said, pointing to Eve. "In birth order, please."

"At the risk of sounding like everyone else in my family," Eve said, her blue eyes glistening as she looked at David, her sons, and then the dumpling in the high chair, "I'm grateful that we moved from Charlotte to be close to this amazing family, and that David is home every evening and on the weekends. And I'm deeply grateful that a young girl named Gabby made a decision that gave us Jacqueline Elizabeth."

She leaned over and kissed her baby's pale golden curls as the room let out a collective, "Aww," for the miracle of her birth. With her blue eyes and platinum curls, the almost one-year-old Jackie looked so much like Eve, it was easy to forget she'd been adopted.

"And you, Angie?" Bitsy asked the second of the three Chambers sisters.

"I have so much gratitude, I could take the rest of the night," Angie joked, butterscotch waves tumbling over her shoulders as she looked from side to side to include everyone. "First, I still can't believe I have a job in the curators department at the Biltmore Estate—my first *real* job other than being Brooke's mother—"

"Which you nailed," her teenage daughter chimed in.

"Thank you, honey. Second, I'm so thankful for this beautiful cabin..." She gestured toward the sun-filled rooms of a two-story mountain retreat that had been in their family for more than a hundred years. "This has become a real home for a couple of California transplants and Brooke and I couldn't be happier here."

"And to think we almost lost this place but for your

tenacity," Eve said, pointing a playful finger at Angie. "Talk about something to be grateful for."

"Amen," Angie agreed. "But I'm not quite done." She squished her features into a typically expressive Angie face. "I probably shouldn't say this, but I have to. I'm grateful my divorce is final. Probably not supposed to be happy, but I am."

They cheered with her, since everyone agreed the end of Angie's rocky marriage was a very good thing indeed.

"Oh, and last but never least"—she lifted her glass toward Brooke—"I'm so thankful for the absolute best friend and darling daughter a woman could have."

"Sweet, Mom," Brooke replied, her eyes suspiciously damp as if her mother's speech had truly touched her. "I love you, too."

"What about you, Miss Noelle?" Cassie called out, clapping a little as all eyes shifted toward Noelle. "I bet you're grateful you married my dad and got me."

Noelle grinned at the little girl. "Yes, yes, and yes, Cass." She reached for Jace's hand. "Most grateful for my new family."

"Well, you know that's what I'm grateful for," Jace said, bringing her hand to his lips to kiss her knuckles. "A soul mate, a mother to Cassie, my best friend, and..." He winked. "We finally made an animal lover out of you."

"Hard to live with a veterinarian and a goat-whisperer and not become one," she said on a laugh. "Yep, I feel buried in blessings this year."

"And even more next year," Cassie added in a strange

stage-whisper, looking down at her plate like no one would notice she'd said that.

"I'm sure next year will be amazing, too," Noelle said quickly. "I'm expanding Mountain Muse and bringing in new artists to the gallery."

But Noelle knew the growth of her Asheville art gallery wasn't what Cassie was talking about.

She wanted a baby brother or sister—almost as much as Noelle wanted to give her one.

But that had not happened yet, and since she and her two sisters would turn forty-one on Christmas Day, it might never happen.

Maybe sensing Noelle's momentary discomfort, Bitsy jumped in with her gratitudes, and Sonny proclaimed their first year of marriage as the happiest either of them had ever experienced.

The glow during the dinner lasted until the last plate was cleared and the family regrouped in the sunroom. They watched the kids run around outside with Lucky, Sonny's golden retriever, while the sun turned the Blue Ridge Mountains into breathtaking shades of silver and gold.

In the kitchen, Noelle helped her sisters arrange the pumpkin and apple pies, the three of them joking around. When Noelle heard the front door of the farmhouse open, she looked into the great room, catching sight of Hannah coming in, looking much sadder than she had at dinner.

She slipped out of a jacket and stood in front of the

fire, letting out a deep sigh that didn't fit the Thanksgiving Day vibe at all.

Still holding a dishtowel, Noelle walked across the wide-planked floors, ready to offer love and support to a woman who'd become as much a sister as a friend. Although they were only related through marriage—Hannah and Caro's father was married to Noelle's aunt—they were all close, but Noelle and Hannah had forged a special relationship.

"You okay?" Noelle asked.

"Oh, yes, of course," Hannah answered, planting a sunny smile that didn't quite make it all the way to her soft brown eyes. "Keith had to go."

"Before dessert?"

"Yeah, he, uh, had—"

"Enough of this family?" Noelle joked, trying to lighten the awkward moment.

"No, he wants to be up at five to go hunting, so..." Her voice trailed off.

"Gotcha," Noelle said quickly. "Well, you can have twice as much pie."

"Just what I don't need." But her humor rang hollow as she put on her "everything is wonderful" face that she frequently wore when the subject of Keith got too personal.

"Miss Noelle!"

Noelle turned to see Cassie tearing across the room. "You're it!" the little girl squealed as she jabbed Noelle in the arm.

"I'm it? I'm not even playing! Who's going to serve pie if I'm it?"

She giggled and waved her hands in the air, oozing joy and childish enthusiasm. "Then you're it, Aunt Hannah!"

"Okay, I'm it!" Hannah took off with the speed and skill of a second-grade teacher who was no stranger to playing tag.

Just then, Jace came up behind Noelle and wrapped his arms around her.

"You *are* it, Mrs. Fleming." He pressed his lips to her hair. "If '*it*' is beautiful, smart, and you control access to pie."

Laughing, she turned in his arms and looked up at the handsome face of the man she'd loved for...well, since they'd been childhood fishing pals on this very mountain and each other's crush.

They'd spent twenty-five years apart, and in those years, Jace had loved, married, and lost, becoming a young widower and single father after his first wife passed away.

But all that pain was behind him now and her husband wore a perpetual smile these days, whether they were hanging as a family or he was busy caring for the cows, horses, goats, and llamas all over this rural area outside of Asheville.

"You all right?" he asked with a slight frown.

"Of course," she said. "Why wouldn't I be?"

"Because you got a little quiet after the Gratitude Attitude thing." He searched her face, and glanced at the crowded room behind them. "Let's talk tonight," he whispered, adding a kiss to her forehead as a round of raucous laughter rose up. "First, the hordes want pumpkin pie. And I include myself in that."

She sighed into his arms, knowing that she could hide her emotions from anyone but Jace. Of course he knew what was bothering her and when they got home, he'd listen and tell her what she already knew. One, she didn't need for Cassie to call her anything—their love was secure. Two, she didn't need to have a baby—her family was complete and perfect.

And three, he'd tell her that Noelle Chambers Fleming would have to stop being an overachiever. She'd achieved plenty.

But would she listen?

"And....she's asleep." Noelle pushed up from the bed, closing a well-loved copy of *The Very Hungry Goat*.

Leaning against the doorjamb, Jace waited until she reached him before tapping the light switch to darken the room. "Didn't take long tonight. Thanksgiving wore her out."

"Wore me out, too," Noelle said, accepting the hug he wrapped her in.

"Too tired for a fireside nightcap?" Jace asked.

"Never." Noelle leaned into a kiss.

A few minutes later, he had a lively fire going and

two small glasses of sherry poured, a tradition they'd started on their honeymoon in the Caribbean. There, they'd shared the drink on their balcony overlooking the water, but here, especially once the weather cooled, they were usually in front of the living room fire.

Jace's spacious ranch had become Noelle's home after they married last spring, and she was as comfortable here as she'd been in an Upper East Side apartment in New York. She'd left her big city life behind with remarkable ease, with Bitsy reminding her all the while that God opens doors when He wants a person to walk through them.

Well, He obviously wanted Noelle Chambers to sell her apartment—it went in one day—and quit her job at Sotheby's, which she'd done easily when her boss showed up at Bitsy and Sonny's New Year's Eve wedding to demand she cut her family time short.

A year later, Noelle was as comfortable in the barn wearing work boots as she used to be strolling down Fifth Avenue in designer heels. And no place in her new life was nicer than right here on the sectional, nestled against the man she loved.

Noelle took her first sip, let the liquid warm her throat, and snuggled closer to Jace, both of them under a fluffy blanket.

"Okay, what's buggin' Miss Noelle?" he asked after taking his own sip.

"That I'm called Miss Noelle," she admitted glumly. "I know, I know. It'll happen organically, but...when? I want to be her mommy."

"She'll get there, I promise. It's a matter of time."

"And I also want to be...someone else's mommy, but..." She made a face. "That isn't happening too quickly, either."

He nodded. "I picked up Cassie's comment at dinner," he said. "But we have to remember that she's only eight—"

"Sometimes I think she's eighteen, she's so mature."

"I know, but she's not. And she shouldn't have overheard us talking about having a baby a few weeks ago," he said. "This isn't a decision we can let her make."

"This isn't a *decision*, Jace," she said softly, staring into the fire. "This is a desire, and a strong one. I really do want to have a baby."

"And I do, too," he said without hesitation. "My position from day one has never wavered. Nothing could make me happier. All we can do is give it to God, relax, and don't let it—or Cassie—control your thinking."

She nodded, considering the advice. "The giving it to God part is new for me, as you know."

She hadn't come into this marriage with faith in a higher power—if anything, having lost her parents at fifteen had left her fairly convinced that no God would let three teenage girls experience such grief.

But out of love and respect for Jace, she'd tiptoed back into church and the message was starting to make sense. Still, she wasn't a "let go and let God" kind of woman. She was a "take control and call the shots" kind of woman.

"I like to make things happen my way," she added.

"Ya think?" he cracked. "But beyond checking the calendar and making sure we have enough time to be alone, there's not a lot we can do to control the process."

"I know," she said on a sigh, picking up her cell phone when it vibrated. She squinted at the text from the woman who owned a bookstore on the same block as her gallery, letting out a little moan as she read.

"What's wrong?" Jace asked.

"Just another one of the retailers in town who turned down my invitation to lunch," she told him. "I'm really trying hard to connect with the small business community but no one seems to want to connect with me. Which is another thing I can't make go my way—people."

He chuckled. "Well, any person who doesn't want to have lunch with you is crazy."

She smiled at the compliment. "Well, they *were* crazy —about the former owner, and they're not happy she's gone. And I guess I have this reputation as a New Yorker who blew in and hasn't paid dues or lived here very long. I don't know what to do, but I do feel like a real outsider in what is a shockingly small and tight community."

He considered that, nodding. "You have to pay dues."

"How? I'm happy to, but I don't know how."

"I do!" He turned and snapped his fingers, pointing at her. "Chair the tree lighting committee. No one wants that job and it will connect you with everyone in town."

"The Christmas tree lighting that we went to last year?" she asked. "That was when Sonny asked my aunt to marry him."

"I also believe it was the site of our first kiss in

twenty-five years," he whispered, closing in for another. "Pure Christmas magic, as I recall."

"Mmm." She smiled and kissed him back, but her mind was on that tree lighting. "What's involved in the tree lighting and shouldn't it be planned by now?"

"I think they've moved it back because the pizza shop owner who has chaired it for the last ten years had to drop out due to health issues," he told her. "They need a local business owner to head the committee that coordinates it, but no one has stepped up yet. No one wants the role because...well, there are strong personalities involved."

She sat a little straighter, visions of tree lights dancing in her head.

"I'm a strong personality."

He snorted. "Understatement alert."

"Doing something like that would be great for business and connections. Not to mention that there's nothing I love more than running a committee and planning an event. I did a zillion of them for Sotheby's. Jace!" She poked his arm. "You are a genius!"

"Just be warned—you might have to tap dance around some powerful people, namely, Edna Covington. She funds the whole thing every year."

"Then give me my tap shoes." She reached to the table for her phone. "Who do I call? Edna who? How do I make this happen?"

He laughed and eased the phone away. "I'll call Tony Jessup tomorrow. He's the police and fire department PR person on the committee, and I know him from church.

He told me they were trying to find a local busi-nessperson to volunteer, but so close to Christmas? Everyone they asked had to say no."

"Noelle Fleming doesn't say no," she joked—*half* joked—picking up the phone again. "What's it called? The Asheville Christmas Tree Lighting?" She tapped the screen, ready to search for more information. "Oh, we could do better than that."

He laughed softly. "Don't try too hard to change things. There's a reason they call it a tradition, Noelle. And, like Sonny said, some of them are sacred."

"I'm not going to desecrate anything," she said. "Just improve it and make it..." She gave a sly grin. "Perfect."

That made him laugh, but she quieted him with a kiss and one led to another and, pretty soon, she forgot about everything but this man she loved with her heart and soul.

She couldn't control what Cassie called her, and she certainly couldn't control getting pregnant. But a little local tree lighting ceremony? Now *that* she could bend to her will.

How hard could it be?

# Chapter Two

## Angie

CHRISTMAS HAD DESCENDED upon the Biltmore Estate and, honestly, there were few things in the world more beautiful. From the main entrance, through the eight thousand acres of winding roads, gardens, and a winery, then all the way to the castle of a main house, Biltmore took the holiday very seriously.

As Angie parked in the employee lot, she took a moment to gaze at the enormous structure that was not only America's largest private home, but also a museum, a significant employer in the area, and a wildly successful tourist attraction. The cream limestone estate with spires and sun-washed windows was stunning all year long, but nothing could equal Christmas.

The house, built and still owned by the Vanderbilt family, was decked, lighted, and sprinkled with holiday enchantment. From the tree-lined entrance to the copper-topped turrets of the centerpiece mansion, every inch of the estate celebrated Christmas, and celebrated hard.

Inside, the sparkle continued with dozens of

Christmas trees, thousands of lights, and enough garlands to wrap all of Asheville in green.

The estate looked just like this one year ago when Angie wandered in with a newspaper article she'd found in the attic at the family cabin. In it, she'd learned that her great-grandmother, Angelica Benson, had saved the life of a baby who was part of a family visiting the Vanderbilts in 1924. The baby's parents had rewarded Angelica's heroism with land in the mountains, and enough money to build the very cabin where Angie and Brooke lived today.

She'd come seeking information about long-dead relatives...and her life had changed.

A full-time stay-at-home mom, Angie had never used her degree in communications to pursue a career until the day Marjorie Summerall, the head curator at the Biltmore Estate, offered her a volunteer position. She accepted the challenge to help put together an exhibit that included Angie's great-grandparents' rich history as beloved staff members for the Vanderbilt family.

That volunteer position had led Angie to a permanent slot as a Junior Curator, which was a very fancy title for a jack of all museum trades. She helped coordinate temporary exhibits and events, conducted tours, stuffed brochures into envelopes, researched art, and lent a hand in whatever capacity was needed.

And plenty was needed. The curator and historian department had a small staff and they were stretched to the nines.

Angie had zero experience but oodles of enthusiasm, and a can-do work ethic. In the past year, she'd said yes to any job, whether it was dragging twenty-pound velvet drapes to a specialty cleaners, brainstorming marketing programs, or helping to set up visiting exhibits that changed every season at the Biltmore.

Heck, she'd sold toys in the gift shop, counted tickets for a summer concert series, and polished a few pieces of silver when no one else was around to do the work.

That eager attitude got her promoted just a few months ago to Associate Staff Curator—or, as Brooke called it, "a *Senior* Junior Curator"—which meant a tiny bit of a raise, more hours, and some additional responsibilities curating temporary exhibits.

Angie didn't care what they called her or what she did, as long as she worked in this beautiful place. Here, she was part of the machine that made a Biltmore visit an unforgettable experience for the thousands of guests who came through every year.

And today was no different, she thought as she entered her tiny windowless office in the first-floor business wing. Humble and cramped, she treasured the space and never minded the hours she spent doing whatever her boss—and many others—asked of her.

She'd barely had her coat off that morning when Diana Kauffman, the department's administrative assistant, stuck her head in the door.

"Don't get comfy," Diana said. "Marjorie is calling a staff meeting to start in..." She checked her watch. "Seven minutes."

"Oh, okay." Angie stood. "What's up? Christmas emergency?"

Diana tipped her head and lifted a brow, as if to say she knew but wasn't saying. And something about that expression told Angie it wasn't great news.

"You'll find out soon enough," the other woman said.

Oh, boy. That sounded ominous.

A few minutes later, Angie grabbed a notebook and pen, stopped for coffee in the employee kitchen, then headed to the one and only conference room. There, six or seven of her co-workers had already gathered. They buzzed with curiosity, but no one seemed to know the agenda for today's impromptu meeting.

At exactly nine, Marjorie Summerall walked in. As always, the sixty-something historian and executive looked completely put together, her silver hair pulled back into a neat bun, her ubiquitous navy blue suit fitting sharply. But her smile, always warm and ready, looked a little...different.

Not shaky, not uncertain, but like she had a secret and couldn't wait to share it.

She wasted no time, flicking her hand to bring the room to quiet, all of her staff watching and waiting.

"I don't really know how to say this," Marjorie started. "So I won't sugarcoat it. I'm leaving the Biltmore."

A gasp whipped through the room, but she stopped any questions with a raised hand and a big smile.

"It's by choice and it's for a very good reason. I've landed a curator's position at the Getty in L.A.—"

"Whoa!"

"Are you kidding!"

"The Getty? That's huge!"

She waited until the reaction died down and continued. "Thank you," she said softly. "It's a great job. But what makes it really wonderful is that I'll be near family. As many of you know, my son and his wife, their baby— and Baby Number Two that was just announced—live in Southern California. I simply cannot wait to be near them and am overjoyed to have such a great job when I move."

Then she let the flurry of questions, congrats, and exclamations of surprise roll through the room, making it very clear this was indeed good news. For her, anyway.

For Angie? That remained to be seen. Still, she reached over to give Marjorie's hand a squeeze.

"Well done, my friend," she said, and meant it.

Not only had they become close this past year, but Marjorie had always been Angie's biggest cheerleader. She'd easily overlooked some very specific requirements to hire, and then promote, Angie. From the day they'd met, Marjorie had nurtured and mentored, helping to foster Angie's newfound ambition and interest in history, art, and all things Biltmore.

In turn, Angie knew that Marjorie ached to be a "present" grandmother. When her daughter-in-law became pregnant for the second time a few months ago, Marjorie had shed a few tears at their favorite table in the coffee shop, crushed by the thought of another baby growing up without her. Maybe Angie should have figured out that this was in the cards then, but she hadn't.

Plus, the Getty! What an honor for a well-deserved and talented curator.

But, *oh*. Where did this leave Angie, who so depended on this strong woman and her support?

"My replacement has been hired by corporate already," Marjorie said when the chatter died down and the most obvious question was asked. "I don't know who it is, but I trust that corporate has selected someone with tremendous experience and skill as a curator and a manager."

A few of the staff members exchanged nervous looks. No surprise, since Marjorie was wildly popular with the people who reported to her. Everyone knew this wouldn't be an easy transition.

And if these extremely qualified people were concerned about their roles going forward—many with advanced art history degrees and years of experience at museums around the country—then what about the most junior of the group?

Angie got the job on guts, grit, and a distant relative who once worked as a parlor maid, with nary an art degree in sight.

Her stomach churned at the idea of a new boss, but she caught sight of Marjorie's warm smile and a look that told her not to worry.

But worry she did.

In fact, she worried all morning, so distracted she could barely work, until a knock on her office door broke into her thoughts.

"Marjorie." She stood and rounded her desk, reaching a hand out. "I know you're flat-out today, so thank you for stopping by."

"I have time for a coffee," she said. "Will you join me? I'm afraid I have meetings all day tomorrow and that's my last day."

"Oh." Angie pressed her hand to her chest, unable to hide her true feelings. "I wish I'd wake up and realize this was a bad dream."

Marjorie laughed. "You have nothing to fear. Come on. Let's find our table and talk."

All the way to the café tucked away in what was once the expansive stables for George Vanderbilt, they talked about her new job at the Getty Museum. In the sunny restaurant, Marjorie got their order while Angie sat at a table by the window, barely seeing the beauty of the grounds and the estate. All she could see was...a pink slip.

"Iced vanilla cream latte," Marjorie announced as she set a cup in front of Angie. "With a side of optimism and good cheer."

Angie smiled at her, trying not to be gutted by the loss. "I'm going to miss you more than words can say."

"I'll miss you, too."

"And I'm going to be lost," Angie added. "You teach me something every day, Marjorie."

"You'll be fine," Marjorie assured her. "You're the great-granddaughter of Angelica Benson."

Angie tipped her head and gave her best "get real" look. "I'm a divorced housewife with a useless degree in communications and no experience. Please tell me the next curator will look past my severe lack of credentials."

"You have the most important credential of all," Marjorie said. "You're a hard worker who loves this place like her last name is Vanderbilt, not Chambers."

"Actually, my legal name is Messina, but I liked using my maiden name here because of the connection. With the divorce, I will probably go back to Chambers, but it's a messy process and with Brooke and— Oh, stop. *Why* are we talking about my name at our last coffee?"

"Because you are endlessly entertaining, Angie."

She lifted her cup. "I should be toasting the woman who gave me one of the best years of my life and the most fun job I ever had, despite a woefully thin resume."

Marjorie laughed and toasted. "You're an asset to the organization. Whoever replaces me will love you."

"You really don't know who it is?"

"I don't," she said. "Trust me, I'd tell you. They did not ask for my input, and I don't have time to train my replacement because the folks at Getty want me, like, yesterday." She let out a little laugh. "I still can't believe I got a job there."

"You? You're so qualified!"

"Thank you. It's a big step up and I'm not a young woman. I don't expect to be there for more than a few years, but I'll make the most of them. And, please, don't worry. You have spirit, you're well-liked and respected, and you are willing to do whatever your boss needs. Anyone would be thrilled to have you on staff."

"I hope you're right," she said, "because this job

means the world to me. Brooke and the Biltmore. That's all that matters."

Marjorie lifted a brow. "No special man in your life still?"

"Nah." Angie flipped her hand. "I dated that lawyer, Max Lynch, for a few months after my divorce was final, but..." She shook her head. "It was too soon. I had too much healing to do after Craig. And I think Max has met someone since then. Lucky lady, but the timing was wrong for me."

"That's a shame," Marjorie said. "I remember you brought him to the Renaissance exhibit in May."

"I brought him to my sister's wedding that month, too. But that event made me realize that while I liked Max a lot, I simply wasn't ready." She shrugged. "I may never be."

"You have a wonderful daughter and a great job, Angie."

"I do...until some new lady blows in here and sends me packing."

"Pfft," Marjorie scoffed. "The new lady—or gent— should watch their back. You are the real deal. Education is great, but it's only a piece of paper—"

"And a brilliant dissertation," Angie interjected.

"But you have practical knowledge, my friend, not the thesis of light and dark shadows of the Baldacchino for a Baroque Art class."

Angie groaned. "I don't even know what you're talking about. I don't know about shadows, except under my eyes. I have no idea what the Balda...keen is, and was

Baroque before or after Renaissance? I can never remember."

Marjorie laughed. "None of that matters when a VIP needs a private tour, or one of the tapestries needs to be cleaned, or some big art exhibit is blowing through North Carolina and needs a home. That's where you shine, so don't worry about a thing."

Angie sat back and smiled, forgetting about herself as she gazed at a woman she treasured.

"Thank you," she said. "For taking a chance on me, for being my friend, and for encouraging me."

"I believe in you, Angie." She put her hand on Angie's, giving it a squeeze. "I am leaving notes in all the employee files and I promise yours will say, 'Don't let this one go.'"

With tears in her eyes, Angie clung to that promise and let the conversation turn to Marjorie's future, which seemed brighter than Angie's at the moment.

ANGIE LOST MOST of the day with a different kind of research than she usually conducted. Instead of perusing museum websites for ideas on how to coordinate a Rodin exhibit they were going to host next year, she'd dug into the org charts of those places to find out what kind of experience was truly required for a job like hers.

The answer was simple—a lot more than she had.

Somehow, she'd have to impress the new head curator

but she could tell that everyone on the staff felt the same way. Her co-workers were wonderful, all laden with accolades and published papers. You didn't just waltz in the back door of the Biltmore Estate and get hired in this department.

Except...that's *exactly* what Angie had done.

At the end of the day, she called Noelle. If anyone could offer art world advice, it would be her sister who'd worked for Sotheby's as an art dealer for years and now owned a gallery in Asheville.

"I've got a client in here right now," Noelle said after they greeted each other. "But Jace is on calf duty—"

"Excuse me?"

"The Robinsons' cow is in labor and having a bit of a time," she explained. "Cassie is having dinner with her grandparents, so I'm free after this appointment. How about a drink at the Montford and we can talk? It's the rooftop at the Hilton."

A cocktail with her sister at a fabulous bar in downtown Asheville sounded dreamy and exactly what she needed. "I can be there in half an hour," she told her sister.

"Perfect. I'll finish with this client and meet you there."

Angie made the short drive into downtown, groaning a little when she realized how packed the streets were. She circled the block around the hotel that housed the bar, annoyed by a complete lack of parking.

The hotel valet line was a mile long, every lot was full, and her only option was to find something on the street and walk. The frustration of a lousy day crawled up her spine, making her squeeze the steering wheel with stress, searching in vain for a space.

"Oh!" She spotted a car pulling out on the other side of the street, so she hit the accelerator, made the skinniest of U-turns, and cut off another car to get to the space.

"Sorry, sorry!" She gave a quick wave of apology and gauged the size of the spot. It was small, but she could shimmy in with a few tries. She pulled up parallel to the car in front of the spot and whipped back and around and—

A blaring horn and the sickening crunch of metal and the crash of glass made her let out a soft scream as she jolted to a stop.

What happened? She pivoted in her seat to see the car behind the empty space must have pulled out just as she tried to back in and...

She muttered a curse at the sight of a shattered right front headlight on the other car, which was, *naturally*, a BMW worth more than she made in six months.

Why was her life a mess today?

For a few seconds, she stayed perfectly still, letting the adrenaline dump and her heart hammer into her ribs. Turning to face forward, she closed her eyes and wished she was a praying woman like her aunt, because right that minute, she needed help from above.

When she opened her eyes and glanced in the rearview mirror, she saw a man slowly getting out of the BMW's driver's side, a scowl on his face as he pulled on a wool overcoat.

He looked to be in his mid-forties, with close-cropped dark hair and one of those neatly trimmed beards that didn't hide the fury and disgust in his expression.

Was it her fault? Probably. Definitely. She hadn't looked to see if the car behind the open spot was even occupied, let alone leaving.

"Dang it!" She opened her door and took one deep breath, hoping Mr. BMW had a heart and felt bad for a woman who'd had a terrible day that had just gotten worse.

He barely threw her a glance as she walked around the back, seeing that the five-year-old GMC Terrain she'd bought to navigate the winters in Asheville was barely scratched. But the Beamer's headlight and front bumper were as crushed as her soul.

"I'm really sorry," she said, not bothering to try and persuade the guy to share the blame. This one was on her. "I just—"

"Didn't look," he said, sparing her a glance. "You never even saw my lights were on and I was pulling out."

She hadn't. "I wanted the parking spot," she admitted. "I was focused on..." Her voice trailed off in shame as he stepped away, crouching down to examine the damage.

"I have insurance," she added weakly when he didn't say anything.

"Good."

"I'll do whatever I can..."

"Try looking before you whip backwards into a parking spot."

"That's how you parallel park," she said.

He took a breath like he was going to say something else, then swallowed it. "Let's just..." He looked side to side, realizing that some traffic was backed up trying to get around them. "I'll pull back, you take the spot, and we can exchange info. And I want to call my insurance company."

At least he was reasonable.

After pulling into the spot—and cringing at the broken glass crunching under her tires—she texted Noelle with shaking fingers. Then she let Brooke know what happened, and finally got her registration and insurance card from the glove box.

When she climbed out, the man was on the phone, so she lingered on the sidewalk while he talked, presumably to his insurance agent. Or maybe his wife, since he looked like the type who had a classy and sophisticated woman at home, waiting for her successful and—*okay, be real, Angie*—kinda handsome husband to come home.

He finished the call and joined her on the sidewalk, tapping his screen.

"I need a picture of your license, registration, and proof of insurance," he told her.

She produced all three and he snapped photos with his phone.

"And do I get yours?"

"Of course." He reached for his wallet and flipped it open, showing a Massachusetts license.

"Oh, you're visiting," she said on a sigh. "I'm sorry to give you such a bad impression of Asheville."

Dark eyes shuttered as he shook his head, clearly not interested in small talk.

"I'm staying here." He jutted his chin toward the Hilton where she was headed. "But give me your number. You'll be hearing from my insurance agent."

They exchanged numbers, his frustration palpable the whole time, though, to be fair, he wasn't rude.

"I had a really bad day," she said softly after they finished. "My boss quit and my job's on shaky ground and...and..." She looked up at him, not seeing even a glimmer of sympathy. "Anyway, bad day."

"Maybe you shouldn't drive when you're that upset..." He glanced at the phone screen. "Angel Messina." The slightest smile threatened as he said her name and she braced for a joke about how she was anything but an angel.

"Maybe I shouldn't," she agreed with a defeated smile. "And I'm sorry again for the inconvenience during your trip here. I, um, know someone who owns a body shop, by the way. My stepcousin's boyfriend?" She wrinkled her nose. "I think that's what she is. Her father is married to my aunt. Anyway, her boyfriend..."

He held up a hand as if he didn't need the complicated recommendation, then took a step back. "It's fine. I'll handle it. Could have been worse, I suppose."

She stayed where she was as he walked toward the side entrance to the hotel, then disappeared inside.

Maybe it could have been worse, she thought as she looked at her own phone screen. How?

Well...she supposed that...she squinted at the tiny

image of his license. Elliott John Quinn of Brookline, Massachusetts could have been a complete jerk and made her feel terrible.

He wasn't, but somehow that made her feel even worse.

As she headed toward the same entrance he'd taken, her phone vibrated with a text from her sister.

**Noelle:** *Still with client at gallery! Sorry about the car! Want to reschedule?*

She typed one word in response: *Yes.*

All she wanted to do was go home and take a hot bath to wash off this utter stinkfest of a day.

# Chapter Three

## Hannah

DESPITE HER EFFORTS, which included a ghastly wardrobe choice, even the annual "ugly holiday sweater" party didn't put Hannah in the Christmas mood. Still, she tried to sink into the spirit in the Copper Creek Elementary School cafeteria, which was somehow different when it was hosting raucous adults instead of starving students.

Cruising through the crowd, Hannah tasted the mediocre appetizers, laughed at some cringeworthy Christmas clothes worn by her fellow teachers, and dug deep for the holiday magic that had completely eluded her this year.

Even the first-year Spanish teacher's knit top featuring dancing Chihuahuas and the words "Feliz Naughty Dogs" failed to do the trick.

Unlike every other year, Hannah was having a blue, blue Christmas and, deep inside, she knew why.

The one thing she'd wanted under her tree—had wanted for nearly a decade—would not be there yet again.

Maybe that was why she'd actually chosen not to get a tree at all, instead encouraging her boyfriend to put one up at his place. That spared her the pain of looking at it for a month and knowing...there wouldn't be an engagement this year, either.

And speaking of Keith—where was he?

He said he'd be here after work at his body shop, and warned her he'd be ten, maybe fifteen minutes late for the seven p.m. starting time.

But it was nearly eight and she hadn't heard a word from him.

"And where's your husband, dear?"

Hannah turned at the question, posed by Nancy Arcuni, the woman who'd run the elementary school front office since Hannah herself had been a student here. That meant she should know that Keith was not Hannah's *husband*.

"You mean my boyfriend, Nancy? He's late."

Her well-creased expression softened. "Honey, you've been with that man forever. Why aren't you married?"

Hannah gave a soft laugh at the unsubtle question. "I'm in no rush."

A gray brow shot up. "I'd tie that man down," she said. "He's not bad-looking, if you like the Prince Harry type."

Prince Harry? Keith had auburn hair and his beard came in red. That's about where his similarity to British royalty ended.

"Don't you want to get married?" Nancy asked.

*Yes*, Hannah nearly screamed over the guffaws of laughter from the music teachers, who always seemed to have so much fun at these things.

"It's a different world now, Nancy," she said instead. "Marriage is merely a piece of paper."

Nancy gave an unladylike snort. "Not for my Frankie. You know, we got engaged after knowing each other exactly one month and five days. It's true," she said when Hannah looked dubious, even though she'd heard the story before. "He came out to my father's farm up near Boone to work one summer. Oh, he was dreamy, too. He was the nephew of a neighbor, an *Eye-talian* boy from New York City. He said he took one look at me in the hayloft and knew he'd met his wife—and we were seventeen years old."

"And you've been married how long, Nancy?"

She gave a sweet smile. "Fifty-two years this January."

"Oh, wow." Hannah sighed. "I'll never see that anniversary." At this rate, she'd never see *any* anniversary.

"Then rope that man down, Hannah MacPherson," Nancy said. "You just tell him that time's a-wastin' and you're not getting any younger."

"It's fine," she said, glancing toward the door again with a kick of frustration—for his lateness, for his unwillingness to commit, and for making her have this conversation.

"Is it fine, though?" Nancy countered. "Because you don't seem fine. I think you're just accepting crumbs and

I guess some women will do that, but if you were my granddaughter? I'd say throw those crumbs in the trash and find something fresh and ready." She leaned in, gray eyes narrowing behind her rimless glasses. "You're a pretty girl with a wonderful personality. Don't take crumbs, Hannah."

Hannah managed a smile and checked the clock to see Keith was officially one hour late. No call, no excuse, no explanation.

"I think I'm going to take off," Hannah said, backing away from Nancy. "We have class bright and early tomorrow and those kids are restless so close to winter break."

Before Nancy could answer, a few other teachers joined them, so Hannah used the chance to slip away. With a few more quick goodbyes, she stopped at the coat room to get her jacket and walked toward the parking lot doors.

Just as she reached for one, it popped open and there was Keith.

"Oh, there you are. I was just leaving," she said.

"You are?" he asked, surprised. "I'm sorry I'm a little late. We got a few last-minute drop-ins at the shop and I stayed open to take care of them."

She'd heard the excuse a million times—the only body shop for miles was always busy and Keith liked to handle his customers personally.

"It's fine," she said, vaguely realizing it might have been the tenth time in an hour that she'd uttered those words. And to be honest? It *wasn't* fine. "I'm ready to leave."

He looked past her, cringing as he scanned the crowd. "Whoa, the ugly sweater brigade is out in full force." He tipped his head to her black and white Santa pullover with a row of tiny red ornaments around the shoulders. "And you're doing your bit, I see."

She wasn't in the mood. "Yeah. Anyway, I'm going home."

"Home?" He blocked her way. "Nope, not going to let you. I know you enjoy this party and I'm sorry I'm late, but I want to say hi to your work friends. Look, I see that P.E. teacher—what's his name?"

"Jack Bellingam."

"Right, right. Jack. C'mon, let's say hi to people."

She took a breath, thought about socializing, but something stopped her.

*Crumbs.*

She was accepting crumbs from him, just like Nancy said. Keith knew when Hannah was disappointed in him, and he always managed to charm or sweet-talk his way out of it. And she accepted crumbs.

"No, let's not," she said. "I'm super tired and I have work tomorrow."

"They all do." He made a face. "Why do teachers have these things on school nights, anyway?"

"I don't know, but..." She gestured to the door. "I'm taking off."

"All right. Suit yourself." He followed her out the door, draping an arm over her shoulders. "Come over to my house for a while. We can chill and watch TV. Or we could finally decorate that dumb tree you made me get."

"I just want to go home," she said, not in the mood for an argument. For anything, to be honest. And *really* not in the mood to hang ornaments on his Charlie Brown Christmas tree.

He walked to her car quietly and when she pulled out her keys, he turned her and forced her to look up at him.

"How long am I going to be in the doghouse for being an hour late tonight?" he asked.

"You're not..." She closed her eyes and let out a sigh. "I don't care that you were late. Well, I do, but it's just indicative of a bigger problem."

"A problem?" He stuck his hands in his parka pockets and stared down at her. "You gonna tell me what it is?"

"You know what it is," she said, knowing that this conversation could only lead to his usual excuses...

*It's just a piece of paper.*

*I want to live with you first.*

*We're together and that's all that matters.*

*My parents' marriage was a disaster.*

He had an answer for every argument, always ending with, "What difference does it make, Hannah, if we love each other?"

"I don't want to fight tonight," she said, eyeing her little hatchback like it was the getaway car from a bank robbery and she *needed* to be in it.

"I had no idea we were in a fight," he countered. "What the heck is eating at you?"

She inhaled and looked up at him, taking in the features she had always found comforting and sweet, if not the most handsome man in the world. She didn't need handsome—she needed a husband.

No, no, she didn't *need* a husband, but she wanted one.

"Keith, I'm thirty-four years old."

"I told you I don't want kids," he shot back, no question at all about why she'd state her age. "You've known that from day one. I had bad, bad role models and I'm not equipped—"

"But what if I do?" she fired back. "What if I want kids and marriage and all that...stuff?"

He studied her for a long time, a little storm of emotion in his eyes. "I'd say you'd changed. You told me you were fine with no kids. Okay with no piece of paper. And I told you I will happily live with you. Move in tomorrow and we can call it."

"Call it...*what*?"

"Living together."

She curled her lip.

"I know, I know," he said. "Your Christian dad hates that. It would break his heart. I've heard it all."

It would break her heart, too. "Aren't I good enough to marry?" she asked on an uncomfortable whisper, the echo of Nancy's love story reverberating in her brain.

"Hannah," he groaned her name. "I love you. You know I love you. I've never been with another woman in, what, ten years?"

"Eleven."

"Even better. That's a long time for me."

"It's called a commitment, Keith. You don't get a medal for not cheating on me for eleven years."

He looked skyward. "It's my way of showing you how much you mean to me, Hannah."

"What about marriage?"

"No," he said simply. "I don't believe in it. Can't do it, don't want it, and won't try it."

She felt her shoulders drop with the weight of his stubborn decision. Yes, she knew his parents had an acrimonious divorce that had gone on for years and made most of his childhood absolutely horrendous. His father had poisoned him against marriage, but in almost every other way, Keith was a good man.

Frequently late and stingy with compliments, but good.

Anyway, if he wouldn't marry her, what other way even mattered?

"I want to go home," she repeated on a defeated sigh. "I'm tired and I don't want to have this conversation anymore."

He stepped back so she could get in the car. As her fingers closed over the handle and she opened the door herself, a bone-deep sadness pressed on her.

Sometimes when he didn't do things like open a car door for her, it hurt in the stupidest and most real way.

"Good night, Keith."

"I'll call you tomorrow," he said as she closed the door.

This was just about the closest they ever got to a real fight. He was too chill to argue, but also too chill to care.

Too chill to fight for her or...marry her.

She got home to an empty apartment, dark and quiet and lonely that night. Why had she given up on the Christmas tree this year? Just because it seemed sad to decorate it alone or hang a star and have no one appreciate the effort? She should have one to make things cheerier.

But there was no tree, no garlands, no Nativity scene, and not a sprig of mistletoe in sight. Hannah had gone on strike this Christmas, and now she was paying the price with sad surroundings and a heavy heart.

So she stripped out of her ugly top, showered, and put on flannel pajamas, taking her laptop to bed.

There, she just made herself more miserable by tapping on the Pinterest icon and revisiting her hidden and old—five years now, at least—fantasy wedding page. There'd been a time when she was certain she'd change Keith's mind about marriage.

Over time, she'd slipped into his mindset, agreeing that they were together no matter what. She bought into the "marriage is only a legality" hogwash, just to please him. And, yes, she said she couldn't move in with him because it would break her father's heart and maybe her mother's—if she was watching from heaven.

But the truth was that living together was a compromise she didn't want to make. So she lived like this, accepting the status quo and surviving on...crumbs.

How could she possibly celebrate the season when her heart was so empty, so heavy, and so sad?

# Chapter Four

## Noelle

PERFECTION.

Ah, yes, Noelle always strived for it and frequently, like this morning, she achieved it.

Stepping back, she eyed the pastry platter and fresh fruit bowl, with a fan of napkins and disposable flatware, all next to a coffee pot, cream, sugar, and cups. The sideboard that lined her gallery loft looked like a high-end hotel banquet, ideal for the tree lighting committee meeting.

Yes, there were only five people on the committee, including her, but she wanted to impress them for this, their first meeting with a new chairperson at the helm.

This was her big opportunity to deepen her relationship with locals and she didn't want to mess it up.

It had been a little more than a week since Jace spoke to his friend at church, who helped persuade the famously difficult Edna Covington to let a "newcomer" chair the committee. Edna had apparently agreed because time was running out and no one else had stepped forward.

Noelle did want to do things a little...well, not differently, but better this year. So she wanted a great atmosphere to present her ideas.

She checked her watch, hoping they'd all be on time at precisely eight a.m. The gallery opened at ten and that gave them two hours to get to know each other, listen to her plans, and finalize an action list for the event that attracted well over a thousand locals and tourists to downtown Asheville.

With five minutes to spare, Noelle slipped down the stairs to her main gallery, glancing around to make sure everything was perfect here, too.

Confident she was ready, she glanced out the picture window to catch sight of a few people approaching the gallery together. Before anyone even knocked, she unlocked the heavy door and greeted the arrivals with a smile.

"Welcome to Mountain Muse," she said warmly. "And the first official committee meeting for Asheville's Night of Lights."

A silver-haired lady who couldn't be ninety pounds or five-foot-two stood in front of two much taller men and an elegant-looking woman.

"Asheville *whats?*" the tiny woman said with nothing but disdain.

Ready for the pushback and the personality, Noelle looked down at her. "You must be Mrs. Covington," she said, extending her hand to the woman with a small frame but a big budget. "What an honor to meet you."

The older woman gave a limp shake and a quick once-over through thick bifocals. "Don't butter me up, doll. And don't even think about changing the name. This whole thing was my late husband's idea fourteen years ago. I'm carrying on the tradition in his name and nothing—and I do mean *nothing*—is going to change."

She muscled her way in, leaving Noelle to try not to make a surprised face as she greeted her other guests.

"I'm Harry Fletcher," the older of the two men said. "We've met up at my Christmas tree farm at the top of Copper Creek Mountain."

"Oh, of course! I remember when I went with my whole family to cut down a tree last year."

"And a long time before that, when you were a little girl." He tipped his head as he slipped out of his parka to reveal a black and gold Pittsburgh Penguins sweatshirt. "I knew your parents, Noelle. And, of course, I'm acquainted with Sonny and Bitsy, too."

The fact that he knew her family and ran such a lovely farm took away Edna's sting. She shook his hand warmly and thanked him for coming and for donating the tree every year.

Next to him was a younger man, maybe forty, with a military haircut and a crisp navy jacket.

"Tony Jessup," he said. "Public affairs for the police and fire department, so I'm here on behalf of law enforcement and order."

"We'll need that, Tony," she said. "And thank you for your help in getting me on this committee."

"Yeah, well, be careful what you wish for," he joked. At least, she hoped it was a joke.

She turned to her last guest, who was a stunning Black woman with natural warmth in her eyes and sassy braids framing her face.

"I'm Joanna Johnson," she said, shaking Noelle's hand. "I'm the local head of the small business coalition in town and I help organize all the other retailers and businesses who run booths. And can I just say thank you from the bottom of my heart for stepping in, Mrs. Fleming? I was beginning to wake up in a cold sweat thinking they'd make me do it."

Was the job really that bad? "It's Noelle," she said. "And I'm thrilled to help."

The other woman lifted a brow and leaned closer to whisper, "We'll see how thrilled you are, hon. But count on my support, because you'll need it."

With that ominous opening, Noelle escorted her guests up to the loft, offered them coffee and pastries, and made some small talk as they took seats around the conference table.

"So," she started as there was a break in the chatter. "We have about three weeks to make this happen, but I'm not worried at all. Today, we'll nail down all the last-minute details. I wanted Harry to tell us about the tree, Joanna to talk booth vendors, and Tony to let us know what role the local police and firefighters want to have."

She glanced at Edna, not wanting to point out that her only function was to write the checks, but that obviously gave her the most power in the room.

"And, of course, whatever you want to discuss, Mrs. Covington."

"I'm here to make sure you don't change anything," she said, picking up a pastry and eyeing it as though Noelle might have dipped it in arsenic. "That's why I let enough time pass so we were on a tight deadline. No changes."

"Nothing major," Noelle said, undaunted by her orders. "For instance, I do think a new name would help us attract local media and—"

"Hold your horses, Noelle the Newbie." Edna leaned forward and sliced her with a look. "We are not changing the name. Period. End of story. Discussion over. This whole event was the brainchild of my Gil, and I made a promise to him—on his deathbed, I might add—that nothing about the tree lighting would ever change."

A deathbed promise? Was she *serious*?

"And nothing will," Edna finished. "In case you're wondering, that's why I'm here. My role is to represent the founder of the tree lighting and to ensure that his vision is protected forever, right down to the last light. May it flicker in his honor."

With that, she bit into the pastry and powdered sugar fluttered like fresh snow on her bosom.

Tony looked at his notes. Harry shrugged a shoulder.

At the end of the table, Joanna smiled and wrinkled her nose. "Pick your battles, hon," she said gently. "We all think the name's fine."

Noelle handed the matriarch a napkin, abandoning her speech about updating the event to attract young people. The place had been packed last year, so did it really matter what it was called?

"Then we will honor Gil's memory," she said sweetly. "And speaking of lights, I'm happy to say I've found a vendor down in Hendersonville who specializes in LED lights, which will be digitally controlled on our phones, so there's no chance of anything going wrong with the power or timing."

Edna choked. "Excuse me?"

"The tree will still be lit," Noelle assured her. "And you can choose the colors to match your husband's vision." That should quiet her down. "But in fourteen years, technology has changed."

"Technology can change all it wants," Edna sputtered. "And you can call your LED man down in Hendersonville and cancel whatever order you placed, because it's not in our budget and we're not doing some newfangled computer thing that will just go haywire if we can't get the internet to work. Am I right, Tony?"

He shrugged, looking trapped between the two opinions. "Of course, Wi-Fi is available in some of the stores and we could do—"

"No, we can't," Edna insisted.

"But it's so much easier to—"

"This isn't about easy, my dear." Edna cut off Noelle's argument. "It's about safety—"

"Nothing could be safer than LED lights," Noelle said. "Or more dependable if the power goes out or a car runs over a wire or—"

"That's not going to happen," Edna said. "Plus, we

have the whole fire department there to make sure we have whatever we need. And the lights need to be white."

"We could incorporate colors for..." Noelle's voice faded out as the other woman peered over a powered donut, a thick discomfort hanging in the air. "Or not," Noelle finished with a chuckle in her voice. "Let's move to the sound system that will pipe in a set of music from..."

Edna stared at her and Noelle let out a sigh.

"Don't tell me," Noelle said. "The high school band plays Christmas carols?"

"No, but there are carolers and they've been prac-ticing for almost a year," Edna said. "They all dress like a Dickens novel and wander through the streets singing beloved songs, and I don't mean 'Jingle Bells.' A...*sound system*?" She scoffed as if the words offended her. "The only system that needs sounds are vocal chords, so you can cut that item, too."

Noelle took a breath, thinking about the playlist she'd been creating to reach hearts young and old. The buildup to the lighting, the drumroll she'd downloaded, and the...

No, this wasn't the battle she wanted to fight, either. Let them carol.

"Harry." Noelle turned toward the older man. "Can you tell us about the tree?"

"It better be a fir," Edna murmured.

Harry just smiled. "Of course, Mrs. C. My son's living here now and he and I went out this morning and marked the perfect twenty-foot Douglas fir, just like Gil preferred."

Edna gave a satisfied nod.

And that, Noelle learned over the course of the next hour, was exactly how the tree lighting would be—the precise tradition that ol' dead Gil wanted fourteen years ago. So much for innovation.

THE MEETING LEFT Noelle on edge for the rest of the day. Frustrated that chairing the committee meant doing everything in a slightly antiquated fashion, she decided to zip over to Red Bridge Farm on her way home. She hoped to get another take on the whole thing.

Sonny and Bitsy were "locals," so they knew the players and the history, and maybe they could give her some ammo for fighting Edna.

Sonny had just come in from a day's work on the farm and was pouring the two of them a late afternoon wine when Noelle arrived, and she happily joined them in a small sunroom that had been added on since Bitsy moved in last year.

The room reminded her of the much larger version at the cabin, a sunny room to stay cozy and warm in but still enjoy the unparalleled Blue Ridge view. Sonny had built the addition himself and situated it to not only offer the mountain vistas, but also the small red bridge over a creek that gave the farm its name.

Settling in and chatting with them, Noelle shared

what had happened at the meeting, giving a colorful account of each player.

"I'm so proud of you, dearest Noelle," Bitsy said, lifting her glass in a toast.

Yes, the elegant New Yorker who was once Aunt Elizabeth might have morphed into a farm owner who wore overalls, boots, and had naturally gray hair, but that didn't change the gleam of love in her eyes when she looked at any of her nieces.

This dear woman had swooped in and eased the pain when the triplets lost their parents in a tragic accident. She would always be Noelle's soft place to fall and a voice of reason and guidance.

"Proud of me for folding like a house of cards when Edna blew on my ideas?" she scoffed. "I'm trying to make friends, not alienate everyone in one fell swoop."

Sonny and Bitsy shared a look, silent.

"What?' she asked, leaning forward. "What don't I know about Edna Covington?"

Sonny tipped his head. "She can be a real piece of work," he drawled, the accent and his expression making Noelle frown.

"Is that...good or bad?"

"It's challenging," he explained. "She not only likes to get her way, this event is her personal tribute to her husband."

"Gil? Trust me, I know all about him." Noelle rolled her eyes. "The tree lighting was his brainchild years ago and nothing can change even though technology has advanced in leaps and bounds."

Bitsy gave a smile. "Well, one thing can't change and that's the row of lights along the bottom of the tree." She shot a look to her husband. "They flickered three times last year right before you proposed, and next time I saw Edna, she told me Gil was thrilled with our engagement."

Noelle nearly choked on a sip of wine. "Excuse me? Isn't he dead?"

"Quite." Bitsy raised a brow. "Except during the tree lighting."

At Noelle's look, Sonny chuckled.

"Let me give you a little history," he said. "Gilbert Covington was a force in Asheville, from a family that's been around forever. He created the idea of the tree lighting, what? Fifteen years ago?" he asked Bitsy.

"I guess," she said. "Sometime in the dark years when the girls and I didn't come up to the cabin, so that seems right. Although I seem to recall a similar event when I was little, but it stopped in the sixties. I can't remember, honestly."

"Well, more recently, Gil threw a couple of tree lightings, and they were resounding successes—except the bottom row of lights didn't work right the first year."

"Which wouldn't be a problem with LED lights," Noelle interjected.

"Then it happened again the following year," he continued. "And Gil was so mad, he climbed under the tree and held the connector himself. They worked, but they flickered."

Noelle looked from one to the other, not sure where

this story was going but nothing about it supported the old-school lights.

"Then he died," Sonny said.

She gasped. "Under the tree?"

"No, no." Bitsy laughed softly and Sonny smiled at that, too.

"He passed away after a brief illness a few months later."

Noelle nodded. "And not without making Edna swear not to change a thing about the tree lighting. She mentioned the deathbed promise, which is why I didn't fight harder."

"Well, it's a little more complicated," Sonny said. "The following year—"

"The bottom rows of lights didn't work," Noelle guessed. "And now Edna thinks that has to happen every year."

"They flickered," Bitsy said. "And they've flickered every single year since then."

Noelle leaned back, hearing the implication in her aunt's voice. "Don't tell me," she said. "Edna thinks...it's him."

"Bingo." Sonny pointed at her. "She's convinced he comes back every year, that his spirit makes the lights flicker as his way of saying he's looking down on his town, his event, and his widow."

She felt her eyes shutter close. "You have got to be kidding me."

"It's sweet," Bitsy cooed. "And that's why the other people on your committee didn't take your side. No one wants to steal that tiny, well, *flicker* of happiness from Edna."

"Okay," Noelle said. "But what if it doesn't happen, even with the old-school lights?"

"It'll happen," Sonny said. "It's sort of a tradition."

"Or maybe someone like Edna's grandson or nephew is flipping the right switch down the street on the breaker panel," Noelle said dryly.

They chuckled. "Maybe, maybe not," Sonny said. "But for the locals—not the tourists or guests who don't even know about it, but those of us who are from around here—it's kind of a sweet tradition."

"You never even mentioned it last year," she said.

"Well, we got engaged," Bitsy explained. "And if you recall, when we got home from the tree lighting last year, Brooke was standing in the driveway, having gotten herself from California to Asheville. We had other things on our mind."

And Noelle and Jace had shared their first kiss—probably at the same moment that the lights flickered, so she probably thought their electrifying attraction caused an outage.

She nodded slowly. "Okay, I get it. Tradition or superstition, whatever you call it, the flicker is important."

"It is to Edna," Bitsy said. "She lives for that moment when her beloved says hello."

"Okay, then, no pressure," Noelle said on a laugh. "Just have to be sure Gil's ghost arrives on time. Just one more thing to control."

Bitsy leaned forward and took her hand. "You know you're not the one in control, baby girl. This event, along with every single thing that happens every day is controlled by..." She pointed to the sky. "The sooner you accept that, the happier you'll be."

Noelle was still a long, long way from believing that. "Well, someone has to do the work down here and for this event? It'll be me."

# *Chapter Five*

## *Angie*

An *egg baby*?

"What the ever lovin' heck is an egg baby?" Angie choked the question, checked the time, and tapped her foot impatiently as she waited for Brooke—who'd literally just rolled out of bed—to tell her what an egg baby was and why she needed one now.

"It's an egg that we're supposed to carry around from now until winter break starts to help us understand the full responsibility of having a child." She rolled her eyes. "As if a few hours of babysitting one of my cousins wouldn't do the trick."

"Seriously." Angie huffed out a breath. "Whose genius idea was this?"

"A teacher, but I totally forgot I'm supposed to make a little carrier for it and name it and give it a face. By first period. In, um, an hour."

"Well, good luck with that, Mama," Angie said brightly, turning toward her bag. "I gotta go because I just checked GPS, and traffic is wretched and today is B-day."

"I think the expression is D-day," Brooke said, her worried look increasing.

"B for New Boss. Starts today. Eight o'clock introductory staff meeting, so I—"

"Mom, *please* help me at least get the gooey stuff out of the egg without breaking it. I have no idea how to do that."

"The egg has to be empty...but whole?"

"Yes, that's the idea. It's fragile, but not, you know, lethal. I have no idea how to do that."

"I think you just poke a hole in it and let it drip. Google it."

"But I have to get dressed and make the carrier for part of the grade today, and I can't do this. Please, Mom."

Angie gestured toward the cream silk blouse and gray slacks she'd picked to make a great impression. "No way I'm dealing with eggs in this."

Brooke snagged a red apron with candy canes all over it, still a tad dusty with flour from cookie-making with the cousins. "This'll cover you. Help me, Mom. I'm desperate. I need you. This is your egg *grand*baby."

Angie groaned and laughed and folded. "Okay, I'll try. Fast. But only for my grandegg."

Four eggs, what looked like a gallon of yolk, and a few not-so-Christian words later, Brooke had an empty eggshell, lovingly named ButtPain. Giving the little guy a face and carrier was her daughter's problem, but the delay had Angie barreling toward the Biltmore with just enough time to sail into the meeting on time.

Until...the highway came to a complete stop.

"What?" She squinted at the unending line of brake lights, calculating how long it would take to get to her exit. Long. Very long.

After a high dose of cortisol and stress, checking the clock forty-seven times, and breaking the speed limit once she got off the highway, she finally blew into the employee lot at exactly two minutes after eight.

*Late.* How could she be late for this, the most important meeting of her career?

She knew nothing about the new boss, but the rumors had flown since the day Marjorie left. A woman from the Met. A professor from Yale. A guy from somewhere in London. And—her most favorite possibility—someone from within the Biltmore organization.

At least that would give her a fighting chance, because the Vanderbilts, who still technically owned the estate, would most likely value her family connections and proven track record.

*Please, please, please let them hire from within.*

She tore into the back entrance, now four minutes late. Maybe New Boss would run behind. Maybe the meeting hadn't started. Without even taking off her coat, she powered down the hall to the corner. Maybe—

"Oh!" She slammed hard into someone coming around the bend, with coffee splashing everywhere.

"Goodness, Angie! Watch where you're going!"

She backed up from one of the tour guides with a gasp, feeling the warmth of coffee all over her silk blouse before she had the nerve to look down and see...

*Oh.*

"Really sorry about that," the other woman said. "It was really both our faults."

"It's okay," Angie said, plucking at the material that was so wet with coffee, you could almost see the lace of her bra underneath. "I'll...manage."

The other woman gave a tight, apologetic smile. "It'll rinse out."

"But what do I wear?" she murmured.

"There are extra tour guide smocks in the break room," she said. "I just saw a few."

A tour guide smock? For her first meeting with a new boss? With one more glance at a stain the size of a small continent—and so ugly and brown—she gave a quick nod and darted to the break room's kitchenette.

There, she pulled on a size large smock that made her look like a human version of Brooke's baby egg, and tore down the hall to the conference room.

The door was closed, so they'd started.

*Son of a...*

Sucking in a breath, she slowly twisted the knob and tried to slip in unnoticed, but every head turned from the conference table to look up at her.

"Sorry," she murmured, glancing around for an empty seat.

There was one, in the front, next to a man standing at the head of the table, and—

No. No. *No, it was not possible.* This was not happening. Her life could not be this cursed.

"Angel," the man said with the hint of a wry smile

that fell somewhere between amusement and disgust. "I didn't know you were a tour guide here."

A tour...oh, the jacket.

"Um, no, I'm not. I just..." With a sigh and a bone-deep desire to scream, run, and possibly hide under the table, she made her way around the room to the only empty chair. There, she sat less than a foot from Elliott John Quinn of Brookline, Massachusetts, owner of one damaged BMW.

And the new head curator at the Biltmore Estate.

"I had a run-in with a coffee cup," she managed to say. "And I..." She fluttered the smock, refusing to look up and meet his gaze. "Covered it up."

"Another run-in?" He lifted a brow. "You must be an expert at those."

She gave a tight smile and glanced across the table, meeting a colleague's very curious gaze.

"Long story," she stage whispered, then let out a sigh. "I'm sorry for delaying the meeting, Mr. Quinn. Please..." She gave a vague gesture. "Carry on."

He cleared his throat and got her colleagues' attention again. "As I was saying, I come here to the Biltmore Estate after many years at the MFA in Boston, with several advanced degrees from a university there—well, in Cambridge—and hope to bring both change and stability to this museum..."

He droned on as Angie's pulse finally settled into something close to normal.

Then his words started to hit her. The MFA? *The Museum of Fine Arts* in Boston? A university in

Cambridge? Did he mean *Harvard*? And...*several* advanced degrees?

And what kind of *change* did he want to bring?

She tried to shake off the insecurities, slipping out a notebook and pen, forcing herself to listen to him talk about building traffic through creativity, attracting major exhibits, and programs to launch the Biltmore Estate as an important national art museum.

Nothing about the Vanderbilt family. Not a word about the annual highlights, like Christmas and summer. No connection to the winery, the history, and he couldn't have cared less how profitable a wedding package could be. No plans to expand the current exhibits like Marjorie had, and not a word about the strong connection to the Asheville community.

The only thing that seemed to excite him was the Monet and a few of the tapestries, making her realize that he saw the place as strictly a museum and not a home. Not only was that a huge difference between him and Marjorie, it was also a disappointment to Angie, who clung to her hundred-year-old familial connection to the place as her only hope of keeping this job.

She forced herself to put that out of her mind and listen to him. He had a vague Boston accent, she noticed, and a slight professorial air that was both intimidating and attractive.

*Attractive? Hold them horses there, Angie.*

Attractive was the last thing he was. Oh, sure, he was a handsome man by most standards. Probably forty-five or so, maybe older. Dark hair with some silver strands, strong features, that sophisticated beard and glasses he wore to read, but casually removed when he looked around the room. His eyes were brown or...no, no. Kind of green with flecks of dark gold, and they were—

Directly on her.

"Wouldn't that be your area, Angel?"

She blinked, frozen, totally busted thinking about the color of his eyes.

Would *what* be her area? What had Marjorie told him?

"Angie," she managed, buying time and hoping to figure out what he'd asked her.

He tipped his head in concession and she saw what she could have sworn was a cloud of quick disappointment in his eyes, no matter what color they were.

Disappointed? Because she didn't go by Angel? Or because he'd have to fire her before the week was over?

"I understand you handled the last two feature exhibitions," he said. "Something with the..." He gestured toward the ceiling. "The upstairs servants' quarters? A walk-through tour?"

"Oh, yes," she replied, back on solid ground. "I helped Marjorie, er, Ms. Summerall, your predecessor, curate the pieces that went in the higher-ranking servants' quarters exhibit on the fourth floor. I have a family connection to the Vanderbilt staff," she added, sitting up a little with pride. "The parlor maid and a footman were my great-grandparents."

He drew back a bit. "Huh. That's...interesting."

Actually, it was, but she didn't need any more attention on her at this meeting, so she just nodded and stayed quiet.

"Then you're the ideal person to help us," he said.

"Anything you need," she said quickly, remembering all of Marjorie's praise for her can-do attitude. "We're sprucing up that exhibit? That's a great idea because—"

"We're taking it down," he said dismissively. "We need space for something that showcases real art and will draw more guests in the spring."

Taking down the exhibit she'd worked so hard to create? For a moment, she was flat-out speechless, but then one of the older curators, Jason Pooley, leaned forward.

"Please tell me we can get Eva Jospin after it leaves Paris," he said.

Elliott gave a dry snort. "Don't hold your breath. But I do have a connection at Versailles and there's a chance on the Frida Kahlo exhibit that's on tour right now."

"Yes!" Jason fist pumped. "Finally, some legit art."

*Legit*? What was not legit about the totally accurate recreation of a room used by beloved staff members? With their actual clothes, bedding, and the very Bible they read on the same nightstand they used? She'd donated that Bible after finding it in her attic.

"The Kahlo news is *not* to leave this room," Elliott warned. "That exhibit is...a longshot. And Eva Jospin?" He shrugged. "She sculpts in cardboard, but does that thrill people? Not as much as the beauty of Kahlo's self-portraits."

The names were a mystery, and Angie felt utterly lost. And more than that, she was frustrated.

Yes, the Biltmore was a museum, but it was so much more than that. The estate had been a home, with children and memories and a deep and beautiful history. Tourists lined up to step into a century-old lifestyle, not stare...wait. Did he say that artist sculpted in *cardboard*?

As the meeting came to an end, it was clear some of the curator staff were excited, and some were wary. Angie was just confused, confounded, and petrified she'd be looking for a new job soon.

In fact, she couldn't wait to get into her office and start a job search, but she knew the polite thing to do was to ask her new boss about his car and try her best to improve her image in his eyes.

She stood as he finished chatting with another staffer, catching his attention. "So, small world, huh?"

He gave her a smile and seemed to relax. "You know what isn't small?" he said with a tease in his eyes. "The dent in my car."

She winced. "Did you find a body shop?"

"Only one but they can't get me in for a month."

"Oh, I can help," she said brightly.

"I remember...you know someone who knows someone."

"I do," she said. "And I'm seeing one of those some-ones this evening. It's my aunt's stepdaughter and her boyfriend owns a great body shop. I'll get your car in lick-ity-split."

He lifted one brow. "Lickity-split? Is that a Southern expression?"

She heard something in the question—not mocking, not at all. Amusement, definitely. A little curiosity. Maybe he was just a fish out of water.

"I'm not Southern," she said. "Well, I was born and raised in North Carolina," she conceded, "but I've been living in California until I moved here."

He nodded. "Great museums out there."

And she couldn't remember visiting one. "There are, but nothing like the Biltmore Estate," she added. "This place is special."

She saw the slightest flash of doubt in his eyes. "It's... different."

"Give it a chance," she said, and meant it. "There's nothing else like it in this whole country."

He studied her, then nodded slowly. "I'll take the name of your body shop connection," he finally said. "Otherwise, I'll be driving with one headlight for a month. Thanks, Angel. Er, Angie. Sorry."

"No, no, it's fine." Truth was, no one called her that and she liked the way it sounded. "Please call me Angel. I *was* born on Christmas."

"Really? Well, we'll have to have a birthday and Christmas drink sometime."

She almost drew back. Was he asking her—

"Mr. Quinn?" Diana poked her head in the room. "There's a call from Paris."

"Ah, thank you. I'll be right there." He turned to

Angie. "The Kahlo exhibit," he said with a grin and then added a finger to his lips as if to say...tell no one.

About the art...or the fact that he'd asked her for a drink?

He stepped out, leaving their conversation unfinished and Angie more restless and itching to get out of the tour guide's smock.

THE THREE SISTERS who loved to gather and catch up on each other's lives had organically grown to the five ladies—sometimes six, if Bitsy came—who now got together nearly every Wednesday night at rotating homes.

With Caro and Hannah added to the mix, it meant more laughter, more conversation, and more Irish coffee. Tonight, they were at the cabin, spread out around the sofa and chairs in the sunroom, sharing life updates.

After Noelle filled them in on the tree lighting committee drama, Angie wasted no time telling them about the changes at the Biltmore and her bone-deep concerns for her job security. She needed advice and the chance to unload with this trusted group.

"He can't just fire you for being late and wearing..." Eve scowled. "A tour guide smock? Seriously?"

"That or a coffee stain," Angie said, glancing down at the memory of the sploosh all over her blouse. "Of all days."

"So he left the Boston MFA to come here," Noelle said, after she took a moment to consider all that Angie had shared. "I actually know someone who used to work there and I can ask for info on him. From the MFA to the Biltmore, though. Huh. That's kind of a..."

"Downgrade?" Angie guessed.

"Not at all," Noelle said. "But it's a wholly different curator experience, so maybe that's what he wanted."

"Somehow, I didn't get that impression," Angie said. "And I don't know how to handle him."

"With kid gloves and no more accidents," Hannah said, looking up from her phone. "Keith says to give the guy his number and he'll do the body work this week with a friends-and-family discount."

"Oh, thank you," Angie said with a sigh. "That might have just saved my job."

"You will save your own job," Eve said. "As soon as he sees your work ethic and attitude, you'll be fine."

"Yeah, if I'm willing to undo the entire exhibit I put together featuring our great-grandparents' room." She groaned and dropped her head back, still not over it. "I hate that he blows in and takes apart the one thing that really had my fingerprints on it. For what? Something called...Kahlo?"

Noelle gasped. "No! Frida Kahlo, the Mexican artist? I heard that exhibit is amazing, and what a coup to get it in Asheville."

"You did not hear that from me." Angie pointed to her. "I'm sworn to secrecy."

Caro leaned in and looked at Angie. "I agree that you

just have to show him your value to the company, Angie. And get to know him."

"He did suggest we get a drink..." Her voice trailed off as all four of them stared at her. "I mean, I guess as an ice-breaker."

"Are you sure?" Noelle asked.

"Was he asking you out?" Eve pressed.

"Is he cute?" Hannah chimed in.

"Actually, he's pretty easy on the eyes, but..." She looked from one to the other. "Stop it."

None of them said a word, but a few fought smiles.

"What could possibly give you the impression I would ever think about him that way?" she asked on an uncomfortable laugh.

"The fact that we haven't talked about anything or anyone else for an hour," Noelle said softly.

"And you've mentioned the color—actually, *colors*—of his eyes three times." Eve made a face and pretended to sip her coffee.

Angie rolled her eyes, utterly disinterested in her boss, but she *had* talked about him a lot.

"Then, by all means, change the subject," she replied, waving toward Hannah. "What's happening in your life?"

"Me? Oh, the fun never stops. The kids have winter break fever, I can't seem to get into the Christmas spirit for love or money, but the last field trip of the semester is a trip to the Christmas tree farm."

"Cassie told me she loved that field trip last year when she was in your class," Noelle said. "Plus, Harry

Fletcher is on my tree lighting committee. Make sure no one steals our twenty-foot Douglas fir or Edna Covington will make my life a living nightmare."

"Will do," Hannah promised with a noticeable lack of enthusiasm.

"But what's up with you, Hannah?" Caro asked, zeroing in on her sister. "You're always so happy at this time of year. Every time of year, to be honest."

Hannah shrugged. "It's just...you know, the life of a single second-grade teacher."

"Single?" Caro narrowed her eyes. "I'd hardly call you that."

"Well, you'd hardly call me married," she quipped, stopping any other comments dead in their tracks. In the uncomfortable silence, she laughed. "But that's the path I've chosen, right? Keith the Non-committer."

No one said a word, then Hannah held up her hands. "Not too much advice at once, ladies."

"Do you *want* advice?" Noelle asked gently.

"I don't know. Do I?" She gave a sad smile. "I know what everyone thinks. I'm a pushover for Keith, who refuses to get married because he doesn't believe in the institution and I should give him an ultimatum or walk."

"You should be happy and comfortable," Eve said.

"You should listen to your heart," Noelle added.

"You should not get married for the wrong reasons," Angie said. "But remember, I'm the jaded divorced one of the group."

"What you should do, my dearest sister..." Caroline

reached over and took Hannah's hand. "Is place a high value on yourself and what you want from life."

Hannah winced at that, probably because it came from the woman in the room who loved and knew her the best.

"It's complicated," she finally admitted on a whisper. "I love him—at least I...yeah. I do. But I do feel like I'm settling for less than I deserve and want."

"What does he say when you tell him that?" Eve asked.

"That we should live together and before you even respond, my answer is no. I...can't."

"Dad could ultimately accept that," Caro said, clearly knowing exactly what was stopping Hannah. "You know he wants you to be happy."

"But Mom..." She gave a tight, teary smile. "If she were here? She wouldn't like it at all. I'm not sure she'd like Keith, but she wouldn't approve of living together and I don't want to...dishonor her. Does that make sense?"

Eve, Noelle, and Angie exchanged knowing looks, nodding and whispering, "Yes."

"The power of a parent is strong, even from the grave," Angie said softly, thinking of many decisions she'd made in life because she thought it would be what her parents would have wanted.

"All I can say is that things are coming to a head with Keith and I'm trying to figure out what to do." She picked up her Irish coffee, staring at the remnants of whipped cream on top. "One of these days, the answer will be clear."

They all agreed and let the conversation shift to Eve and Caroline, who commiserated about the challenges of being baby-moms again.

"It's not easy," Eve said. "Nothing about being a parent is easy."

"No kidding!" Suddenly, Brooke came bounding into the sunroom, holding out her hands, the cracked shell of an egg baby in her palms. "I accidentally dropped my phone on ButtPain and she's done for! I have to make another one and give her the same face or I'm doomed."

"I know how to make a perfect egg baby!" Eve announced, popping to her feet.

"Of course she does," Angie joked. "Why didn't I call you the other morning? I wouldn't have been late and put my career in jeopardy."

"Just get me one of Aunt Bitsy's old knitting needles," Eve called as the women walked into the kitchen to watch the master at work.

Next to her, Noelle put her arm around Angie and squeezed. "You'll be fine," she whispered. "Just do your job and it'll all work out."

She glanced at her sister. "Should I have a drink with him?"

"Sure. Just don't go any further than that."

"I wouldn't think of it," she said, but even as she said the words, she realized that deep, deep down? She was still thinking about those green and gold eyes.

*Oh, Angie. There is dumb and there is really dumb.*
That thought was really, really dumb.

Which didn't exactly make it go away.

# Chapter Six

## Hannah

As THE SCHOOL bus chugged up the side of Copper Creek Mountain, patches of snow grew thicker from the dustings they'd had every day this week.

"More snow than I expected." Amy, a first-time chaperone, inched down to get a better look out the bus window next to Hannah.

"Which is perfect," Hannah told her. "You might think the trees are the highlight of the Christmas tree farm field trip, but trust me, it's the snow tubing at the end."

"Oh? I doubt Riley will do that." She tipped her head toward the shy little girl across the aisle. "Unless I do it with her."

"You can. The students go down the slope in pairs, but..." She lifted her brow. "I'd sooner run screaming naked down the side of the mountain than tube. But the kids love every second."

She turned from her seat to check out the twenty-seven little passengers, plus three parent chaperones.

Chaos mostly ruled the day, with lots of noise, laughter, and a hum of excitement louder than the motor working its best to make it up the side of the mountain.

"Is this safe?" the woman next to her asked, concern in the young mother's eyes as the bus took one of the famous hairpin turns that got them near the top.

Hannah lifted her brow with a wry smile. "The bus? Absolutely. The kids? If they follow the rules. The adults? We'll need wine tonight," she joked. "But don't let that stop you from chaperoning, Amy. We need all the parents we can get."

"I should have done this sooner," Amy said. "Riley missed me so much at the pumpkin patch in October, I realized it was more important than work."

"You'll love it," Hannah promised. "This field trip is always a blast for the kids. They get to see at least one tree chopped down by Harry Fletcher, the owner, and he gives them a wonderful tour. They'll get hot chocolate and pizza, run around until they're exhausted. Then—the highlight of the day—they get in an inner tube and fly down the back hills of the farm."

"It sounds wonderful," Amy said.

Wonderful? It usually was. But this year? The trip felt more like a chore.

Taking a deep breath, she eyed the weathered sign that said Fletcher's Farm, a landmark that had been here as long as she could remember to mark the entrance to what everyone called "the Christmas tree farm."

"Oh, we're here." She stood and tried to get the chil-drens' attention. "Ready or not, it's field trip time."

When nothing changed or maybe got louder, she clapped a few times, calling, "Class! Class!"

Failing that, she lifted both hands and put them on her head, ballerina-style, and opened her mouth to bellow, "Hands on top, everybody stop!"

Almost everyone did stop, then imitated her pose. All but Nicholas Venema and Daniel Duncan, who were in the last row, howling with laughter and jabbing each other. She took a few steps down the aisle, eyes on her most behavior-challenged duo.

"Nick, Dan. We're waiting for you."

The boys exchanged a look, rolled their eyes, and raised their hands with half-hearted enthusiasm.

"Boys and girls, we have arrived at Fletcher's Farm," she told them once she didn't have to yell. "And we have a very exciting day planned." She waited through a soft rumble of response. "We're going to tour the farm, watch a tree being cut down—"

"With a *buzzzzzz* saw!" Nick hollered, getting the expected response—all of the kids in the class buzzing like noisy bees.

She waited through that, too, throwing a wry look at one of the chaperones. After a minute, she put one finger to her lips and gave her sternest look. Most of them settled down.

"Before we get the tour, before we get hot chocolate and pizza—" She held up her hand to stop the cheer. "And *if* you want to go snow tubing..."

She couldn't stop that cheer, but let out a sigh and a laugh, knowing some joy couldn't be contained.

"We are going to follow the rules!" she exclaimed. "And that means when you hear my instructions, you obey them."

They finally quieted so she could finish the speech. "If you want to go snow tubing," she said, softly enough that they had to be still to hear her, "you will not let go of your partner's hand. You will not go anywhere alone. You will not touch anything without permission, and you will not use any language or actions that offend your friends or our hosts."

Behind her, she heard the bus doors open and a footstep, knowing Harry Fletcher must have arrived. She didn't want to turn and lose their attention, but a few of them were already staring at the new arrival.

"Boys and girls, we will be kind, we will be mindful, we will be respectful, and then we will…" She gave them a look they all knew and got a chorus of, "Have fun!" in response.

"Now, this farm is privately owned and also functions as a community farm, and that will be explained to you by a man named Mr. Harry and…" She turned, ready to introduce the older man who always made the day so special. "He is…"

*Not* Harry Fletcher.

She blinked in surprise at a man she'd never seen before leaning over the railing, his arms crossed as he braced himself and listened with more attention than any of these kids were giving her.

He wore a red-checked flannel shirt that pulled over broad shoulders, with silky brown hair that brushed the collar and fell over his brow. Piercing blue eyes pinned her with a gaze of interest, amusement, and warmth.

"Hello," she said, her voice suddenly tight. "Are you going to give the tour today?"

"I am," he said, coming up a step to fill the space on the bus with what had to be a six-foot frame. "But I'm not Harry, so sorry to disappoint."

Disappointment would not be her first response.

"That's...fine," she said. "And you are..." *Also fine.*

"Harry's son and replacement," he supplied. "He sent me to stand in and—I'm quoting him—'delight' the children."

"That sounds like Harry," she said, offering her hand. "I'm Hannah MacPherson, the teacher."

"Brandon Fletcher, the tour guide."

Brandon Fletcher. She'd heard that name before, hadn't she? Well, if he was Harry's son, that made sense.

Before she gave it more thought, his smile grew, which gave him—no, that wasn't a dimple. It was a scar right along the side of his mouth, jagged, curved, and a shocking imperfection on an arguably perfect face.

As they shook hands, the noise on the bus grew, forcing her to turn to the chaos behind her. Nick and Dan were snickering, and a few of the kids were already standing up.

"Hey, hey," she called, but things only deteriorated. With three loud claps, she called out and held up three fingers. "One, two, three!" She brought her hand down to point to her face. "Eyes on me!"

That always worked and today was no different, and

sudden silence reigned. Thank goodness, since she wouldn't want to look like an incompetent teacher in front of...

She glanced over her shoulder, but the good-looking tour guide had disappeared out the bus door. She flicked her hand to the first row, giving them permission to rise and leave the bus.

"Hold your partner's hand," she instructed the second row. "Line up outside the bus."

She couldn't help looking out the window, scanning the group for the flannel shirt-wearing Brandon Fletcher. He certainly made the trip less of a chore.

"You two behave today," she said as Nick and Dan lollygagged, last in line. "No shenanigans today."

"No she*what*agans, Ms. MacPherson?" Nick joked, his eyes dancing with the spunk he could never hide.

She tapped his shoulder, laughing. "You heard me."

They giggled their way off the bus, so Hannah grabbed her jacket and purse and stepped down. She instantly spotted Brandon making his way up and down the double row of children, arms locked behind him like a pretend drill sergeant.

"All right," he called out to them. "We're gonna have some fun today! Who likes fun?"

A cheer went up.

"You can call me Fletch but only if you know...how many days until Christmas?"

He got about twenty different shouted responses, only a few with the correct number, which, for some reason, cracked him up.

"And who has been very, very good and will not make an appearance on the naughty list?" he asked, his magnetic presence somehow calming all the ants in their pants.

Every arm shot up. Well, except Nick and Dan, who poked each other and instantly got Brandon's attention.

"Coal for you two?" he asked, stepping toward her only real behavior problems. And, honestly, they weren't bad. Nick was super smart and always bored, and Dan loved to instigate trouble, but never anything serious.

Brandon leaned closer and had an exchange with the boys that Hannah didn't hear, but Dan straightened and Nick's eyes grew wide and he nodded fast. And both of them fell into line as the group started walking.

Hannah stayed close to the middle, watching Brandon lead the line like the Pied Piper.

"Fletcher's Farm has been in my family for sixty-seven years," he told them and, somehow, miraculously, they listened.

Taking a break from leading the class, she took a moment to consider this Brandon "Fletch" Fletcher.

She'd heard the name somewhere, yes, but how could she have been coming to this farm for years and never met Harry's son? He looked to be in his mid-thirties and she'd lived on or around this mountain her whole life.

How could she not know him? She knew his father and mother and...didn't he have an older sister who'd known Caroline?

But where had Brandon been all these years?

Her curiosity piqued, she stayed close to the kids and

listened as he explained how the community aspect of the farm worked, that the locals were allowed to take a tree every year in exchange for planting a new one. She knew it was a wonderful way the Fletcher family had given back to the area for years, but still couldn't imagine how or why they'd never met.

He walked them by the tiny trees in the "nursery," making silly jokes about tree babies that the kids loved. And he grew more serious when he told them about the year they'd had a blight and lost all the trees.

"But now it's time to cut down a tree! Who can yell, 'Timber' with me?"

The reaction was loud and instant, with twenty-seven little voices—and one booming above them all—calling out, "Timber!"

"All right, now, boys and girls. I want everyone way over there, lined up so you can see."

His instructions were completely ignored as they danced around the tree, called, "Timber," and pretended to fall, and Dan and Nick made the loudest chainsaw noises they could.

Over the much shorter heads, Brandon caught her eye and mouthed, "Help."

With a smile and a nod, she gave a two-fingered whistle.

That quieted some of them, then she held up her fingers. "One, two, three! Eyes on me!"

Instantly, they stopped and locked their gazes on her, but the one she felt was Brandon's. He looked impressed and, for some reason, that gave her a little thrill.

"Boys and girls, I want all of you to listen to Mr. Fletcher."

"It's just Fletch," he said. "Or Brandon."

Some of those locks tumbled with the humble shake of his head. "Mr. Fletcher's my dad and he's better at this than I am."

She walked along the line of the kids. "Take the hand of the person next to you and make a line over there so you can see the tree coming down."

Dan and Nick led the march into line, surprising her so much, she didn't realize Brandon had come right up next to her.

"You're good," he whispered.

"I'm trained."

He studied her for a minute as if he had more to say, but then a younger man who worked at the farm came bounding up holding a chainsaw. She stared at it, then at him.

"Your dad uses an old-school saw."

"This is not my father's tree cutting," he said with a wink that really should have been illegal.

*Illegal...because I have a boyfriend*, Hannah reminded herself, stepping back to the kids.

"Everyone!" he called, tugging at the sleeves of his flannel shirt in a way that made him look well-built and masculine. Of course, he was both of those things.

"Stay back and get ready to yell!" he called to the kids.

Once again, her two most rambunctious students fell right into place and, in fact, instructed the others what to do. As she watched in amazement, Amy stepped up next to her.

"He's cute, huh?" she whispered.

Hannah glanced at the chaperone, surprised and maybe a little guilty. Had she been ogling the tree farmer?

She gave the most casual wave of her hands that she could manage. "He won't be if a tree falls on one of these kids."

Amy chuckled. "That tree's not big enough, but I love how he's making the kids think it's a huge deal."

"He's good with them," she said.

"He's also not wearing a wedding ring," Amy teased. "And neither are you."

Hannah let out a sigh. The words, "I have a serious boyfriend and I don't notice other men," were on her lips, but something stopped her from saying them. Something like...the fact that Hannah MacPherson didn't lie.

Because she did notice Brandon Fletcher. Which basically made her human and female. Who could miss that smile made distinct by a crooked scar or those eyes the color of a Carolina winter sky or that long hair that fluttered in the wind like golden brown silk?

*Yeesh. Hannah Jean MacPherson. Get a grip.*

She managed to, but honestly, had she ever enjoyed watching a tree being chopped down quite this much?

"Dɪᴅ you get enough hot chocolate, Miss MacPherson?" Brandon Fletcher dropped into the chair across the café table and slayed Hannah with a sweet, semi-scarred smile. "It is *Miss*, right?"

Hannah looked up and managed to not react. She'd done such a terrific job of avoiding close contact with him through the rest of the tree cutting, the Q-and-A session, the short video and a long, noisy lunch. Now, the adults were in the café, looking out the windows at the kids who were running off their pizza and hot chocolate.

But here he was, unavoidably close.

"I did, and thank you. Oh, it's Ms. Just...*Ms*, Mr. Fletcher."

"It's just Fletch, or Brandon. Whichever you prefer."

She preferred not to be this close and tempted to flirt with him, but he seemed settled in and interested in talking.

"So, how'd I do?" he asked. "Can I replace Harry the Ham for the annual kids' tours?"

She smiled. "Your father is irreplaceable, but you'll do."

"He has to be replaceable," Brandon said with a quick smile. "Because he's retiring after this Christmas and you, *Ms.* MacPherson, are looking at the third generation of Fletcher to run the joint."

She inched back, surprised. "I didn't know Harry was retiring."

"They're moving to Florida because my sister is having Baby Number Three, and the first two are small and wild. April needs help and the cavalry is on the way to Tampa and I'm taking over the family business."

"Well, congratulations. Is that something you're happy about?"

He tipped his head, then shifted his gaze out the window, looking at the farm and rolling hills. "It's a big change, but one I've known my whole life I'd make."

"What were you doing before?" she asked.

"Hockey," he said.

She blinked at him, inching back, something way in the recesses of her brain coming back to her.

"Oh, oh!" She snapped her fingers as she remembered some family history she'd completely forgotten, and a vague memory of hearing one of Keith's many hockey games on TV. "You're that Fletch. I *have* heard of you! You played in the NHL."

"Yep, that's me." He gave a toothy grin. "And before you ask, these pearlies are all mine." He touched the jagged scar. "Puck hit me here once and gave me a ton of stitches, but I'm proud to say I never lost a tooth. Loosened a few, but not gone."

"I was wondering why I'd never met Harry Fletcher's son all these years."

"Oh, we've met," he said. "You're Sonny MacPherson's daughter, aren't you?"

"Yes...I'm sorry, I don't remember..."

"One year I was injured and came home for Christmas—it's a holiday I frequently missed due to games—and you came and got a tree."

"You remember that?" she asked, a little stunned.

"Yup. You were—um—with a guy, but I did notice how cute you are." He winked again.

She felt a flush deepen her cheeks. "How long were you in the NHL?" she asked, digging for a natural question that couldn't be construed as flirting back.

"I went to a sports training high school up in Vermont, then played in some smaller semi-pro leagues, then ended up playing for a few teams, finishing my career with the Pittsburgh Penguins."

"Wow. I've never met a professional athlete," she said, leaning back. "If the kids knew that? They'd go crazy."

He waved off the comment. "Well, I already bribed Frick and Frack with hockey pucks if they fell in line."

"Oh!" She let out a soft hoot. "Is that how you got Nick and Dan to behave? Well done, you."

"I don't know," he teased. "Your 'one-two-three-eyes-on-me' trick is pretty effective."

She laughed, a little flustered that he paid that much attention to her.

"Like I said, I'm trained," she said. "And I'm happy to hear that the Christmas tree farm is staying in your family. Live trees from this place is a big tradition for people around here and, really, all through Asheville."

He nodded, a glimmer of pride making his eyes even bluer. "My grandfather planted the first tree on the side of this mountain in the late 1950s. My dad has run the business since I was a kid. So now, these one hundred acres are my legacy."

One hundred? She had no idea it was that big. "It's

an important business," she said. "But I'm still surprised..."

"That I'd walk off the ice to be a tree farmer?" he chuckled as if he'd heard the comment many times before. "I always knew I was coming back, it was just a matter of when." He leaned forward, his gaze so direct it curled her toes in her boots. "So, Hannah. I hope you don't forget meeting me this time."

As if she could. Unable to form a response, she searched his face, lost for a minute in the warmth of his gaze and the angles of his cheek and that curved scar.

And only then did she remember...Keith.

*Holy moly—this is wrong.*

She shouldn't be staring at this guy, practically drooling in her hot chocolate. She should push away from the table, check on the kids, stop tempting fate.

Just then, the same young man who'd brought him the chainsaw saved her when he hustled up to the table.

"Snow tubes are ready, Fletch," he said. "I'll handle getting the kids out at the bottom if you can put them into the tubes. They're little, so two at a time."

"Let's do it," he replied, standing up and giving Hannah a look. "I could probably use a little of your teacherly discipline and rules at the top of the slope."

She opened her mouth to say no, they'd be fine, but then she closed it again. Watching the children was her job. She'd just have to control herself from watching *him*.

"I'm happy to help," she told him.

They rounded up the kids and marched them around a huge lot of trees and brought them to the top of an embankment. There, a few dozen oversized inner tubes were piled up at the top of a wide trench dug into a snow-covered hill.

After giving the kids instructions that they probably didn't need, Hannah and Brandon faced each other at the top of the hill, ready to help place each team in a tube.

"One in front, holding the handles," he said as he guided a little boy into the tube. "Another in back, arms around his waist."

With the team loaded up, Brandon held the inner tube in place.

"Have you been naughty or nice?" he asked the two boys.

"Nice!" they both answered.

"Then have a nice ride!" He gave them a solid shove and got a noisy scream in response as the tube went flying side to side and down the hill, making Hannah laugh.

"Next!" she called to Layla and Corinne, two little besties who never parted.

"Climb up," Brandon said, helping Corinne into the front and giving the giggling girls the instructions. "Now, what's your favorite Christmas song?"

"'Jingle Bells'!" Layla called out.

"Jingle bells, Santa smells, now you're on your way!" he sang, then pushed the tube for a wild, loud ride.

Riley and her mother, Amy, were next.

"Can I go with my mommy?" Riley asked him shyly.

He grinned at her mother. "You're in the back, Mom, and hang on."

When they sat in place, Amy turned to Hannah and

mouthed, "You gonna ride...or scream naked down the mountain?" she teased, then tipped her head toward Brandon. "I know which one I'd do."

Laughing, Hannah gave her a shove without any fun Christmas questions and got a quizzical look from Brandon.

"Secret stuff," she replied, making him chuckle.

The hilarity and screaming, the silly Christmas puns, and a barrage of jokes from Brandon continued until the very last two kids—Dan and Nick, naturally—went sailing down the track to the bottom.

"All right, Ms. MacPherson," he said, reaching around for one more inner tube. "It's our turn."

"Us?" She practically choked the word. "Oh, no, I'm not. I can't...I don't want to."

He leaned in, close enough that she could count every unfairly long lash around his eyes. "Are you scared, Hannah?" he whispered.

She couldn't breathe. "Petrified," she admitted on a whisper.

"Come on, just hold the handles...and I'll hold you." He reached for her hands and easily guided her onto the waiting inner tube, her heart pounding so hard she could barely hear what he said. Except the "I'll hold you" part.

That she heard loud and clear.

"I'm really not a fan of—"

"In you go!" And then her bottom was in the tube and strong, jean-clad legs were lined up next to hers and his arms were around her waist.

He gave a squeeze. "One, two, three...eyes on me."

She looked up and over her shoulder, locking on his mesmerizing gaze, so lost in the momentary connection that she barely felt the inner tube tip and twist and twirl down the trench. The wind whipped her hair, and his, singing in her ears.

For the space of four or five heartbeats, she couldn't think about anyone or anything but this moment and this man.

They hit the bottom with a thud and she scrambled onto the snow, pushing to get to her feet and, hopefully, hiding how much her whole body was trembling.

"Okay, kids, time to line up and get back on the bus!" she called out, waving her hands to get order but also to shake off the nerves that gripped her whole body.

Somehow, she managed to end the field trip, sit on the bus, and get them back to school. And the minute she was alone, she called Keith and left a message to say she wanted to plan a nice date, just the two of them, because...well, just because.

But no matter how hard she tried, she couldn't forget what Brandon's arms felt like when he took her on that ride. And she had to forget. She had to.

# Chapter Seven

## *Noelle*

WHEN NOELLE PULLED up to the ranch house, she took a moment in the driveway to drink in the place she now called home. Draped with Christmas lights, dusted in snow, and silhouetted against the sunset on the mountains, she certainly couldn't think of a prettier place to live.

Knowing that the man she loved and the step-daughter who'd stolen her heart were inside waiting for her just made it all better.

She climbed out and grabbed her bag—an inexpensive one she'd taken to carrying after someone in the gallery had a made a comment about her New York designer purse.

Then she let out a big enough sigh that she could see her breath in the chilly mountain air.

The fact was, she'd come a long way since her New York days, since she had Sotheby's on her business card, Louis Vuitton on her shoulder, and limos as her mode of transport. And it had been such a good journey.

Until a year or so ago, she'd come home to an empty

Manhattan high-rise, pour a glass of wine, and think about the success of her day as an art dealer.

Some might say how the mighty had fallen...or that she didn't belong here.

And they'd be wrong, since she'd never been more at home.

As she opened the front door, she looked past the entryway to a den lit by a TV and the golden glow of a Christmas tree that Cassie had insisted they put up and decorate the day after Thanksgiving. She heard a little girl's giggle over the TV and smelled the delicious aroma of Jace's spectacular red sauce simmering on the stove.

The whole moment just infused happiness in her heart.

"Oh, Daddy! Miss Noelle's here!"

Miss Noelle, not Mommy. Okay, *that* didn't infuse her with happiness, but the sound of Cassie's voice always did.

The little girl came darting out, arms extended, followed by Jace wearing jeans, a dark T-shirt, and a heart-melting smile.

"I'm sorry I'm late," she said, taking the hug Cassie offered first. "Christmas traffic in town is crazy."

"It's fine." Jace's hug was strong, warm, and accompanied by a kiss. "We're watching *Elf.*"

"Without me?" Noelle laughed. "Let me change and I'll be right with you."

Cassie danced around, then looked up at Jace as Noelle took off for their room on the other side of the house.

"Can I ask her now?" she asked in a whisper loud enough to be heard down the hall.

"Give her a chance to breathe, Cass. I told you—talk to her over dinner."

Noelle stepped into the main bedroom as a frown pulled. Ask her...about calling Noelle Mommy?

She squeezed her eyes shut, hoping that's what their little girl wanted.

But Cassie didn't ask anything, lost in the hilarious holiday film that made them laugh and wipe happy tears. When it was over, they headed into the kitchen, where the red sauce was ready. Noelle made a salad while Jace boiled the pasta, and Cassie flitted around the room repeating her favorite jokes from the movie.

Whatever she wanted to ask, it was either forgotten or she was being uncharacteristically patient.

Noelle was neither. All she wanted to do was scoop that child into the air and say, "Yes! Please call me Mommy!" But that didn't happen.

They sat at the table together, held hands, and closed their eyes as Jace led them in a prayer before they ate. The words were starting to hit Noelle's heart, though she still didn't have the rock-solid faith that quietly guided her husband. She was closer every day, that was for sure.

"Hand me your plate, Cass," Noelle said. "I'll fill it up for you with extra sauce, just how you like it."

Cassie did, but her gaze was on Jace, a question in her eyes. "Now, Daddy?" she whispered. "Can I ask now?"

Noelle looked from one to the other, surprised by the quiver of joy the whole conversation gave her. "You can ask me anything, Cass, and the answer is probably going to be yes."

"Really?" She practically climbed out of her seat. "Okay, then."

"At least let Noelle have a bite before you descend," Jace muttered.

Cassie frowned. "Descend? I don't know what that means."

"It means..." He threw a look at Noelle. "She can be relentless, so brace yourself."

Setting down her fork, Noelle leaned back, curiosity winning over dinner, somehow knowing this couldn't be the way he'd act if Cassie wanted to call her Mommy. For one thing, Jace knew what it meant to her. For another... this was just weird.

"I'm braced. What is it, Cass?"

Cassie slurped up a long spaghetti strand and gave a red sauce-enhanced grin. "It's about the tree lighting."

"The...wow." The thud of disappointment surprised her. "Didn't see that coming."

Cassie practically crawled out of her chair. "I have *ideas!*" She dragged out the word, accompanied by a gesture so sweeping she nearly knocked over her water. Jace easily snagged the wobbling glass before it fell.

"What are your ideas, Cass?" she asked.

"Well, you might want me on your committee," she said with far too much seriousness for an eight-year-old.

"I would but..." Noelle leaned in to whisper, "They aren't exactly an adventurous or forward-thinking group."

"Ahem—*Edna*—ahem," Jace fake coughed.

"Ahem, no kidding," Noelle agreed. "I can't even change the lights."

"But my ideas are wonderful!" Cassie exclaimed, on her knees now, visibly aching to hold their attention.

"Talk to me, baby," Noelle said, putting a gentle hand on her arm to guide her safely to a seat. "I promise you *I* am adventurous and forward thinking."

"Okay," she said, settling in to be serious. "First, the entertainment." She put her hand on her chest with a noisy thud. "Me."

"You?"

"You saw me last year at the church play," she replied, eyes wide. "Everyone said, 'My, that kid has a set of pipes.'"

Noelle almost choked on her next bite, but somehow managed to swallow. "You did sing like an angel."

"Which I was not," she reminded both of them. "I was an ugly sheep."

"Because you gave the angel part to another little girl," Jace said, smiling at the memory. "I was so proud of you, Cass."

She waved off the dad pride with a casual flick of her wrist.

"But this year, I *do* want to be an angel, or at least the soloist. And maybe I can be lifted to the top of the tree with that same contraption they used at the play. Then I could float over everyone and sing!"

Her whole face lit with the idea and it took everything Noelle had not to burst out laughing or throw both arms around her.

"*Oookay*," she said instead. "Well, I don't know about a contraption—there has to be insurance liabilities for that—but there is a small riser for speakers and the officiant of the lighting ceremony, which, at the moment, is me. So, thank you for your ideas, Cass. The committee will take them under consideration."

"That's not all," Cassie announced excitedly. "How about...an animal parade? And not just any animals, but the ones from here and Daddy's best patients—the healthy ones, of course—and...and...and..."

They both stared at her, mesmerized and waiting.

"They are dressed as elves!" she announced, dead serious and so proud of her idea, she was bursting.

"Oh. Elves?" Noelle looked at Jace, who could barely hide his mirth.

"Elves," he confirmed. "Goats, sheep, and the occasional farm dog all decked out as elves."

"Right?" Cassie exclaimed, their amusement lost on her. "What's Christmas without an elf? Animal elves? How super-duper would that be?"

"So...super-duper," Noelle agreed. "Like you, Cass."

Again, she swiped away the love, far too invested to give up. "And guess what else?" she asked. "Just guess."

"I...can't," Noelle admitted. "You tell me."

She stood now, next to Noelle. "Wish cards!"

"Wish..."

"Everyone gets a card and writes down their Christmas wish," she said. "Then they put them on the tree!"

"Does someone...make the wishes come true?"

Noelle asked, the question probably far too pragmatic for this child.

"Someone could make them come true," Cassie replied, clearly not having thought that one all the way through. "Or not. Not every wish is granted, you know."

"Prayers," Jace corrected. "Not wishes."

"But wouldn't it be fun?" Cassie pressed.

The truth was, she didn't actually hate these ideas—except the flying contraption. Edna, however, would *weep* at the animal elves, unsanctioned by Gil the Ghost.

"All of those ideas are fun," Noelle said, glancing at Jace, who was obviously loving this exchange. "I just have to tell you that the whole thing about the tree lighting is... tradition. Everything has to be the same every year or—"

"Well, that's a dumb tradition," Cassie said, giving perfect childlike clarity to exactly what Noelle thought.

"Cassie," Jace reprimanded softly. "We don't say things are dumb and stupid. You know that."

"But can't traditions get better every year?" Cassie asked.

"You, child, are too brilliant and mature for your own good," Noelle observed. "But we do have to respect them and the people who make the traditions happen. However, if you want to have an elf parade right here at the ranch—"

"Glow sticks!" she exclaimed, talking right over Noelle.

"Glow sticks?"

"You know, the long glowy necklaces that you wear and wave and they come in all different colors."

Jace made a face, shaking his head. "That stuff inside them is suspect, if you ask me."

"But just think about it," Cassie said, still bright with her own enthusiasm. "Everyone waves sticks at the same time, maybe before the tree is really lit, and, you know... while I'm singing in the air."

Noelle let out a sigh and gave her a big smile. "I love all your ideas, Cass."

"Can we do them?" she begged. "Any of them? Since you're the boss of the whole thing?"

"I'm not really," she said. "I don't make the final decisions, sadly. But I promise you, I will suggest some of these things to the committee."

Cassie finally settled down, satisfied with her stellar pitch.

"I do like the wish cards," Noelle added. "I'll run them by the group."

"Well, I think I should sing," Cassie said as she rolled up a long strand of spaghetti. "Since my mom is running the whole thing."

Her...mom? Noelle waited for more, but Cassie was downright breathless after her heartfelt presentation.

Later, as they cleaned up, Cassie slipped out to finish her final chores with the animals.

"Did you really love those ideas?" Jace asked when they were alone.

"I really love that child," she replied, pressing next to him at the sink. "She's the most extraordinary little thing."

He chuckled, looking out the kitchen window toward

the light by the barn. "She is that. And she won't be crushed if nothing happens, but she had to plant the seed."

"Who knows?" Noelle said on a shrug. "Edna might like something. And I need an excuse to go see that woman and smooth things over with her. Cassie deserves something for her creative thinking. Starting with a bath," she added as she caught a glimpse of Cassie hugging her favorite goat, Sprinkles.

But Jace was looking at his phone, his broad shoulders dropping. "Tom Bertram's brand-new mare is struggling," he said. "She has a respiratory illness and isn't responding to the meds. I have to get over there and monitor Goldie, maybe give her a stronger shot. I'm sorry."

"Sorry you're going to drop everything and save a horse?" She looked up at him, knowing he had to see the love in her eyes because she felt it so strongly in her heart. "Get over there, Dr. Fleming, and do your large animal vet thing. Just don't bring Goldie back dressed as an elf."

He laughed and kissed her lightly. "What are you going to do while I'm gone?"

"Be a mom," she said, unable to hide the smile. "I will make sure our daughter is bathed, brushed, and read a wonderful book before she goes to sleep."

With a soft grunt, he pulled her closer. "What did I do to deserve you?"

"Oh, please. I could ask the same thing." She got on her toes and gave him the kiss she could see that he wanted more than his next breath.

"You are a wonderful mother, Noelle."

She tried not to let her disappointment show, but she didn't hide anything from this man.

"I wish she'd call me Mommy," she admitted. "And I also wish..." She touched her stomach and smiled. "Guess I should be filling out some wish cards of my own."

"Prayers," he corrected in the same kind tone he used with Cassie. "We say prayers and sometimes they are answered the way we want, and sometimes they're answered the way God wants."

She smiled. "Well, Cassie didn't pray for her ideas. She asked me because she thinks I'm in control."

"And are you?'"

She laughed and tapped his chin. "I try."

WHEN BATH TIME ENDED, and Cassie's long wet hair was brushed, dried, and braided, the two of them propped on the bed for the nightly reading of *The Very Hungry Goat*.

"Don't you ever get tired of this one?" Noelle asked as she flipped open a book she now knew by heart. "And aren't you outgrowing it?"

Looking up at Noelle, Cassie's face grew serious. "I read it every night. It's tradition."

That made her laugh. "I thought you said some traditions should change."

She tapped the book. "Not this one. But I would like to sing at that tree lighting. I dream about it."

Noelle's heart folded. "I will work on that, Cass. I promise."

"We can make my singing every year a new tradition."

"I love that idea. Did you know there's a song about tradition? It's from a famous play called *Fiddler on the Roof*." She sat straighter and cleared her throat before belting out, "Tradition!" and raising a hand like the lead on stage.

Cassie giggled and imitated her. "Tradition!" Somehow, she hit the note and held it longer than Noelle.

"You are a really great singer, Cass."

"I know," she said with that guileless lack of humility that children had. As if she suddenly realized it wasn't right to be prideful, she pointed to Noelle. "And you are a really great..."

Noelle held her breath for a second but when Cassie didn't finish, she whispered, "Art gallery owner?"

"Yeah, that." But Cassie's eyes told her everything and she knew that the little girl wanted to say, "Mom," but either couldn't or wouldn't. She still wasn't sure which.

Cassie knew Noelle's parents had died when she was a teenager, but it wasn't a subject they'd discussed at length. She and Jace both felt it was too much for her to handle at her age, especially having lost her own mother. They didn't want her to live in some kind of fear that "mothers die," and she was just imaginative enough to go there.

"Well, I think this goat is still hungry. Why don't you read it to me?" Noelle asked, leaning back and closing her eyes as Cassie started to recite as much as read.

As she listened, Noelle thought...some mothers *do* die. Hers did. Cassie's did. And wanting this little girl to use some arbitrary three-letter word didn't change that. She wasn't kidding when she said all that mattered was their love.

Somehow, she would prove that to Cassie and to herself.

She knew exactly where to start...with a slight change in "tradition."

If only Edna Covington would let her.

# Chapter Eight

## *Angie*

HE REALLY WANTED to take this exhibit down? Angie studied the restoration of a servants' quarters that she— and Marjorie—had worked so hard to build last year. Her connection to every item on every shelf, the soft chenille bedspread, even that well-loved and much-read King James Bible that rested on the nightstand, was so strong, she could feel it in her gut.

This was the very room where her great-grandparents lived together until they built the house she and Brooke now called home. She could practically feel their spirits, imagine them discussing some Vanderbilt family gossip, or snuggling in for a good night's sleep after a hard day's work as a parlor maid and a footman.

Why would Elliott Quinn undo this display?

But the hall leading here was silent, without any tourists, even during this busy season. Granted, these fourth-floor exhibits weren't decked out like the rest of the Biltmore for Christmas. Plus, this section of the tour was optional for a higher entrance fee, so many people skipped so they could spend more time on the far more spectacular parts of the estate.

But...*no one* came up here? She wasn't aware of that, to be honest.

If it didn't generate interest or additional revenue, she kind of understood ditching it. Kind of. That way, some obscure artists might have an exhibit here and visitors would likely pay the extra fee.

On a sigh, she pulled out her tablet to start an inventory of every piece in the room so she could recommend an exhibit-dismantling schedule and figure out where in the vast estate they would store the artifacts.

That was her job, like it or not. And she'd better do it well because—

A text flashed in the corner of her iPad.

**Marjorie**: *How's it going?*

Only training kept Angie from dropping onto the bed with a noisy sigh at the sight of her friend's name. She stared at the text and considered how to answer, then simply pulled out her phone and tapped Marjorie's cell number.

"Well, hey there," the other woman answered with a smile in her voice. "Something tells me that if you're calling in response to my text, it's not going well."

Sliding her tablet in her bag and settling the phone against her ear, Angie walked down the dim hallway toward a window with a wooden bench at the end. She didn't want one of the few tourists who visited this exhibit to have the experience wrecked by the discovery of a Biltmore staffer chatting on a cell phone, killing the historic vibe completely.

"It's going," she said. "But, sadly, I'm up on the fourth floor starting the process of undoing all we did. The additional servants' quarters displays are coming down."

Marjorie groaned. "I feared that might happen. It's in line with what I've heard about him."

*Him* being Elliott Quinn, Angie imagined. "What have you heard?"

For a moment, Marjorie was quiet, probably deciding how to navigate the fine line of inappropriate gossip with a former employee and giving up helpful information to a friend.

"He's an art guy," she said carefully.

"I got that," Angie said. "I'm not sure he really grasps the essence of the Biltmore."

Again, Marjorie was quiet, then she said, "No one is sure of that."

"Really?" Angie sat up. "Then why did they hire him?"

"He's a catch in the museum world, with excellent credentials," the other woman said. "Apparently—and you didn't hear this from me—there were two strong candidates and he won out, but not without a little contention. So, I guess that means he wants to make his mark, one way or the other."

"By taking down my exhibit," she said glumly.

"Well, it's been there for year," Marjorie reminded her. "And I'm sure you can find some uses for the pieces we had and you donated, including that Bible."

Angie smiled that Marjorie remembered the details and still cared. "How's it going at the Getty?"

"It's ...interesting," she said, sounding far less enthusiastic than Angie expected.

"How so?"

"I wasn't prepared for the enormous corporate machine I need to navigate or the number of layers just to get something done. I admit to being a bit homesick for the charm of the Biltmore."

"Come back!" Angie exclaimed.

"Don't tempt me. But, tell me what's the issue with your new boss,"

"We got off to a bad start," Angie admitted. "Turns out he's the man whose headlight I took out a week or so ago."

Marjorie gasped. "Oh, dear. That's unfortunate."

"And he has to realize that I'm only here because you liked me and my long-dead relatives worked here. I'm about as relevant to the Biltmore as a parlor maid." She cringed in the direction of Angelica Benson's old room. "Sorry, Great-grannie."

"Stop it," Marjorie chided on a laugh. "Any manager worth his weight recognizes that sometimes enthusiasm and grit beat out fancy degrees."

"Not sure he's there with me yet. The only thing he's asked me to do is to undo what I did last year. Other than that, he hasn't given me a single new assignment."

"Then get one," Marjorie said, with the firm voice of a mentor. "Volunteer, get in his face, find an opportunity for something and ask him to give you the responsibility."

Angie considered that advice, nodding. "I guess I could."

"And if you're smart, you'll help him keep the job, because I honestly think he's on a bit of probation, and one major screwup and he's gone. But, again, you didn't hear that from me."

"Of course not." Marjorie was not a gossip and had always done a great job of keeping a wall between the curators of the estate and the more distant corporate executives. Because of that, Angie knew very little about those people, the departments they ran, or how the business was structured. "But...why is he on shaky ground?"

"Oh, you know, corporate warlords, vying for power."

"But the Biltmore Company is family owned, still run by the Vanderbilts."

"It is," Marjorie agreed. "But remember, it's still a conglomerate of brands. Yes, the estate is the largest and most well-known, but there are numerous businesses under the Biltmore umbrella—hospitality, wine, even home goods. All those little fiefdoms are always jockeying for budget, power, and attention."

Was Elliott Quinn caught in the middle of that? "So what should I, a lowly associate staff curator, do?"

Marjorie chuckled. "You're not lowly. But my advice would be to find out his pet project and get on it and while you're at it? Let him in on the best-kept secret in the art world."

"That the Biltmore Estate is heaven on earth?"

"Exactly," Marjorie agreed. "If anyone can make him fall in love, it's you."

"Fall in love?" Angie choked. "I mean, he's good-look-ing, but—"

"With the Biltmore!" Marjorie hooted a soft laugh. "Anything else is on your own time, Angie."

She chuckled as she noticed a small group of tourists entering the hallway. "I better go," Angie said.

"Okay. Hang in there. Let me know how it goes."

After they said goodbye, Angie passed the exhibit, glancing in at the group milling about her great-grandparents' room.

"Yeah, this is boring," one woman said to another.

"I want to go back to the library and look at those insane trees."

"And the tapestries," a third woman added.

Angie hurried down the stairs, feeling her heart drop with each step. Of course, Elliott was right, and the exhibit needed to go, but could she suggest something in its place? And then, could she make whatever it was his pet project and then get involved?

She was still wondering when she got back to the long hall that led to her department.

"Oh, there you are," Diana called as Angie passed her desk. "Just in time."

"For what?" Angie asked.

"I sent you an email that Mr. Quinn just called an emergency meeting of curators in the conference room. It starts in ten minutes."

Emergency meeting...to fire people? She hoped not. But at least this time she wouldn't be late. And the minute he hinted at a pet project, she'd be the first to volunteer her time. Hopefully, Marjorie was right about that.

Elliott Quinn was beaming as the other staff curators—four in all, counting Angie—came into the conference room at the appointed time. Angie was by far the lowest in seniority and experience among the group. None of these other people would be considered for cutting, she decided.

Elliott wouldn't look quite so happy if he'd brought them in here to announce mass layoffs and he certainly wouldn't fire her in front of her colleagues.

So she relaxed, opened a notebook, and made small talk with a co-worker until their fearless leader cleared his throat and opened the meeting.

"I have four words, my friends," he said with an air of excitement that couldn't be ignored. "And you'll never guess what they are."

"Take this Friday off?" a woman named Pamela joked when he waited a beat.

He didn't seem thrilled with that answer.

"We got Eva Jospin," Jason chimed in.

"Even better, but no." Elliott glanced at Angie, no doubt expecting a guess.

"Um...brand-new latte machine?"

He gave a smile and shook his head. "Forget it, because in a million years, none of you will guess. But you will be happy." Still standing, he pressed his hands on the table top, leaning in an inch. "*The Adoration of the Magi,*" he said, keeping his voice low, as if saying the words too loud would be more than they could handle.

And it was, based on her colleagues' response.

"Da Vinci?"

"Are you kidding me?"

"That's unbelievable!"

"No way!"

Again, he looked at Angie, who hadn't reacted because she was mentally digging through her minimal knowledge of...da Vinci? What had he called it—*The Gift of the Magi*? No, no, that was a short story she'd read in high school. Panic nearly broke her into a cold sweat.

"Amazing," she managed, sounding far calmer than the rest.

"You don't even believe me," he countered, with a half-twinkle in his eyes.

"Well, it *is* kind of unbelievable," she said.

Almost as unbelievable as sitting in this room with a bunch of art historians—supposedly one of them—and having no idea what this piece of art actually was.

"I know," he conceded. "But here's the deal—I arranged to get it for the MFA before I left, as part of their Christmas event. But I just got a call that there was a glitch in the paperwork and it's going there *after* Christmas. So that leaves the *Adoration* with no home for three weeks this month—until now. It's coming here."

She joined in the celebration and high-fives, certain

she'd identified his pet project but not sure how to get involved as Marjorie had suggested.

"So, ladies and gents," Elliott continued when their excitement died down, "we have our work cut out for us. I'm going to need someone to draft an immediate press release and get on the phone with every local media outlet to drum up excitement. Pamela?"

"On it," she said.

"And Jason, would you be my liaison with the Uffizi in Italy? They have mountains of customs forms and admin that needs to be handled—correctly, this time—to add us to the list of guest museums. And, of course, you can manage all the Biltmore issues, communicating with PR and the tour staff. We'll need you to write up an exhaustive description of the work, including its history, and get that on the audio tour. Oh, and programs."

"Done and done and done," Jason said, gobbling up all the good assignments, as he so often did. "I'm a huge fan of the Uffizi myself."

Of course he was, since he was the original teacher's pet.

"Louisa?" Elliott looked at the other woman. "We'll need to prepare a space for—"

She held up a hand. "Mr. Quinn, my vacation starts Wednesday and I'm out until next year."

"Oh." He drew back, obviously not expecting—or liking—that. "Then we—"

"I'll handle it," Angie said before he could finish. "I know exactly how to set up a temporary exhibit."

"But this is *The Adoration of the Magi*," he said, as if she didn't quite grasp what he was talking about.

Okay, she didn't. Was it a sculpture? Painting? Tapestry? A Nativity scene from Leonardo da Vinci's front yard? Why didn't she know this?

Her whole body tensed with a flash of anger, entirely aimed at herself. She had to fake it and if she got caught... she might as well pack her bags and print her resume.

"We can make a special area in the tapestry room," she said with remarkable calm for a woman who literally had no idea what she was talking about.

He looked at her for a long moment, then nodded. "That is perfect," he finally said. "The painting can go directly in front of the center tapestry, which will be great for traffic and viewing, plus a place of honor. Absolutely perfect."

She literally had to keep herself from collapsing with relief.

"But it will take some feats of logistics—"

"Not a problem," she interjected quickly. "Feats of logistics are my specialty."

"Good. Then we're set." He lifted his hand to dismiss them all. "Time is of the essence, so, please, everyone should make this project your highest priority and plan on daily updates and a very active and busy workflow. I realize this is the holidays, but having a da Vinci in-house will put this place on the map."

It wasn't the first time he'd used the expression, which irked, because not only was the Biltmore Estate on

the map, it was the crown jewel of Asheville. But not to
Mr. Boston.

The others left on a cloud of genuine excitement,
clearly thrilled about the new arrival. Angie couldn't wait
to book it to her office and search *The Adoration of the
Magi*, so she could—

"Angel?"

She turned, still not accustomed to anyone using her
given name—or how much she liked it. "Yes?"

"Can I see you in my office for a moment?" he asked.

Oh, no. That couldn't be good.

"Of course," she said, tempted to ask what it was
about. But she resisted the urge and gave him a minute to
gather his pen and paper, round the table, and hold the
door open for her.

As she passed by him, she stole a look into his eyes,
trying to determine if she was headed to the chopping
block, but all she got was a whiff of musky cologne and
that twinkle again.

He wasn't firing her, was he? Or asking for that
drink? Maybe it was a test to see how much she really
knew about *The Adoration of the Magi*.

Whatever it was, she followed him into the only
spacious, windowed office in the department. There, she
slipped into the guest chair while he stayed outside,
talking quietly to Diana at her desk.

Angie sat across from a sizeable mahogany desk,
marveling that the office had such a different feel than
when Marjorie worked there.

For one thing, he'd replaced Marjorie's light oak parsons table with a heavy mahogany and very manly desk.

The family woman kept pictures of her grandchildren in one corner, a gold antique clock in another, and more than a few files open and spread across the surface.

Elliott had no personal pictures, but a very expensive pen holder and a glass paperweight with the skyline of a city, which she presumed was Boston. No files were open, though two folders were squared on one side. The only personal item in the whole office was a baseball in an acrylic box, of all things, sitting on the windowsill.

It seemed so odd for such an art lover that she couldn't help walking over to it, peering at the blue ink on top. Autographed? She picked up the box and gasped as she made out the signature.

"Drop it and you can pack up and leave," Elliott said, enough humor in his voice that she instantly knew he was kidding. Kind of.

"Yaz?" she asked, holding the box with reverence. "You have a baseball autographed by Carl Yastrzemski?"

"I do, and he gave it to me himself just last year after an event at the MFA. You a fan?"

"Not really, but my dad was. He loved baseball—like crazy loved—and he had a few favorite players. Yaz was one." She set it down gently and went back to her seat.

"Was he a Red Sox fan?" Elliott asked.

"Just all baseball," she said, glancing at the paperweight. "Are you homesick for Boston?"

His eyes flickered a bit, probably at the personal nature of the question, or maybe because she'd hit a target.

"I'm getting used to it here," he said.

"Still living in a hotel?"

"Well, my car's in the body shop..." He lifted a brow. "And I hate that rental, so I haven't driven around to look for a home. Haven't driven anywhere at all, other than town and here."

She smiled. "But Keith took you right away at his body shop?"

"He did," he acknowledged. "And gave me a discount, so thank you for being friend or family. Which is it?"

"Kind of both, but I promise my insurance will cover whatever it costs." She shifted in her seat, regarding him. "Is that why"—she gestured vaguely—"I've been called to the principal's office?"

He laughed. "No, not at all. I just..." He let out a sigh and opened one of the files on the desk. "I've looked at your personnel information and I was just wondering..."

"How the heck I got this job," she finished for him, anxious to have the truth out and quit worrying about it.

He looked surprised, then eased into a smile. "I admit, it crossed my mind that your background is different from some of the other curators." He tapped a page in the file. "But then Marjorie spoke so highly of you," he said as he fluttered a piece of paper, making her wonder what was on it. "I really don't see relevant experience, so I wondered if you could enlighten me. So I can put you on the right projects," he added.

She nodded, feeling another adrenaline rush of relief at not being fired.

"My degree is in communications," she started, having practiced this conversation a few times in front of the mirror. "But I have taken some art history classes."

Not enough to know what *The Adoration of the Magi* was, she added silently.

"I also bring a skill set that allows me to..." Her voice faded out as she looked at him, then smiled, dropping back in the chair in surrender.

No. She wasn't going to try to be something she wasn't. She'd be honest and let the ol' chips fall where they may.

"I've basically been a stay-at-home mom for sixteen years," she admitted. "I stumbled into this place by accident after discovering a familial connection."

"The parlor maid and the footman were your great-grandparents."

"Yes. And that got me in the door last Christmas. Marjorie was in the middle of planning that fourth-floor exhibit—the one you hate, and for good reason, I suppose—and so short-staffed that she let me volunteer. And then..."

"You stayed."

"Well, it was a little more complicated than that," she said. "I discovered my husband was cheating on me, my teenage daughter followed me here while I was on vacation, and then I found out our family cabin was going to be taken away, so I had to fight for it and..." She caught her breath and laughed. "Yeah, Marjorie really liked me and offered me a job."

"Well, that's quite a..."

"Non-resume," she supplied.

"Story," he finished.

"Except it's true and I hope my lack of credentials doesn't go against me."

"On the contrary," he said slowly. "I have, uh, also been through a divorce, so if nothing else, I can empathize."

She nodded. "Sorry."

He let out a breath and turned the paperweight. "Also...infidelity. Hers, not mine."

"Ouch," she whispered. "It's awful."

"It sure is," he agreed, then looked up. "And I felt I had to leave Boston, which is a place I love very much."

"And come to a small town in the mountains that you don't love at all," she surmised.

"Is it that obvious?"

She lifted a shoulder, silent.

He winced. "I'm sorry. I want to like the place, but I don't know where to begin."

"Well, begin by looking around the Biltmore Estate," she said without hesitating. "This place is heaven on earth. The views will steal your soul and just wait until spring and summer. And, oh, my gosh, the autumn leaves. You've never seen anything like it."

He looked skeptical.

"Okay, okay, I guess New England can hold its own in the fall, but this place is magical."

He inched forward. "Maybe you could..."

She held her breath, not sure what he was about to ask her.

"Help me see the beauty of it all," he finished.

"I'd love to," she replied. "As soon as we finish getting ready for the uh...*Gift of the Magi.*"

He laughed, and she nearly cringed at her error.

"It's a gift, all right," he said, letting her off the hook, intentionally or not. "And I will personally help with the placement and preparation, which you so enthusiastically volunteered for."

"Because I might not have an advanced degree in art history, but I know every worker on staff, how to get the tapestries safely moved and stored if we have to, and how to set up a temporary exhibit, which has an enormous amount of moving parts. The whole thing takes a different skill set, and I happen to have it, I promise."

"You have that and much more, Angel," he said with a warm look. "I look forward to working with you on this."

She stood slowly, feeling that that was the end of the meeting. "Same, Mr. Quinn."

"Call me Elliott, please. Since I, uh, can't seem to call you what everyone else does."

She smiled. "It's fine. I, um, I kinda like it."

She went back to her office with a bounce in her step, diving right onto her computer to research Leonardo da Vinci's *The Adoration of the Magi.*

And then she stared at the single ugliest mess of a mustard-yellow blotchy painting she'd ever seen.

*Seriously, Leo? You couldn't do better?*

Chuckling, she texted Marjorie and thanked her for the advice. *Today*, she told her friend, *was a win.*

Then she went back to the painting and tried to find something she liked about it.

# Chapter Nine

## Hannah

ADDITION AND SUBTRACTION was so much harder a week before winter break. Twenty-seven little faces stared back at Hannah with no interest—zero-plus-zero interest, to be specific—in learning today.

"I wonder if we could sneak into lunch early," she mused, getting the first glimmer of enthusiasm from any of her kids.

Several cheered. A few sat up straight. Nick and Dan high-fived each other and closed their math books so fast, Hannah could feel the breeze.

She killed some time putting books away, letting some kids go to the bathroom, making order in the classroom, and lining them up. By the time they reached the cafeteria, they were only five minutes before the bell, so she played a Christmas word game in line and, finally, a break.

Anxious for the pasta salad she'd made the night before, Hannah headed toward the teachers' lunchroom, reaching the door at the same moment as Nancy Arcuni.

"Hello, beautiful," the older woman greeted her with a smile. "You're in a hurry."

"I'm starved and my kids have..." She glanced at her watch. "Forty minutes. I need every one of them."

Nancy put her arm around Hannah and guided her into the room where about a dozen teachers were scattered around a few round tables, some in conversation, some on their phones, some reading. Tinsel hung haphazardly around the window behind an artificial tree in the corner.

"Eat with me," Nancy said. "I have a surprise for you."

"A surprise?" Was this going to be another dressing down on her marital status? Hannah considered begging off, but she respected the older woman and had known her too long to be rude.

So, she got her Tupperware and a drink and settled into a round table with Nancy, joining a music teacher named Maggie Burns and a first-year third-grade teacher, Tianna Dupree.

After some chatter and jokes about how ready they all were for a month off, Nancy scooted closer and put her hand on Hannah's arm.

"Ready for my surprise?"

Hannah nodded slowly, not sure where this was going.

Nancy brought out her phone, clicked a few times, then turned to show her a picture of a man in his thirties with short brown hair and a sweet smile.

"This is Luke."

"Okay. He looks...nice. New teacher?" she guessed.

"New love interest." She grinned. "You're welcome."

"New...interest..." Hannah sputtered, looking at the other two teachers, who leaned in, curious to see the phone.

"That's my nephew," Nancy told them, showing him off like a new car. "My youngest sister's oldest son, who will be here for the Christmas break." She squeezed Hannah's arm. "You should marry him!"

The other teachers laughed, not sure if she was kidding or not, but Hannah felt her heart drop down to her feet. She wasn't kidding—Nancy was serious.

And that meant instead of enjoying her pasta salad for forty minutes and making small talk with her co-workers, she'd be defending her eleven-year relationship with a man who couldn't commit.

*Really?*

"Thanks, Nancy, but I'm—"

"Oh, I know what you are—a sweet girl with a good heart and no backbone. And I am offering up Luke, the most wonderful man, who is completely single, makes six figures, and is looking for a good woman to have by his side."

"Aren't too many of those around," Tianna said. "I'd grab him, Hannah."

"No kidding," Maggie chimed in. "I've been married for, what? Two years now? I am so glad I'm done with that rat race of being single."

"I don't mind it," Tianna said. "But I'm only twenty-four. I think it stops being fun at twenty-seven."

Hannah almost groaned, not wanting to admit she was ten years older than Tianna. "I really appreciate the offer, Nancy, but—"

"It's not an offer, it's a done deal," she said. "I sent him a picture I took of you at the Christmas party and he was *so* interested." She leaned in and tapped the phone, showing a text string. "Look, he said, 'Ugly sweater, pretty girl. Please set up a date.'"

Hannah just stared at her, pasta salad turning to cement in her mouth.

"Do it, Hannah!"

She whipped around to Tianna and managed to swallow. "I have a boyfriend. I've been with him forever."

"Exactly," Nancy said, pulling Hannah's attention back to her, but not before she caught the look that passed between Maggie and Tianna. "But you don't have a ring, so there really isn't a forever, is there?"

Hannah let out a sigh, furious that she felt she owed these women an explanation. "I'm very happy," she said.

"Are you?" Nancy countered, clearly not ready to back down. "Is this what you want from your man? Because I happen to think you're worth more. And I bet if you ask your sister or your new stepsisters or whatever they are, they'd all agree."

"They love Keith," she said.

"They love *you*," Nancy countered. "And they don't want to hurt your feelings. But I am not family, just an observant old woman who happens to think you have a light in your eyes and a sweet soul. All of it is being wasted on a man who won't make you his wife. And frankly, at this point, I'm not sure I'd want him."

"Well, I do," she said.

"I understand that," Nancy said. "You've made a big investment. How many years together? Ten?"

"Eleven."

Nancy winced. "Ouch. That's a lot of time, Hannah, but, honey, you're still young. There are terrific men out there." She tapped the phone she'd set face down. "Men like my nephew."

And men like...Brandon Fletcher.

As she had since the field trip, Hannah pushed the memory of the hockey player-turned-tree farmer from her mind. Keith was her boyfriend, and she was committed to him.

"So, can I tell Luke you'll have lunch or coffee? Just meet and see if there's a little spark." Nancy leaned in. "You know, the spark? It's a delicious feeling, isn't it?"

And once again, she thought of Brandon Fletcher, who sparked so much he darn near lit her on fire.

Now the pasta salad threatened to come back up.

"Well, thank you for your advice," Hannah said stiffly as she closed the container and started repacking what was left of her lunch. "The fact is, I'm very comfortable in my relationship. I know Keith so well, and he knows me. We love each other. We..." She looked from one to the other. "We're not up for discussion."

With that, she rose and put her food back in the fridge, taking the rest of her lunch break outside, listening to kids scream on the playground the way she wanted to scream into the air.

She wasn't happy and she knew exactly what to do about it. But for some reason, she couldn't bring herself to give Keith an ultimatum.

Maybe because *an ultimatum* wasn't the answer. Maybe the answer was to give Keith...the big goodbye.

And she could barely stand the thought of that, which was probably why of all the ways Nancy had described her—good heart, sweet soul, pretty face—only one was indisputable: no backbone.

WHILE HANNAH WAS HOME ALONE WRAPPING Christmas presents that evening, the inevitable "come on over" text came from Keith. She stared at the words for a long time, and thought of all the ways she could say no.

He wouldn't be that upset. Because if she didn't go to see him tonight, she would the next night. Or they'd go out on the weekend, or spend time with her family— although he'd probably be late or leave early—and then more of the same next week.

She was in a deep, deep rut. And as comfortable as that might be, she had to climb out. She knew because the blues had pressed on her all day, alternating with bouts of anger. Stress crawled through her as she considered what she'd say to Keith, and how.

It wasn't anything she hadn't said before, but this time...she meant it. Or did she?

She texted back that she would be over in a bit, then she finished wrapping some presents for her nephews, dressed and freshened her makeup, and got in the car with all the enthusiasm of someone headed in for a root canal.

Letting herself into his small house on the outskirts of Asheville, the first thing Hannah heard was the sound of a hockey game on TV.

*Hockey.*

Instantly, she conjured up images of blue eyes and long hair and strong arms wrapped around her while they sailed down the side of a mountain.

"Babe, guess what?" Keith called. "Hurricanes are up by two goals and I put twenty on them at work today."

"That's great," she said, putting her purse on the kitchen counter and slipping out of her jacket. It smelled like eggs and onions, which was probably what he'd made for dinner. Keith never cooked, but loved it when she did. "How much will you win?"

"Two hundred smackeroos." He patted the empty leather sofa next to him. "C'mere and bring me luck."

She joined him, shared a quick kiss, then stared at the TV. The hockey players whipped back and forth on the ice, but suddenly—for the first time ever—she was interested and actually wanted to watch the sport.

It was better than that ultimatum she should probably deliver.

"Oh, man!" Keith shot off the sofa. "How'd he miss that goal?"

Better question: how could he be so clueless as to not realize the woman he allegedly loved was sitting right here next to him thinking about giving him an end date. Engagement, marriage, or...

Or what? What if she said "it's now or never" and he said...okay? They'd get married. And that would be—

"And that is the game, baby!" He jumped up and fist-pumped the air. "Two hundred for me!" He leaned over to kiss her. "Someone is going to get a very nice Christmas present."

But not the ring she...

*Wait a second.* Did she even *want* a ring?

Or did she want a backbone?

It felt like her blood was running ice cold, enough that she shivered. Not that Keith noticed. He was already texting someone—presumably whoever would pay him that two hundred dollars.

Taking a deep breath, she realized her throat was dry, so she pushed up from the sofa and went back into the kitchen for water.

"Get me a brewski, babe," Keith called. "And get one for yourself! Skinner's gonna pay me tomorrow."

She cringed at the mention of Ron Skinner, a man who worked at Keith's body shop who gave her a total ick. She hated the way he looked at her, hated his unsubtle comments about her body, hated...him.

Was Keith...much better?

As she stood at the sink getting water, she looked into

the den at the man she thought she loved. They'd shared a lot—laughter, travel, good times and bad. He'd been a solid boyfriend for most of their time together, but the older they got, the more he...wasn't what she wanted.

So why should she push for a ring or a proposal? Why not just...leave?

Oh, *my*.

The thought had grown from a mustard seed to a much larger kernel today and now? It was sprouting and rooting and about to wrap around her until it strangled her.

Break up with him? How *could* she? Hannah was *horrified* by the idea of being alone.

Ever since her mother had died when she was thirteen, Hannah had been terrified to be alone. Not long after her sister got married, Hannah met Keith and it was easy to be with him. He made no demands, so neither did she.

"Brewski?" he called, a note of impatience in his voice.

She grabbed a bottle of light beer from the fridge and walked slowly toward the den, where Keith was grinning on the sofa. "Man, I shoulda put fifty on the Hurricanes. I knew they'd win this game." He took the beer. "Thanks. You okay?"

Finally, he noticed her.

"Yeah, I'm fine. Long day. Kids are antsy. So am I."

"Oh, I get that. Time for Christmas and—oh, here's the MVP. Look at that dude. He's a beast."

She turned to the TV, mostly for a distraction from

the terrifying thoughts plaguing her. The hockey player didn't look anything like the one she'd been flirting with— he had blond hair and a beard that covered any scars. But still, his slightly long hair and confident attitude reminded her of—

No. She couldn't sit here and think about another man. She had to think about this one and what she was going to say. She couldn't take this anymore.

The truth was, she didn't want to give him an ultimatum.

She wanted...out.

She didn't want crumbs from Keith Kelly. Or beer or two-hundred-dollar bets or *anything*.

Now what?

She could barely breathe just thinking about it.

The hockey player on the screen was talking fast, looking around, and finally turned right to the camera.

"I gotta do something," the player said, wiping his brow. "Marissa. Babe. C'mere!"

The way he called off-camera got her attention, mostly because it sounded just like Keith with the "Babe, c'mere" demand.

*Don't do it, Marissa. Don't jump when he tells you.*

But all of a sudden, a beautiful blonde was on the screen, laughing, showing off a set of blinding, perfect veneers and a body that Hannah would kill to have as her very own. Was that the kind of girl Brandon Fletcher dated?

The hockey player pulled the woman closer for a kiss, making the interviewer laugh.

"We really wanted to hear about that last goal," the reporter said, holding the microphone closer.

"I only have one goal," the player said, looking into Marissa's lash-extended eyes. "One goal. One love. One question to ask."

"Oh, man," Keith groaned. "Can we talk about that last near-miss, dude?"

But Hannah was mesmerized, watching the interaction frozen in her seat, gasping when the hockey player dropped to one knee.

"Babe!" the girl squealed. "What are you doing?"

"I'm asking you to marry me, Marissa Wilding. Right now, in front of millions of fans. I love you and want to spend my life with you."

Hannah pressed both hands to her lips, tears springing forward.

"Seriously?" Keith grabbed the remote and smacked it, turning the beautiful moment to a black screen. "What a bunch of—"

"I thought it was...lovely," she whispered, her voice tight.

"Lovely?" He mocked the word. "I think it's a candy ass move, if you ask me."

"Why?" she demanded as he took a long swig of his beer. "He loves her and wants to marry her."

He put the beer bottle on the table with a thud. "I know that's what you want, Hannah," he said softly. "And Christmas is—"

"No." The word was out before she could stop herself.

"'Scuze me? Did you just say no? You don't even know what I'm going to say."

She inched back, looking hard at him. "Just...no. Don't...say it or ask me or...anything."

He snorted. "Well, if that's how you—"

"I'm serious, Keith. Don't do it."

"Please." He flicked his fingers in her direction. "Never even thought of it. You know where I stand on the subject. I'm glad you agree. Save me the cashola of buying a ring for—"

She held up both hands, not surprised they were trembling. "Stop. I don't know if you were or you weren't, but..." She swallowed hard and all humor left his face as he stared at her.

"What?" he croaked the word.

"I want to end this."

His brows furrowed. "This discussion? This night? This—"

"This relationship," she whispered. "I'm done, Keith. I want to move on. I don't..." She took a deep breath. "I don't love you that way anymore. I'm sorry. I really am. I just—"

His whole face screwed up and for a second, she thought he was going to cry. Then he pulled it together and picked up his beer, taking a deep drink while she stared at him.

When he finished, he put it back down and nodded. "Fine. Do what you gotta do, Hannah. I won't stop you."

She didn't move for a moment, then stood up very slowly, walking to the kitchen like she was wading through water. Part of her hoped he would come running after her.

But a much bigger, stronger, better part of her hoped he wouldn't.

That part won.

She didn't even cry, which was the strangest part of all. She got her coat, purse, and keys, and went home alone.

Just Hannah and...her backbone.

# Chapter Ten

### Noelle

Edna Covington had been out of town for a few days, so it took her a while to respond to Noelle's text asking for a one-on-one meeting. But she finally agreed to one—on her terms, of course. It would be that very day, at her house, promptly at 11:00 a.m.

The meeting was important enough that Noelle canceled a gallery walk-through with a new buyer and shortened her morning session with a local artist. It was a shame, because the Brazilian woman's portfolio of stunning watercolors was impressive and she hoped to carry her work.

With half an hour to spare when the floor manager clocked in, Noelle took off, driving to an address in South Asheville, arriving with five minutes to spare at a tidy brick house that she suspected belied Edna Covington's true wealth.

Small and tucked into a sweet residential street, with a hand-painted "Santa Stop Here" sign in the driveway, the home was decked out with garlands wrapped around a quaint front porch.

As she walked up to the door, Noelle realized she didn't really have a game plan for asking if any of Cassie's ideas might be implemented. She hoped that a warm and friendly conversation would soften up her adversary, at least enough that she might consider a small change. If nothing else, she wanted to forge a better relationship with Edna, certain they'd gotten off to a rocky start.

Edna opened the door after the first ring, surprising Noelle again with just how diminutive she was.

She gestured her into a dimly-lit entryway where an endless array of Christmas decorations started and didn't appear to stop.

"Is there a problem with the tree lighting?" Edna asked without much of a greeting.

"Absolutely not," Noelle said, sliding out of her coat to hang it on a stand by the door without being invited to do so. "I just thought you and I might get to know each other a little bit so I can really understand your—well, Gil's—vision for the event."

That earned her a flick of an eyebrow and a nod to the kitchen. "I made coffee and store-bought cookies," she said as they walked into a maple-and-Formica-heavy corner kitchen. "Not your fancy buffet setup, but never let it be said I can't show Southern hospitality. Do you take cream and sugar?"

"Yes, both, please." Noelle settled into a chair at a dated kitchen table. "Have you lived here long, Mrs. Covington?"

"Longer than you've been alive," she said, coming over with two steaming cups on saucers.

The old-school coffee service made Noelle smile. "Thank you."

"Gil and I got married in 1963 and moved in here not long after. Bought for a song, we did, though I don't know what it's worth. Don't care because I'll never leave."

"What a wonderful history," she said, looking around and wondering, had the kitchen been updated in those sixty years?

"Which is your way of saying it's an old house. Yes, it is. But I'm an old woman—gonna be eighty-four on my next birthday—and I don't like change. But you already knew that."

"I know you like...tradition." She clung to Cassie's new favorite word.

"Well, I don't like these big modern houses with no walls and a piece of marble in the middle big enough to skate on," she scoffed. "If I wanted an island in my kitchen, I'd move to the Caribbean."

Noelle chuckled at that.

"And I like my furniture, which is as old as the hills. Just like I like my bouffant hairdo, my handbag that doesn't have sixteen zippers so you can't find anything, and all the other old stuff. I like things as they are and so did Gil." She gave a tight smile and maybe stole a breath after her speech. "So, honey, if you came over here to sweet-talk me into your silly lights or piped-in music, you wasted a drive to South Asheville. I don't like change, period, end of story."

Noelle leaned back, eyeing her and trying to figure out some way to win this ornery little lady over.

"I understand that you aren't interested in those ideas," she said, and meant it. "I came to get to know you and maybe have you know me, too."

She snorted. "A busy woman like you with a successful art gallery just dropped everything to have coffee with an old lady? No agenda? I don't believe it."

Noelle also knew that you had to give information before you get it.

Taking another sip of coffee that tasted like it had been brewed yesterday, she slowly lowered the cup to the sweet saucer and looked across the table.

"I have a problem," she started. "And I'm hoping to get your advice."

Edna looked over the delicate rim of her cup. "I'll do my best, but I won't change a thing at the tree lighting."

"I can't seem to find a way to connect with the other retailers and shopkeepers in town," she said. "I feel like an outsider and I know they all loved Sherry Kinsell, the former owner of my gallery."

"And her husband," Edna added.

"Of course, Zander. A true talent and his death was a huge blow to the art gallery."

"It was a bigger blow to his friends and family," she said dryly. "But you're right, Sherry was a friend to all and a local girl. Zander opened the gallery decades ago and he was actually one of the first real famous artists to come out of Asheville. They were a source of pride and you are...a New Yorker."

She said it as though it was a disease.

"Well, I'm actually local, too."

"I know," she said. "I know your parents came here in summers and at Christmas, and that your family has had that place up on Copper Creek Mountain forever. That doesn't make you a local."

Noelle nodded. "I get that. What would?"

To her credit, Edna considered the question carefully, taking a drink before answering.

"Well, for one thing, you don't swoop in and change things just because you're young and new and...hip."

Noelle smiled. "I wouldn't describe myself like that."

"Lots of people have," she countered. "And for another, you need time. So take it." One more drink and she finished the coffee. "Was that all?"

Noelle nearly choked. No, that wasn't even close to all. Talk about not connecting.

But Noelle Chambers Fleming didn't give up that easily and at this point? She had nothing to lose.

"I have another little problem," she continued.

Edna tried not to react with disdain, but she failed. "And that would be..."

"My daughter—my stepdaughter, to be precise— would like to sing at the tree lighting."

Edna blinked and drew back. "Excuse me?"

"She has a beautiful voice," Noelle said quickly. "Really a remarkable talent. She sang the solo in the church play last year—"

"Then sign her up for *America's Got Talent*, dear, but she isn't auditioning at Gil's tree lighting."

"It's so important to her," Noelle insisted. "She's such a good girl and hasn't had a mother for her whole life—"

"Oh, please. No." She crossed her slender arms and sliced Noelle with a look. "Any other problems you want to drop on me?"

Was she really that heartless?

"I guess a parade of animals dressed as elves or letting people post wish cards on the tree or waving glow sticks is out of the question."

Edna choked a laugh. "You guess right."

She let out a sigh and pushed her coffee away to signal that she understood this little meeting was over. "I'll be on my way."

They both stood and Noelle looked down on the woman, a hundred different parting shots in her head. A wry comment about Gil and his flickering lights. A little joke about not liking change...even in her décor. A crack about anything from her nasty attitude to her bitter coffee.

But Jacqueline Chambers didn't raise that woman.

"Thank you for your time," she said instead, turning to walk toward the front door and retrieve her coat. She considered not even putting it on so she could make a quick getaway from the meeting that had blown up in her face.

She did slide her arms in, though, and reached for the doorknob just as a small but surprisingly strong hand landed on her shoulder.

"Wait."

She froze for a second, then turned to the other woman, bracing for another dressing down and a reminder of all her flaws and how unfit she was to be a mother or store owner or committee chair.

Then she gasped softly at the tears filling Edna's eyes.

"I think you should know something," she said on a ragged whisper. "The Asheville tree lighting didn't start fourteen years ago. It started a second time fourteen years ago."

Noelle stared at her, silent and not sure why Edna was telling her this.

"It was a big deal back in the fifties and sixties," she said. "Folks around here forget that, but when Asheville was a very, very small mountain town, we'd have a lighting right there on the same intersection, at the same park. Smaller tree, smaller crowd, but same atmosphere."

"I...didn't know that," Noelle said.

"I had my first date there with a handsome boy named Gilbert Covington. And it was in front of that tree, on December fourteenth, in the year of our Lord nineteen hundred and sixty-two, where he kissed me as the tree lights came on. All white lights, which was unusual back then."

"That's...amazing," Noelle said, and meant it, thinking of her own kiss at the tree lighting last year.

Edna gave a smile. "Gil called it my last first kiss. And it sure was. The tree lightings stopped in the sixties when hippies showed up and took over Asheville for a while. Then fifteen years ago, I think my Gil knew he didn't have a lot of time left. He decided to start the whole thing again and...do it just like it was back in our day. All white lights, with the carolers, and everything the same. I think he wanted to recreate the moment for other young couples."

"Oh." The word slipped out as Noelle covered her lips. "I kissed Jace there last year for the first time in twenty-five years. It was…a last first kiss, too."

"Well, there you have it. We were married less than six months later," Edna said.

Noelle gasped. "So were we!"

Edna's expression softened. "When those lights flicker…" She swallowed and forced herself to continue through a thick voice. "I know he's watching over me. Every year at the tree lighting, he…shows up. Oh, I know people think it's silly folklore, but it's not…silly or folklore."

She blinked, sending a tear over her crinkly cheek. "It's the highlight of my year, Noelle. Please don't take that from me. Don't change the lights or the music or entertainment or…wait. Did you say an animal elf parade?"

Noelle let out a little laugh at her tone of disbelief. "That one's a stretch."

She blew out a sigh. "You tell your little girl I'm sorry but I can't. When I'm dead, you can do all the changes you want. I'll be with Gil. But until then? No changes. Glow sticks? What in tarnation are they, anyway?"

Noelle laughed, her whole being lighter. "Nothing you have to worry about, Mrs. Covington."

"It's Edna. Goodbye, dear."

"Goodbye…Edna."

Noelle had no idea why, but she left with a much happier heart than she'd had when she arrived.

Somebody else might have their last first kiss at that tree with the flickering white lights, and Noelle wasn't going to be the person to bring that tradition to an end.

NOELLE FOUND Cassie singing in the barn late that afternoon. She was belting out her favorite Christmas carol, "O Holy Night," and sounded even better than she had last year on stage, dressed as a sheep next to the manger.

It was time to break the bad news.

"Need help?" Noelle asked, reaching for her mucking boots that sat in the corner of the small structure that housed Sprinkles, two cats, and Tom Bertram's mare, who was still struggling with a respiratory infection.

The horse, a stately dappled girl, stood looking out of her stall, watching Cassie work and no doubt enjoying the song.

"Yes, please," Cassie said, holding out her muck rake. "I'm ready for a break."

She rarely complained about her chores, so the comment surprised Noelle. "You okay?"

"Yeah...I just..." She folded onto a hay bale and looked up, her big blue eyes wide and genuine. "I don't have enough money."

Noelle almost laughed at the incredibly mature

admission, but she could see that Cassie was serious. "What do you need money for?"

"Christmas presents!" She sounded shocked that Noelle didn't know that. "I have cousins now—"

"You don't have to buy them presents, Cass."

"Oh, I do. I have a big family now that Daddy married you." She held out her hands and started counting on her fingers. "Three boy cousins, a baby cousin, a teenage cousin, two new aunts, and Uncle Sonny and Aunt Bitsy!" Then she waved the one finger left over. "And you and Daddy. I don't have enough money even after I get paid for all my chores."

"I could...lend you some."

"Nope. Not for gifts. It's a rule."

"Well, you certainly don't have to get me a present," Noelle said, getting a dropped jaw and an "are you kidding" look in response. "I'm serious, Cass. Save your money on me. And what if we set up a Secret Santa and you and your cousins pull names and only get a gift for that one person?"

"I already got Sawyer a paperweight with a bear inside and I found barrettes for Brooke."

"You shopped?"

"We have a gift thing at school where kids can buy presents for people," she explained. "But I'm running out of"—she rubbed her fingers together in the universal sign for money—"moolah, as Daddy says."

"Well, we'll figure something out." Noelle dragged the rake over the hay and thought about the real reason she'd come out here—to break the news to Cassie. "So I had a meeting with the lady who controls the tree lighting ceremony today."

"I thought that was you."

"Well, she's the lady with..." Noelle mimicked the moolah gesture. "And she gets the final say. Sadly, none of your ideas passed muster."

"Why would you pass mustard?"

Noelle chuckled. "It's an expression and it means we got shot down. I'm sorry, Cass."

She made a face as she considered the news. "She didn't like any of them?"

"She...wants this event to never change. It's tradition, you know, and part of the tradition is that it's the same every year."

Cassie rolled her eyes. "Why?" she asked, proving that she might not know what "pass muster" meant, but this child was wise beyond her years. Edna's motivation didn't make sense...unless she knew the truth.

On a sigh, Noelle leaned on the rake and studied her little girl, making a decision to share more than she might with the average eight-year-old, but absolutely nothing about Cassie Fleming was average.

"Her husband, who died years ago, came up with the whole idea a long time ago, and she made him a promise that she wouldn't change a thing," Noelle explained. "So it's very important to her that nothing new or different is introduced at the tree lighting."

"Huh." Cassie thought about that for a minute, then squished her face. "That's kind of sad, because sometimes new is better."

"I'm with you, girl, but she calls the shots."

Shaking her head, Cassie huffed out a breath. "I mean, I get the elf parade. But why would he care if I sang? People sing at that thing all the time. And they dress weird. I could be an elf..."

Noelle could hear the ache in her voice, and it touched her. Leaning the rake against the rough-hewn wood, she crouched down in front of Cassie on the hay bale.

"Every year, since even before he died, the tree lights along the bottom two rows have flickered, turning off and on really fast. It happened when old Gil was alive, and it's happened every year."

"Then they need new lights," she replied, making Noelle smile. So wise.

"Except that Mrs. Covington thinks those lights are a sign from her husband that he's watching her from heaven and he completely approves of the tree lighting."

She inched back with an expression of total disbelief. "That's..." Then she thought about it for a second. "Wait. Can that happen? Can dead people do that? Daddy says we don't believe in ghosts. They're not in the Bible."

"They're not and we don't, but this is very comforting to Mrs. Covington because she's very, very sad that her husband died."

"Maybe it's true."

"No, no," Noelle insisted. "That's not how it happens. Things can remind you of someone you lost— like when I see cardinals in the winter, I always think of my mother. But it's not...her."

Cassie looked just uncertain enough to make Noelle think she might buy the Covington Theory of seeing dead people.

"But Cassie—"

"It's fine, Miss Noelle. I won't sing and I won't do anything to change the tree lighting. That old lady should...see her husband."

Torn between fighting her on logic and hugging her for having such a soft heart, Noelle just nodded. "I think that's the best gift we can give her. And speaking of gifts, maybe I could take you shopping for some of the ones you're missing and we could make them from both of us."

"Daddy would say you're bending the rules."

Noelle just smiled. "Bending, not breaking. Come on, let's finish mucking so we have time to watch another Christmas movie tonight."

"Yay!" And proving she was still a very little girl, Cassie easily moved to the next highlight in her life and hopefully let go of this one.

# Chapter Eleven

## Angie

THE WORK CREWS were only able to move art and furniture after-hours—after VIP tours and official closing—which was at nine o'clock tonight. That meant that Angie had to wait all day and much of the evening to supervise the dismantling of her favorite exhibit, although, in truth, she didn't need to be here at all.

Carlos and Company, as she thought of the skilled moving crew, were pros and wouldn't hurt a thing. She'd had her storage plan approved, had marked and categorized every item in the three-room exhibit, and had taken a few final pictures for her department files...and her family.

Knowing that this was the last time anyone would ever be in the oversized servants' room, Angie took the liberty of sitting on the edge of the bed and closing her eyes for a moment. She imagined a conversation between Angelica and Garland on their own last night in the room.

They left these sleeping quarters—though not the life of service—to move into the small cabin they'd built on land they'd been gifted by friends of the Vanderbilts. What did they talk about that night, she mused.

Did they read this Bible? She reached for the leather-bound King James version, grazing her fingers over the initials GB—Garland Benson—embossed on the cover.

"Not sure I took you as a Bible reader."

With a soft gasp, she looked up and did a double-take at the sight of Elliott in the doorway.

Instantly, she stood. "Oh. I was expecting the moving crew."

"I figured I'd find you up here."

He was looking for her? At this hour? "Did you need something for the *Magi* project?" she asked, suddenly worried she'd forgotten a task on the tight and complex timeline.

"No, no, but I enlisted the help of Carlos's crew moving a few pieces down in the sub and threw my weight around to get it done before this. He's going to be delayed."

"Oh, okay," she said, knowing that most storage was in the sub-basement. "Thank you for letting me know. That wasn't necessary."

He angled his head in concession and took a few steps into the room. "I've only been in here once, but it's a fine exhibit. Well thought-out."

"Thank you," she said softly. "It was my first and, as you know, personal." Still holding the Bible, she lifted it. "I wasn't reading. I found this in my attic."

"You donated it? I didn't know that."

"I found it when I was looking for the deed to our

cabin," she told him. "Relatives of the original owners were threatening to take it away, since it is evidently built on a goldmine."

His eyes widened. "The plot thickens."

"Not so much. We're not interested in mining, and I found the deed, and now, as you know, I live there, so the good guys won." Realizing she was talking too much, she placed the Bible back on the nightstand. "Anyway, I'll wait for Carlos if you want to head home."

He gave a nearly imperceptible shrug, as if he didn't want to leave. Instead, he crossed the room and went to the dresser, where a few old pictures rested and some very simple jewelry that belonged to Angelica.

"My car's fixed," he said, surprising her with the topic that had nothing to do with the exhibit.

"I'm so relieved to hear that," she said. "Did Keith do a good job?"

"He did." He turned to her. "But no friends-and-family discount."

"What? That's not right, because he—"

"It's fine. He said something about not being family... or friends."

"That's weird," she murmured, wondering if something had happened with Hannah. "Whatever the cost, my insurance will cover it."

He held up a hand. "It's all done, Angel. No worries."

*Angel.* Dang, she could get used to that.

"So...did you have any questions about the exhibit?" She couldn't resist a sly smile. "Change of plans?"

"No, sorry. I know you love this one."

"I do, but I understand you want space for...art."

With a soft laugh, he slid his hands into his pockets and regarded her with that look of interest and amusement that always felt just a little...personal. "Why is it so many people are opposed to art in a museum?"

She considered her response and the things that Marjorie had told her about how not everyone wanted to hire him. Was she witnessing a division in the company? And was he in the middle of it—or causing it?

"I'm not opposed to art," she finally said. "I just love the history of the home more than the valued art pieces. I see them as part of the whole thing."

He nodded, then smiled. "You just don't care about art that much."

She laughed. "My daughter occasionally calls me Saran Wrap because it's so easy to see through me."

"Nothing wrong with transparency," he replied. "So, I'm right?"

She shifted from one foot to the other, really not wanting to step into anything but also wanting to make her point.

"I didn't come to the Biltmore Estate because there's a Monet on the floor," she said. "I came because this was —is, actually—the vibrant, gorgeous, shockingly beautiful home of a family."

He listened, studying her and seeming to be waiting for her to elaborate.

"Yes, two members of the staff happened to be in my own family tree, but the family that lived here—and still owns it—has touched a chord in my heart. I'm sure you know the fascinating history of the Vanderbilts, but what I think is amazing is how you can experience that just by walking through these halls and rooms. They *lived* here," she added, a little breathless. "They had children and issues and parties and quiet conversations. They prayed and they worried and they stared out the window and solved their problems. Yes, they were wealthy, but they were also...a real family. Quite frankly, that's the true appeal of this place to tourists and guests. Not the art. But the art, I guess, is why you took the job."

He surprised her by taking a few steps closer and sitting on the edge of the bed where she'd been earlier. "I'd have taken any job to get out of Boston and the MFA."

The admission threw her. Not only was it unexpected, even the tone was raw and real. "Why?" she asked.

"It's complicated," he said. "She was a colleague in the very small world of Boston museums, working with the Institute of Contemporary Art. The town just wasn't big enough for the both of us."

"So she won your beloved town in the divorce. Not easy."

"Not at all," he agreed. "And to make matters worse, she's getting married and they're having the reception at the MFA. Truth was, I just couldn't get away fast enough."

"So you took a job at the Biltmore even though it wasn't exactly...your cup of career tea?"

He lifted a brow. "It could be," he said. "I can see

your perspective but..." He shook his head. "You know, Carlos is going to be an hour or more. I have an idea, if you would be so kind."

"Sure. What do you need?"

"A tour."

"A...tour? I have to believe that by now you've seen every inch of the place."

"Not through your eyes," he replied. "I'd like the family tour, not the art tour. The one that showcases the people, not the stuff."

She stared at him for a moment, liking a person willing to consider changing their opinion. It really appealed to her.

"I'd love that," she said, waving around the room they were in. "We can start right here with the lovely secrets of Angelica and Garland Benson, our Bible-reading parlor maid and footman." She took a step back and pointed at him playfully. "Fun fact? Garland was an expert in the art of mimicry and used to entertain the staff for hours by doing dead-on impersonations of the Vanderbilts and their guests. Once, George Vanderbilt overheard him and Garland was certain he was going to be told to leave immediately, fired for impudence."

"Was he?"

"No. George loved the imitation so much, he had Garland come up and do a private show in Mrs. Vanderbilt's secret salon, known as the Louis XV room." She gestured him out of the room. "Where we are going next."

Elliott threw her a sideways glance, holding her gaze

for a heartbeat or two. "See the lesson in that story?" he asked.

"The lesson?"

"Some people think they're getting canned and, in truth, they're trusted more than anyone else."

She slowed her step. Wait a second. Was he...

*Yes, he was.* Elliott Quinn was not so subtly giving her the message that her job was safe, and that he trusted her.

That put a smile on her face for the rest of the private tour.

As ANGIE PULLED up to the cabin several hours later, she let out another long breath, trying to center herself after the late evening of touring, laughing, talking, and— she glanced at the box on the passenger seat next to her— surprises.

Everything about Elliott Quinn surprised her, she had to admit, but nothing as much as the look in his eyes when they were both back in the fourth-floor exhibit watching Carlos's crew gingerly carry hundred-year-old furniture.

He genuinely felt bad about having to dismantle the exhibit, and proved that by...

She slipped the lid of the box wide open to look at the leather Bible he'd given to her, remembering his warm look.

"It belongs in your home, and with your family," he'd said. "Not in a sub-basement storage facility."

She'd been touched by the gesture, and had to fight the urge to hug him in gratitude. Because they got along nicely and had gone a long way to building a rapport, but that would be—

"Mom!" Brooke appeared out of nowhere, yanking open the driver's side door. "I've been so worried about you!"

Angie gasped at the sight of her daughter in the driveway. "Oh! I didn't see you come out."

"What about the texts I've been sending you? Did you see them?"

She grimaced. "I honestly haven't picked up my phone since..." Since before she started the "family" version of the tour for Elliott. "Is something wrong?"

"It's after midnight," Brooke said. "I was worried."

"Aww. That's sweet. But you're the kid and I'm the mom. All is well." She gathered the box and handed it to Brooke. "Don't drop that, please. It's a hundred-year-old Bible."

"The one you found in the attic and donated?"

"Elliott gave it back to our family," she said, grabbing her bag and climbing out. "Oh, Brooke, I made such progress with him tonight."

Brooke eyed her with suspicion. "What does that mean?"

"It means my job feels so much safer," she said, navigating the steps up to the front door. "I don't think he's going to fire me."

"Are you sure?"

"Yes." She let out a soft laugh, thinking of how they'd actually joked about it a few times. "On the contrary, I think he wants me to be his eyes and ears in the department. He really opened up about his life and career. His job, although he didn't come right out and say this, isn't that secure. Oh, and he had a terrible divorce—almost as bad as mine. We both—"

"You told him about Dad?"

"Sure. And about moving here." She opened the front door, surprised to see a fire roaring. "You've been up waiting for me?"

"You didn't answer my texts. I was, to quote a mother I know, 'waiting for that call from the hospital.'"

Angie snorted at the words she'd said plenty of times when Brooke was out past curfew.

"I'm so sorry, honey." She dropped her things on the entryway table and let out a happy sigh, looking around the cabin. "I'd love some tea. Join me. Or is it way too late for you?"

Brooke was still looking at her oddly.

"What's wrong?" Angie asked.

"You're all flushed. Your eyes are bright. You look... different."

"It's late and—"

"You're crushing on this guy," Brooke announced as if the very idea had just landed in her head. Where it did *not* belong.

"Brooke, he's my boss."

"I know." She took a step back and narrowed her eyes. "But you are definitely interested."

"No, I'm..." She made a face. "I don't *want* to be." She laughed. "See why you call me Saran Wrap?"

"As if we have any control over crushes," Brooke said with wisdom beyond her years. "I'll make the tea. And then you will spill some because I want to know everything."

"Deal. Maybe." Angie plopped onto the big sectional in front of the fireplace, dropping her head back. "There isn't much tea to spill."

"Oh, please. Start with what you've been doing with the guy all night."

"Touring. And talking. And laughing. And..." Angie squeezed her eyes shut.

"Crushing?" Brooke guessed.

"Ugh. Maybe a little." She put her feet up and let out a groan. "Maybe more than a little. I had no idea he was so...nice and funny."

A few minutes later, Brooke handed her a steaming cup of Sleepytime tea and snuggled under a blanket on the sofa next to her. "Okay, tell me every gory detail and leave out nothing, no matter how inconsequential."

"There's nothing to—"

"Mom."

Angie blew on the tea, considering what to share and what it meant. "Nothing—"

"*Mom.*"

"*Nothing* is going to happen with a man I work for," she finished. "It would only put my job in more jeopardy and you know I don't have the qualifications expected for that position."

"You just said you feel safer than ever," Brooke countered.

"I do feel like he took the time to get to know me and appreciate whatever it is I bring to the job."

"And your pretty laugh, sweet smile, gorgeous hair, and inimitable wit," Brooke added. "Also a bangin' bod for forty."

"Forty-one in a few weeks," Angie reminded her. "Do you really see me that way?"

"Everyone does, Mom," she said. "You're all that and a bag of chips. Why do you not recognize that?"

Probably because her husband annihilated her self-confidence, but Angie hated to say anything negative about Craig. While their relationship was strained and their marriage was over, he was still Brooke's father.

"I don't know how people see me, but..." She tested the tea for heat with a baby sip. "This guy is very..."

"Attractive."

"Well, yeah. I mean, he's not a smoke show, as you would say—"

Brooke snorted on her first sip of tea.

"But he's good-looking and surprisingly warm and very smart. But not the uber-intellectual, uptight guy I thought he was. He really opened up to my way of thinking about the estate." She stared into the fire and remembered how his eyes lit up when they slipped through the secret chamber in the library as she explained how the Vanderbilt children used the passageway for epic games of hide and seek. "I think he caught the vision."

"How about the feels? Did he catch them, too?"

Angie laughed before her smile faded. "Romance would really, really complicate my job."

"It would also really, really spice up your life."

"My life is plenty spicy." At Brooke's look, she added, "I like my life just as it is."

"Sure. Boring and lonely. That's great, Mom."

"I'm not lonely! I can't even stay out until midnight without my seventeen-year-old daughter pounding the floorboards and sending a million texts. How's the egg baby?"

"Four texts and I didn't pound anything," Brooke said. "Even ButtPain. But Mom, the most important thing you said in that sentence was *seventeen*. This time next year I'll be in college, coming home for Christmas break. You don't want to be alone."

Angie turned to study her beautiful daughter, reaching over to brush back a few dark strands that had escaped from a sloppy bun to fall like wisps around her achingly beautiful face.

"I have family and a job," she said. "And I don't care if you go to the moon, we're going to talk and text all the time every day."

Brooke rolled her eyes. "Says the woman who didn't answer my million texts."

"Sorry about that." Angie took another sip of her tea. "Anyway, tonight was fun, I feel good about my job, and as far as Elliott, there's nothing to—"

"Text him."

She almost spilled the tea—literally this time. "What? Now? Are you crazy?"

"He's still up if you are, and you can keep it super professional but...why not send him to bed thinking about you?"

Angie blinked. "Why would I do that?"

"Mom, don't be lame. You like the guy. If you want to know where you stand, send him a nice text. Nothing gooey. Nothing personal. Just something that lets him know he's on your mind, too."

And he was, Angie hated to admit. He was all over her mind. "I don't know, Brooke."

But her daughter was already up and digging through Angie's purse to get her phone. "Let's just draft something."

"Don't send it!"

"I won't. Is this him? E Quinn? What? No heart-eyes?"

Angie chuckled. "When did you say you're leaving again?"

"Please." She plopped on the sofa. "You love me."

"So much," Angie whispered, reaching for her daughter's hand. At the break in her voice, Brooke looked up. "Really, Brookie." They both smiled at the childhood nickname. "We've come so far here at our cabin in the mountains. I have great sisters and good friends, but no one—absolutely *no one*—gets me quite like you do. I do love you, more than I can say. And more every day as you grow up into a woman."

Brooke's expression softened. "And I worry about you when you're out past curfew," she teased. "Also, I love you just as much, Angel."

"Angel," she sighed. "That's what Elliott calls me."

"Oh, boy." Brooke handed her the phone. "You better text him."

"And say what?"

"Something warm and professional and funny and sweet and completely like the Angel you are."

Angie sucked in a breath and typed...

*Hey, Elliott. Just want to thank you for the opportunity to let you see the Biltmore Estate through my eyes. Thank you for the Bible and for the opportunity to work on the da Vinci project with you. It's going to be great!*

"How's this?" She handed the phone to Brooke.

She read it and nodded. "Perfect." And moved her thumb. "Sent."

"What?" Angie practically leaped off the sofa. "You *sent* it? I wasn't ready! I didn't give permission! I have to edit it and get the message right. That was wrong, Brooke!"

Her daughter laughed. "So much for, 'I love you, Brookie.'"

"I do, but it was—"

"Oh..." She stared at the phone. "He texted back. Lightning fast, too."

"What?" She lunged for the phone, but Brooke held it away, laughing so hard her eyes were bright. "Let me see it, Brooke!"

After a second, Brooke released the phone to Angie,

whose heart was pounding way too hard as she read, with her daughter leaning in to see it, too.

*Loved every minute, Angel. Looking forward to more.*

"Oh, that's..." Angie didn't know *what* it was.

"That, my friend, is man-speak for, 'I caught feels, *Angel*.'" Brooke's grin shifted into a giggle as she rubbed her hands together in anticipation. "Oh, wow, this is going to be fun."

Angie read the eight words again and again. And one more time just to let them sink in.

Yep, it would be fun. Scary as all get out, and dangerous to her heart and career. But fun.

# Chapter Twelve

## Hannah

DRIVING up the winding mountain road to the Christmas tree farm for the big family outing, a cocktail of mixed emotions had Hannah's stomach in knots. Dread. Sadness. Uncertainty. And just a splash of... excitement.

All the feelings that had been rocking her since she'd broken up with Keith five days ago were rising to the surface, and her always astute and loving family would surely notice that he wasn't there...and that she was emotional. Even if they didn't, it was time to tell them the news, and she wasn't looking forward to it.

There hadn't been any way to get out of the Chambers-MacPherson family trip to pick out the tree for the cabin, nor did she want to. The three sisters had organized the event and pronounced it a restart of an old family tradition, following the tree cutting with a party at Angie's to decorate, bake, sing, and laugh.

Hannah didn't feel like doing any of those things, but she also didn't want to wallow in the post-breakup blues and ruin the holidays. Plus, she knew her family would be understanding and encouraging—maybe too encouraging. She didn't want to hear a single person she loved confess that they had never really liked Keith.

So all that was where the dread came in.

And the sadness? Well, it hurt so much to think she'd wasted eleven years, which was really the only thing that made her shed a tear. Why did she stay so long? Why hadn't he come after her? Why didn't she miss him more? Everything about Keith made her sad.

The uncertainty was because Hannah had to face facts: she was well into her thirties and basically starting over as far as her future husband was concerned. The very idea kicked her in the gut and made her wonder if maybe her path was one of a lifetime of being single. Which wouldn't be so bad, except, deep inside—she didn't want to spend the rest of her life alone.

Which led to the splash of excitement and a slightly giddy feeling she tried to ignore. That could be explained in two words: Brandon Fletcher.

Chances were good that he'd be here tonight. She wasn't sure what she'd say—if anything—but the spark of anticipation couldn't be denied.

But first, family.

They were easy to spot as she drove up to a caravan of familiar cars, trucks, and a van waiting in the lot. The crew of Eve and her four kids, Noelle with Jace and Cassie, and Angie and Brooke, plus Dad and Bitsy. Caro pulled up next to her, waving wildly from the front seat, with Joshua barely waiting for Nate to park before he tried to climb out and join his cousins.

Hannah shook off all the swirling emotions and got out of the car, giving her sister a hug and a helping hand with baby Tyler in his car seat.

"Haven't seen hide nor hair of you lately, Hannah," Caro said as she eased Tyler into her arms. "What's new?"

"Oh, you know, end of semester craziness. Holiday madness. Shopping insanity."

"So basically, you've lost your mind." She hoisted the baby on her hip.

"No I haven't," she said. "I've lost—"

"Where's Keith?"

"Him."

Caro angled her head and frowned. "'Scuze me?"

"I've, um—"

"There are our MacPherson girls!" Noelle came right up between them and put her arms around Caro and Hannah. "I feel like I haven't seen you guys in ages." She squeezed Hannah's shoulder. "Check your texts once in a while, will ya?"

Hannah shot her a guilty look. She'd seen Noelle's breezy messages and cute memes, but she knew if she replied, the truth would come out.

It had to sooner or later.

Caro brushed back some hair as she looked at Hannah. "So I shouldn't take your ignoring me as a personal affront? Everyone's being ghosted?"

"I broke up with Keith," she said on just enough of a whisper that both women had to lean in as if they didn't quite hear her.

But their dropped jaws said they had.

She braced for a barrage of questions or, worse, congratulations, but both of them simply wrapped her in a hug without saying a word.

"Can I get in on this?" Angie called.

"Me three," Eve added.

They expanded the circle and soon it was a five-way hug, and Hannah murmured the news again. Eve and Angie looked as shocked as Caro and Noelle.

Hannah inched back and held up her hands. "Can I share all the deets later? I'm sure the kids are chomping at the bit to cut down a tree, and everyone is here. After we decorate the tree?"

"Of course!" Noelle gushed. "Just tell us how you're doing."

"Yes, please," Caro said. "That's all we care about. Not how it happened, or why."

"How is uneventful, why is..." She gave a dry laugh. "You *know* why. And I'm fine, really. A little shell-shocked, but I'm good. And I just want to have fun tonight and talk later."

Everyone agreed and hugged her again, moving in a pack toward Bitsy and Sonny, who were surrounded by the younger boy cousins, all bouncing with excitement.

With the babies in strollers and all the jackets and gloves on tightly against a chilly mountaintop wind, they headed down a snow-crusted path toward the entrance. Just making the walk had Hannah thinking about the last time she was here, on a field trip, flirting with—

"Welcome, everyone!"

*Him.*

Hannah hung back as Brandon greeted the gang with high-fives for the kids, handshakes for the adults, and a smile that...that she hadn't forgotten. She listened as he explained where to go for the larger trees to cut—that got a big cheer from the boys—and that he and his dad were here to help if they needed it.

Still lingering behind Noelle and Caro, Hannah tucked her hands into her parka and looked around the rolling hills of the farm. The sun hadn't quite set, giving a golden glow to everything as she turned, taking in a deep breath of the crisp air.

"Hey, I know you."

Despite the coolness, a low-grade heat bubbled as she met the blue eyes she'd thought about more than a few times since she'd been here.

"Hello, Brandon," she said with a smile, tipping her head toward the gang. "My second field trip in a week."

He laughed and followed her gaze to Eve's boys, who'd already taken off. "I have a feeling you're not in charge of this bunch."

"Not a chance. This is my family, as you might have guessed. Oh, Caro." She eased her sister closer. "Have you ever met Brandon Fletcher?"

"You're April's little brother," she said brightly. "How is your sister? We had some classes together in high school and I liked her so much."

"She's good. Lives in Tampa and is four months from Baby Number Three," he told her. "Don't make me whip out pictures of the other two. I'll go all Uncle Brandon on you."

She laughed and gave Hannah a playful elbow jab. "Just like our Aunt Hannah, here. Tell April I said hi."

"I will." He turned as Noelle and Eve stepped closer and, once again, Hannah did the introductions. Then one of Eve's boys called, and they all said a quick goodbye and started off. Hannah hadn't made it five steps when a light hand landed on her parka sleeve.

"Making another quick getaway?" Brandon asked with a tease in his voice.

She dug around for a quip that would be the perfect response—funny, light, flirtatious but not too much so. Instead, she stared at him like a fool.

"I guess you're terrified I'll make you face your fears again."

"Face...my fears?" She had a feeling she *was* facing them.

"Snow tubing."

"Oh, yeah." *Geez, Hannah. Get with it.* "But that was fun."

"The tubes are out if you want a nighttime run. No screaming kids. Well, none that you have to keep track of."

"Oh, I...well, I'm with my family."

"Another time, then?" he asked, looking hopeful and sweet and...way too real. Yes, he was attractive, but Hannah was barely out of a long relationship. She...*couldn't.*

"Maybe," she said quickly, glancing at the group and

noticing Noelle had hung back to wait for her. "I better go."

He gave a smile and a nod and she walked across the frozen grass, squeezing her eyes shut and wishing she could have done that whole exchange over again.

"Did you want to stay and talk to him?" Noelle asked.

Not yet. It was too soon. Much, much too soon. "Oh, no. I met him when I had my class up here for a field trip last week. He was just...asking about one of the kids who was scared to go tubing."

"Oh, gotcha. He's a cutie. Love the long hair, huh?"

"It's too soon, Noelle," she said quickly. "I know he's great-looking—hard to ignore that—and he's really nice, and I would like to talk to him but I honestly don't even know how and I'm scared and it's just so soon."

Noelle stopped and gave an amused look. "I only said he was cute."

Hannah laughed. "And I spewed all my churned-up emotions and complicated feelings and...stuff."

"Relax and breathe, hon," Noelle said, sliding an arm around her. "No pressure on you or anyone else."

Hannah sighed, nodding. "Yeah, you're right."

"Come on. Let's cheer on the tree cutting."

They let the subject drop as they made their way to an orchard where most of the family—the boys, especially—had surrounded a beauty waiting to be cut.

"I think we'll need a good electric saw," David said as they gathered around the biggest one.

"I've got that right here." Brandon joined them,

carrying a chainsaw as if it were as light as a pair of scissors.

"Oh, he reminds me of Jace," Noelle whispered to Hannah.

"He doesn't look like Jace," Hannah replied.

"No, but I remember when we were here last year and Jace showed up with his saw looking like a hunk of a mountain man." Noelle's gaze shifted to her husband, who had just hoisted Cassie onto his shoulders so she could have a great view. "And now he's mine."

"It happened fast," Hannah reflected. "I guess when you know, you know."

"Oh, we knew when we were fifteen," Noelle replied. "But, yeah, when you know, you know." She turned and looked at Hannah. "You also know when it's not right."

She gave a sad smile. "Uh, it took eleven years to face that particular music. But I finally listened to the tune."

Noelle leaned into her. "You okay, really?" she whispered, her voice nearly lost as the saw started screaming.

"I am, I promise. Tough time of year but it had to happen." She let out a sigh. "You're right, Noelle. When you know, you know. I'm just scared that...I'll never know."

"Stop it. I was older than you when I stumbled into Jace on Creekside Road, still certain I would spend my life alone in a Manhattan high-rise. Now?" She stuck out her boot. "I'm a ranch girl in love with a man I never saw coming."

"Oh." Hannah squeezed her eyes. "You've been an

inspiration, maybe more than you know. I want that same happy ending, but I don't even know where to look."

"Well, I don't know where *you* should look..." She said with a tease in her voice and the most imperceptible elbow jab. "Because we're up to eight, no, make that nine times that cute guy has looked over here hoping to get your attention."

"Really?" She felt her eyes widen but purposely didn't look at where she knew he was standing. "He's just being..."

"Interested," Noelle said. "I know, I know, too soon. Oh, here comes the tree."

Hannah looked up at the pine but met those piercing blue eyes pinned directly on her instead.

"Timber!" Sawyer screamed as his father stretched out his hands to keep everyone clear. "Somethin's gonna fall!"

The pine landed with a noisy thud, a puff of powder, and a loud cheer from the family. But through it all, Hannah and Brandon held that gaze, only breaking when someone walked between them.

They cheered and gathered round while Brandon and two of his employees helped lift and carry the felled pine. As he passed, his arms around the trunk, he glanced at Hannah.

"Meet me at the sales shack in the front," he said. "I want to show you something."

He was gone before she could answer, moving rapidly in time with the three other men, leaving her standing to watch him disappear into the orchard.

When they left, she turned to Noelle, who wore a slightly smug "I told you so" smile.

"Tim*ber*," Noelle whispered. "Somethin's *definitely* gonna fall."

Hannah laughed as a shudder of that giddy excitement rolled through her.

SHE TRIED TO WAIT. Tried to play a teeny bit hard to get. Tried to give the unexpected invitation a few minutes, so Hannah lingered with the family, enjoying the company and the air.

The kids wanted to go snow tubing, so taking a deep breath, she headed to the sales area of the farm. There, a wooden structure where precut trees were lined up for purchase—a temporary outdoor "shack" that went up every November and, she assumed, disappeared in January—was lit with vineyard lights and heat lamps.

Harry, his wife, and a few employees chatted with customers near a table with free steaming cups of coffee and hot chocolate.

She spotted Brandon, who was finishing tying a small tree to a minivan parked about twenty feet away. With her heart pounding more than it should, Hannah waited, leaning against a wooden railing, inhaling the scent of fresh-cut pine and winter air.

He jogged back as the van disappeared down the hill, giving her a wide smile of greeting.

"I need a break," he said as he reached her, the tiniest bit breathless from carrying trees. "Take a walk with me?"

"Sure."

He gestured for her to follow him through the parking area to a hilly area covered in snow.

"I know you don't want to snow tube," he said. "How do you feel about ice skating?"

"Now?"

"Well, it's a busy night, so later, if you like. Or another time. I wasn't sure you knew we have a skateable pond."

"I know there's a small lake here," she said, remembering Eve had talked about skating there when the triplets were little.

"Different pond. Smaller, and secret." He led her down a slope and around a curve to a path that seemed to hug the side of the hill. "You might want to plan your third field trip out here."

Was that why he was bringing her out here? To plan another field trip?

No. He would have let go of her hand if that were the case.

As if he read her thoughts, he took a few steps ahead, holding back a tree branch that hung over the path.

"Okay, this part is steep, which is why not a lot of people know about it. Be careful, but it's worth the risk."

He put his arm around her and slowly led her down an embankment. With the waning light, she had to squint to see where they were going, but at the bottom, he guided her around a large grouping of thick pines.

"Look," he said in a voice rich with reverence.

She exhaled at the sight. "Oh, wow." Rolling hills, covered in trees and dusted in snow, surrounding a frozen pond that glistened in the fading light. The moon rose over a cabin tucked into the woods near the pond, offering up a scene that looked like someone had painted it.

"This is gorgeous," she exclaimed.

"I live here now." He gazed at the vista, pride in his eyes. "My parents' house is up closer to the orchard, and I might move there after the holidays when they go to Tampa. For now, I'm here and I love it."

"It's spectacular," she said, drinking it all in. "Is this... what you wanted to show me?"

"Yeah, this is my pond. Well, I guess it's technically my dad's, but I learned to skate here when I was really little, like two or three. Pushed my first puck over this pond, and got hockey fever."

She split her attention from his delighted and proud expression to the icy pond, imagining him as a child learning to skate, then a young man gliding down the ice with a stick and a puck ...then playing professionally.

"I know it's not a great time to skate," he said. "But I thought I'd have a better chance of getting you to say yes if I showed it to you before I asked you to come back sometime and ice skate with me."

Her eyes widened as she realized he was definitely asking her on a date.

"It's shallow and completely safe," he said quickly, misreading her reaction. "I know you're...scared." At her look, he added, "I mean, you were a little cautious on the snow tubing."

"I am scared," she admitted on a whisper. "But not... of ice skating."

"Oh, good, then maybe..." His voice faded as he studied her face and no doubt was smart enough to read her expression. "Of me?" he guessed.

She laughed softly. "Of..." How did she describe it? "I, uh, just broke up with someone."

He lifted his brows hopefully. "I love it when I have good timing."

"But I'm not sure it is," she said. "I mean, it just happened, like five days ago, after...a long time together." She grimaced. "Eleven years."

"Whoa." He drew back. "I guess I should have done some homework, but when I saw you tonight, I kind of... decided to try. You're not ready to dip your toes in the water yet?"

"Or on the ice," she said on a laugh. "But...wow. Thank you."

He searched her face for a long moment, his own thoughts impossible to read. "Was it bad? Like cheating bad or...God, never mind. None of my business."

"No, nothing like that," she said. "I just wanted more than he was willing to give. You know, the whole thing... till death do us part and all that nonsense."

"It's not nonsense," he said, shockingly serious. "And I'm sorry for the breakup. Rough time of year, too." He kind of shuffled a little, with a glimmer of shyness that just made him that much more attractive. "Guess we better get back. Our field trip's done."

Oh. Was it? She didn't want it to be over. She didn't want to leave him or turn him down or end this moment in the snowy valley.

She stayed stone still as he started to walk. After a few steps, he turned back and looked at her.

"I understand if it's too soon, Hannah. But when you're ready, I'll be here. Skates are hanging beside the cabin door and if I'm not cutting down trees, I'm inside with a fire and a good book."

She still didn't move, frozen by fear and uncertainty going to war with how much she wanted to say yes.

Fear won, sadly.

A few hours later, with carols echoing through the cabin and the laughter of her family adding to the music, Hannah was still thinking about Brandon Fletcher and his invitation.

She'd filled in Caro, the triplets, and Aunt Bitsy on her breakup and not one of them said they were relieved or happy. No surprise, all they cared about was Hannah and if she was all right with things.

As the evening ended, Noelle got her alone in the kitchen, giving her a very expectant look.

"What?" Hannah asked on a laugh.

"You know what. You disappeared with cute tree farmer guy."

"Brandon," she said. "And we just took a walk."

"And..."

"And he asked me to go skating with him and I..."

"Told him it was too soon," Noelle guessed with a sad and frustrated sigh.

"Because it is."

Noelle looked like she didn't agree but understood. "Just be careful, Hannah."

"I am," she insisted. "Why do you think I said no?"

"I mean be careful you don't protect your heart so completely that no one can get to it."

The words hit that protected heart, and she knew she'd be thinking about that wise warning for a long time to come.

# Chapter Thirteen

## Noelle

The morning had flown by at the gallery with so many customers, two meetings with artists, and a shipment that had to be handled, all before lunch. Noelle was ready to head out for something to eat when she heard the front door open.

So much for eating, she thought as she pushed up from the conference table where she'd been working and leaned over the railing to see who'd come in. As soon as she did, she let out a squeal of delight at the sight of her sister, Eve, with little Jackie in a stroller.

"This is a surprise!"

Eve looked up and beamed at her. "Hello! We come bearing sandwiches and love."

"Nothing I want more." She hustled to the steps and darted down, arms extended but not sure who she wanted to hug first—the angel looking up at her with a sweet smile or the sister gazing back with a hesitant look on her face.

"You don't mind us barging in?" Eve asked, taking the warm embrace Noelle offered.

"Are you kidding? I'm alone on the floor, so I might get pulled away but I was just about to get something to eat. Perfect timing." She bent down to kiss little Jackie, getting a gooey hand on her face and a big smile with those four little teeth they'd all gotten so excited about.

"Hello, my sweet niece! I love you!"

Jackie answered by flexing her fingers, silently demanding to be picked up.

"Can I?" Noelle asked.

"At the risk of getting a Cheerio or two on that silk blouse, knock yourself out."

"I do not mind a Cheerio," she said, half in baby talk as she kissed the soft cheek she loved so much. "I do not mind it, Sam I Am."

Jackie giggled, probably having no idea what she was saying, but she was a sweetheart of a child, affectionate and happy.

Once Noelle had her settled on her hip, she turned to Eve, who had a goofy look on her face.

"What?" Noelle asked.

"Oh, nothing. It's just that you're a natural."

She pushed her lip out in a sad face. "Not that natural."

Eve drew back. "What does that mean? Are you okay?"

"I'm fine," she said, trying to sound bright but the disappointment she'd just felt was way too fresh to fool her sister. "What brought on this surprise visit?"

"I have time, for once in my life," she said on a happy laugh. "Time to visit and Christmas shop and enjoy my baby. So, I decided we needed some Aunt Noelle time. It was so fun the other night at the tree thing, but we didn't really get to talk."

"Aw, I know." She kissed the baby's head. "And I need some Gallagher girl time."

Eve reached down to the back of the stroller to pull out a bag with the Loretta's Café logo on it. "Split a Big Lo with me?"

"With fries?" Noelle's voice rose in excitement.

"And banana slices for the under-two crowd."

Noelle punched the air with a victory fist using her free hand, scooting Jackie higher on her hip. "Let's set up a picnic in my meeting loft while I still have one. Next year, it'll be another gallery."

"That's exciting," Eve said, snapping the stroller closed with the ease and proficiency of a seasoned mother.

Back upstairs, Noelle cleared her laptop and work off the conference table with her one free hand while still keeping the other comfortably around Jackie.

"Look at you," Eve joked. "You really are a natural with that baby on your hip."

Noelle shot her a look. "You're killin' me, Eve."

"Why?"

Noelle didn't answer until they'd laid out the food and had the delightful sandwich divided between them, with fries and drinks, and a paper plate with a banana cut up for Jackie, who stayed firmly planted on Noelle's lap.

"I might have to toss you to Mom if someone comes in wanting to buy art," she said to the baby, punctuating it with a kiss. "But until then, you're all mine. Maybe the only baby I'll ever bounce."

Eve lowered the sandwich, glanced at Jackie, who was preoccupied with her banana, and leaned closer. "What's going on with you, Noelle?"

She sighed. "You really don't know?"

"That's why I asked, although I do know you well enough to recognize that something is bugging you, dear triplet of mine. We did share a womb."

"That," she said softly.

"The...womb?" Eve asked, frowning and not following.

"I haven't told you and Angie yet, but..." She made a face and stage whispered, "We're kind of trying to have a baby."

Eve gasped softly.

"And failing," Noelle added. "Some days I really worry that it's just a dream that will never happen."

"Oh, wow." Eve abandoned the sandwich completely and scooted closer. "David and I were just talking about that."

"Another one?" Noelle asked, a little horrified but laughing, too.

"No, about you and Jace. I suspected you might be thinking about it."

Noelle shrugged. "We're doing more than thinking, but..." She lifted a hand in resignation. "December twenty-fifth looms and we'll all be forty-one. Closer to menopause than pregnancy, I'm afraid."

"Oh, I so remember thinking about this," Eve said. "It

scared me, too. So much that I jumped on the chance to have someone hand me that baby in your arms."

"And I love this baby in my arms," Noelle cooed, smashing kisses on Jackie's soft curls.

In response, Jackie whipped around and slapped a playful hand on Noelle's chest, slathering her silk blouse with banana.

"Oh, no!" Eve said, sitting up.

"It's fine." Noelle glanced down at the mess and just smiled. "I have a change of clothes in my office."

"Wow." Eve dropped back, gazing with a little wonder in her eyes. "You are ready for this."

"Ready, willing, and wildly disappointed every month," she said glumly. "But there's nothing I can do about it, so—"

"There's plenty you can do about it," Eve countered as they both took bites of their sandwich. "Aren't you the original control freak?"

"I am, but I'm not going to adopt a baby," Noelle said. "I have Cassie and she's like having ten of any other child."

Eve smiled. "She's amazing, it's true. But there are other things you can do to...well, not take matters into your own hands, but exercise some control over the situation."

Noelle studied her, always interested in exercising control. "Like..."

"Have you seen a doctor?" Eve asked.

Noelle shook her head. "Not since we started seriously trying. I haven't even found a gyno yet, which I should do, but...everything's normal, you know? I'm as regular as a Swiss watch, no pain or problems, and obviously Jace can make a baby, so..."

"You still should get checked. Why not see a fertility specialist?"

Noelle inched back, considering the question. "I guess I thought it was too soon and also, I don't want to take drugs or start fertility treatments. I like control, yes, but I don't want that. If that's my only option, I'll accept the fact that I'm not going to have children."

"There are a lot of..." Eve lifted a shoulder. "Nuances in infertility. Something could be wrong that's an easy fix."

"Like what?"

"A tipped uterus or a mild asymptomatic case of endometriosis," Eve said, sounding very much like a woman married to a doctor. "I'm just talking first-line checkup to make sure everything is in perfect working order."

"And if it isn't?"

"Cross that bridge when you come to it, but peace of mind is worth a lot."

Noelle nodded, liking the suggestion a lot. "I do want a baby," she said softly, bringing a banana-filled spoon to Jackie's mouth. "But that doesn't mean I'm not happy and I don't want Jace or Cassie or anyone to think that everything I have isn't enough."

Eve reached over the table. "No one thinks that. What you want is natural. You love Jace and Cassie and a baby would make all your lives even better." She glanced at the banana stain. "Maybe not cleaner, but better."

Noelle smiled and fed the spoonful to Jackie, loving the feel of the child in her arms. "You're right. I'd like to know if there's anything wrong. I'll find someone—"

"No, no. *I'll* find someone." Eve already had her phone out, tapping the screen. "Let me text David. He's on a local medical board with a fertility specialist. He'll be able to get you in right away."

"You do not let grass grow, Eve Gallagher."

Jackie pushed the spoon away and stretched both arms out toward Eve.

"Oh, she wants her mama," Noelle said, finally relinquishing the baby.

Eve took her with that same effortless grace that she showed with the stroller, as though navigating motherhood was her first language.

"Now *you* are a pro," Noelle said longingly.

"I better be after four of them. Eat your sandwich," Eve said. "And then you will definitely want to change your shirt before another customer comes in."

"I will, but—"

"Oh, he wrote back." Eve tapped her phone. "Here's the name and number. I'll forward it to you. It won't hurt to find out if anything's wrong. If it is, you might want to fix it. If it isn't, then maybe you'll relax."

"That's what I'm supposed to do—relax. Which is easier said than done for a person like me."

"Exactly, so call." Eve pointed to Noelle's phone, which sat face down untouched on the table. "Make the appointment and you'll feel like you have a little control, anyway."

"You know me so well. Now?"

"Is there a better time? David said he'd text the doctor and her staff can be notified to squeeze you in as soon as possible."

Noelle's eyes widened. "What's the rush?"

"Asks the woman about to turn forty-one."

Noelle grunted, knowing she was right. Picking up her phone, she opened the text and read the name Dr. Marcia Andrews.

She touched the phone number and the screen flashed, ringing on speaker so Eve could hear, too. A receptionist answered on the second ring, all bright and efficient. As though God Himself were moving the pieces on the chess board of life, Dr. Andrews just had a cancellation for her four o'clock appointment.

Could Noelle come in this afternoon?

The two of them shared a look—Noelle feeling conflicted, Eve looking encouraging. Doing her part, Jackie snuggled closer to Eve's heart and let out a shuddering sigh, murmuring, "*Mamamama.*"

And that was game over.

"I can definitely be there at four," Noelle said, not even a hundred percent sure what she'd say to the doctor.

She hung up and stared at her sister, a little stunned by her spontaneity.

"Good job," Eve said.

"I have to call Jace and tell him. He might be able to meet me there."

"Perfect. Oh—" Eve turned at the sound of the gallery door opening. "You have to work."

Noelle brushed at the banana stain, which really wasn't that bad, still thinking about what she'd say to the doctor.

"Let me see if they need help," she said, pausing next to Eve, then bending over to kiss her sister's head. "I love you."

Eve looked up at her and smiled. "Jackie doesn't have any sisters, so...have a girl, okay?"

Noelle lifted a shoulder. "Now that much control, I don't have."

But the appointment made her feel like she had a little, so that was good.

A LLAMA with a blocked esophagus kept Jace from coming to the appointment, but he'd been strongly supportive of the idea. Noelle had gone alone and now, she was slipping into her clothes and inhaling the antiseptic scent of the doctor's office, not sure how she felt about what all had occurred.

After a blood test and an ultrasound, the doctor had done a pelvic exam, asking many questions as she proceeded. But, through it all, Noelle had been tense, which made no sense considering how kind and welcoming everyone had been. Nothing that should make her nervous or tense.

But...she was. A baby wasn't a pipe dream—this was a real dream. And Noelle always got what she wanted. And wasn't that why Eve sent her here in the first place—to know?

She looked up at the tap on the door, which opened to reveal the warm smile of the nurse.

"I'll take you to the doctor's office now," she said. "If you're ready."

A minute later, she stepped into a sunny and spacious office, greeting Dr. Andrews as she looked up from an open file. The woman was in her early fifties, with keen dark eyes and an easy laugh, and Noelle imagined she was well-regarded for her lovely bedside manner.

"Have a seat, Noelle." She gestured to the guest chair and Noelle made herself comfortable.

"So, am I in good working order?" she asked.

The doctor's eyes flickered for a nanosecond, instantly replaced by a smile. "You're a healthy woman, Noelle."

*Oh, boy.* Her heart dropped. "But?"

She angled her head in concession. "I believe you have a structural abnormality in your uterus."

Wincing, she inched back. "Like a 'tipped' uterus?" she asked, remembering that was one thing that Eve had mentioned.

"It's a little more complicated," the doctor said. "We've ruled out a lot of issues such as PCOS and thyroid or hyperprolactinemia."

Noelle made another face and Dr. Andrews chuckled. "Fancy word for hormone issues. Your blood work is fine, your cycles are normal, you have no visible polyps or fibroids, no endometriosis, and your overall health is excellent. No reason you shouldn't get pregnant. I do think I see a septate uterus, which means a band of tissue has formed in the uterine cavity. But you said your periods aren't painful."

"Not the kind that put a woman in bed for two days, but I get cramps."

"And you power through."

Noelle smiled. "It's kind of who I am."

"I get that. A septate uterus can prevent any fertilized egg from implanting."

She bit her lip. "You mean I can't get pregnant?"

"I don't know that yet, but it certainly explains why you haven't. You may have actually conceived, but the egg won't take hold. Eventually, it miscarries without you even knowing you were pregnant."

"Can it be fixed?"

"Possibly."

She didn't sound that certain, which deepened the pit in Noelle's stomach.

"First, we'd need to do an MRI and an HSG, which is essentially a minimally invasive X-ray using contrast fluid in your uterus."

Noelle grunted. "That doesn't sound fun."

"It's painless and easy, but if we do have a septate, the solution is surgery to correct it."

"What kind of surgery?" she asked.

"Hysteroscopic metroplasty, which sounds far worse

than it is. HM isn't a terribly complicated surgery and it has a high degree of success, but..."

Noelle inched closer, all the blood in her body pooling low in her gut, somewhere in the vicinity of her imperfect uterus. "But what?"

She shook her head. "Every year you age makes it more complicated, and the success rates are higher with women under forty. This doesn't mean you can't do this, Noelle. You can start the tests, meet the surgeon, and schedule the procedure, recover and heal and—"

"Then will I get pregnant?"

"Your chances are higher, yes."

Higher, but not...high. "Oh." She closed her eyes as the whole thing pressed down on her. "It's...a lot."

"It is," the doctor agreed, and Noelle appreciated her not sugarcoating the truth. "You need to think about it, talk to your husband, and decide if you want to go through something like this—again, not terribly complicated, but it is surgery—and miscarriage rates are still higher than average. That means, it could take several—"

"Years," Noelle finished.

"Tries," the other woman corrected with a smile.

Noelle swallowed, her head swimming with it all. "And if I don't have the surgery?"

"Conception is unlikely, to be honest. If it happens, the chance of miscarriage is high, even with bedrest or precautions."

"And if I don't do this? Could I be in pain or..."

"Absolutely not. There are no effects of this situation if you don't want a baby. You'll continue your cycles until they get irregular, then you'll enter menopause at the normal time and will go the rest of your life with no issues."

And no baby.

"Then...I have to think about it," she said.

"Yes, you do. And I'll be here when you're ready to talk about the next step, whatever it is."

She nodded, shook hands, and left the office with a lump in her throat and an ache in her chest.

In the car, alone, she let the tears flow even though she wasn't exactly sure why.

As she reached for the ignition, she closed her eyes and for no reason she could really understand, she saw her mother's face. Well, maybe she understood the reason.

If Jackie Chambers were still alive, she'd know what to do. She'd take Noelle's hand and tell her exactly what was the right thing to do.

For now, Noelle had no idea. She could talk to Jace—of course she would—and her sisters and Bitsy and doctors. But the only person who could make this decision was Noelle, and she had no idea what to do.

It gave her some of the control she craved, but no guarantees. And surgery was always a risk, no matter how routine. She'd always been a risktaker, but now she had Jace and Cassie to consider. If anything happened to her and that sweet angel lost *another* mother?

She swiped her tears and started the car, not even wanting to think about that.

# Chapter Fourteen

## Angie

"You picked the perfect spot, Angel."

Try as she might, Angie could not get used to anyone calling her Angel. So that must be the reason why every time Elliott said her name, she got a little kick out of it.

Or maybe because he always said it while those indescribable sometimes brown-sometimes green-and occasionally gold eyes were leveled on her with a glimmer of delight and a glint of interest.

Or—this had to be it—he was so frequently complimenting her on her work or ideas during the hours they'd worked together preparing for the *Magi* event.

Whatever it was, when he called her "Angel," it made her happy.

"Yes," she agreed, stepping back to the large gallery where tourists were usually gathered in groups, gawking at the three masterpiece tapestries that covered the limestone walls.

It was nearly midnight, since it took hours for the crew to wrap and carry the numerous settees and tables that furnished one-third of George Vanderbilt's famous tapestry gallery. The massive estate was dim, lit by just essential lamps, and eerily quiet now that the move was complete.

"I know it blocks the *Triumph of Faith* tapestry," Angie said as she and Elliott stood side by side and imagined the layout when the painting arrived. "But this site is central and dramatic."

"You're right." He took a few steps closer. "You really have an eye for placement, Angel, and that's a huge skill in curatorship."

"Thank you. It made the most sense, considering the painting isn't that big or…" Her voice trailed off and he turned to her with a question in his eyes.

"Or what?" he asked when she couldn't come up with something better than what she was thinking.

It wasn't that big or *beautiful*.

She didn't dare admit that to him.

"Well, it's not that big," she said. "But very famous," she added. "So famous."

His lips tipped up in a smile. "What were you really going to say?"

"Nothing."

"Angel."

A laugh bubbled up, as it often did with him. "It's just that it's an, um, unusual color."

He pretended to look horrified. "The color? First of all, there are many, and they are muted, earthy, and, sadly, faded by time. I think the tones convey a sense of humility and the theme of worship, which is what the Magi did."

She stared at him. "Yes, of course," she finally said.

"But you hate it."

"I just think it's very, um, yellow."

"Yes, the base level is painted with a lead-tin yellow, and brown ochre." He took a step closer, his eyes narrowing playfully. "Which, let me guess, is not Christmasy enough for you."

Biting her lip to keep from laughing, she half-nodded, half-shrugged. "Art is subjective."

"Are you sure you're talking about da Vinci's *Adoration*? There are many, many paintings that bear the same name."

"This would be...the yellow one?"

He choked a laugh. "Uh, yes, that would be one way to describe one of Leonardo's greatest works of art. It's unfinished. Still stunning in its composition and message, and the work is, well, da Vinci. You know that, don't you?"

"Yes, yes, but..." She crinkled her nose. "It's just not a really happy moment, is it?"

"There's a baby and a virgin, three wise men—"

"And some really creepy folks all around."

He threw his head back and laughed. "Yes, there are. They symbolize war and famine and death, with the hope of Jesus in the midst of it all."

"Oh. I hadn't thought of it that way." She pointed at him. "Good thing I picked a good room or you'd fire me right now, wouldn't you?"

"I'd be crazy if I did," he said. "No one knows this place like you do, at least not on the curator staff. Yes, they know art, but there's a lot more to the Biltmore Estate than art."

She lifted both fists. "Hallelujah! He sees the light."

"I'm serious," he said with a beaming smile. "You're a valued employee. Maybe more than I am."

It wasn't the first time she'd heard him make a veiled comment about his job, but it was the most obvious one he'd ever let slip. Surely that meant he wanted to, or would, talk about it.

"I guess Marjorie left big shoes to fill," she said, purposely vague.

He huffed out a breath. "It's not the size of the shoes, it's the direction I want to walk." He stared at the spot where *The Adoration of the Magi* would be placed, quiet for a long time.

"Something you want to share?" she prodded gently.

"Yes, but I'm not sure where to begin or if I should burden you with...things."

"I love burdens," she said quickly. "I love things. And I love gossip, so spill."

He turned to her. "You know what I love?"

"Da Vinci?" she guessed.

"Funny women."

Some blood warmed her cheeks. "Well, be wary of them because we hide all manner of things with humor."

"That's the challenge," he said. "Trying to figure out what you're hiding."

"You're the one hiding something," she countered. "What are the burdensome things you're not telling me? The exhibit broke the bank and you can't give out

Christmas bonuses? Don't worry, I wasn't expecting one."

He glanced around left and right. "Guess you can't really sit and talk in this room, huh?"

"We can find somewhere that isn't a hundred-year-old antique," she said, sensing he really did want to talk. "Because we're done and the painting is being delivered tomorrow."

"Panel," he corrected. "The work is not technically a painting, but a section of fresco."

"Oh, I...didn't know that," she admitted sheepishly. "And here I go again displaying my ignorance."

He shook his head. "You're the opposite of ignorant, Angel. You're actually the very person this museum is trying to attract—families, mothers, people who can appreciate the home that we're in more than the museum."

She smiled, grateful that she'd made that point with her boss.

"But I'm not," he added. "And I think I've made a few decisions in my very short time here that have ruffled more feathers than yours."

"You haven't ruffled my feathers," she said. He'd ruffled...other things. But no feathers. "Who's ruffled?"

"Your instinct is right. Corporate is very iffy on... this." He gestured to the space they'd been preparing. "There's been zero uptick in ticket sales since we announced it, the PR has been lackluster, and I'm afraid the average estate visitor is here at Christmas for the ribbons and lights and not..."

"Not the yellow panel that Leonardo da Vinci never finished," she supplied.

He laughed softly. "And yes, the budget to rent it broke the bank or at least ate into next year's bottom line."

She felt a teeny bit vindicated by the news, but the fact was she liked him too much to gloat.

"I'm sure the exhibit will be a big success," she said.

"It better be."

The tone surprised her. "Don't worry, Elliott. Visitors will pour through this gallery and absolutely love seeing something that came all the way from the Uffizi in Florence."

He angled his head, looking unconvinced. "If it gets ignored, overlooked, or panned in reviews and the press? I might be looking for another job."

Wow. It was bad. Marjorie wasn't kidding.

"Never mind," he said quickly, swiping his hand as if he could erase what he'd just said. "Not your problem."

"If you get fired, it is," she countered. "You just said I'm a valued employee. You think I want to do a song and dance for yet another boss?"

"You're a good singer and dancer," he said, holding her gaze. "I bought into the Angel Chambers musical, starting with a...crash in Act I."

She cringed. "Again, sorry about that."

He didn't answer for a minute, then leaned in a little closer. "And speaking of Christmas bonuses..."

Chills tiptoed up her spine, lifting the hairs on the nape of her neck. She had no idea where he was going, but chances were pretty strong right then that she'd follow.

"I should use mine before they yank it away when some influencer goes on social media and says they hated the yellow blob by da Vinci."

"Use yours? How?"

He reached into his pocket and pulled out a noisy key chain. "I have the keys to the kingdom—well, the winery, where I have been told I'm allowed to pick any bottle of wine—within reason—for my very own as a Christmas gift. Want to share it with me?"

Her jaw loosened. "Now? The winery's closed and..." She laughed at his look and the delicious sensation when he reached for her hand. "Of course. Let's go to the winery."

APPARENTLY, the keys to the kingdom included a golf cart, parked in the employee lot. Laughing, with jackets open to the cold night air, Angie and Elliott hustled to it, and then rumbled out of the lot and onto the road that meandered through the whole estate.

Tucking her hands into her pockets, she let her body lean into his when he took a tight bend, inhaling crisp air when the moonlight spilled over the woods, then onto the rolling mountains beyond.

"That's pretty," he said, shifting his gaze from the dark asphalt ahead of them to the glorious view.

"Like a little piece of the Blue Ridge Parkway," she agreed.

"Which I haven't seen yet."

She turned to him, agape. "And you've been here a month?"

"My car was in the shop for most of it."

"Okay, my bad," she acknowledged, laughing. "We'll take a drive there soon."

He tossed her a sideways glance, that amusement glinting again.

"I mean...if you want to and..." She just rolled her eyes and shook her head. "If you haven't been canned."

He pulled up to the very back of the winery, a major attraction at the estate, but it looked closed tight for the night. He didn't seem bothered by that. Feeling adventurous and daring, she climbed out and followed him to a side door even she hadn't known about.

"This leads to the cellars and a tasting room," he told her.

"Well, membership certainly has its privileges," she joked. "I've never been to the wine cellar and thought you had to get to the tasting room from the front."

"Different tasting room," he told her. "This one is where I closed the deal on my contract," he said, his voice sounding wistful.

She followed him down a dimly lit hallway and stone stairs, reaching an open door at the end.

He touched the switch to spill a soft golden glow over the room, which was small and furnished only with three high-tops and a few barstools.

"Ah, the speakeasy," she said, glancing around to see a wine bar along one wall with a bottle-filled rack on the opposite side.

"This room is for Biltmore execs, VIPs, and their guests," he said, gesturing for her to join him at the wine rack. "It's run by the honor system. And, as I said, I get a bottle for Christmas, and one for my one-year anniversary." He leaned closer to her, dipping his head to whisper, "If I make it."

She almost laughed but his voice was way too serious. "You don't really think..."

"No, not unless there's a catastrophe with one of my major projects. Red or white?"

"Definitely red."

He ran a hand over the wax-covered corks. "These are all Biltmore Estate label and I think every one is excellent. Pinot Noir? Cabernet?"

"I love a good cab or merlot."

"Perfect." He pulled out a bottle and blew on the dust. "How about a Biltmore Reserve, 2021? Looks like a nice rich merlot with..." He turned the bottle over to read the notes on the side. "Approachable flavors of raspberry under a warm blanket of pomegranate." He lifted a brow. "Who writes this stuff?"

She laughed. "Are you sure we can be here? We're not going to get arrested and then fired?"

"We can be here and no one will arrest us." He slid the bottle back and chose another. "Ah, full bodied and fruity, with blackberry notes and a lingering finish. I like it."

"I'll take it."

Snagging a corkscrew that hung on the wall, he brought the bottle to a high-top table in the middle of the room and set it down, gesturing for her to sit, then walked behind the bar and found two crystal goblets.

As Angie settled onto a barstool, she said, "This feels very much like something I'd kill my teenage daughter for doing."

"As you should, but I promise you, we're allowed to be here and we can drink this wine." Still standing, he twisted the cork and popped it with the ease of someone extremely adept at uncorking wine.

"Taste?" he asked, hovering the bottle over the glass.

"I'm sure I'll love it and I won't pretend to know what I'm doing, but yeah."

He poured a small amount in the glass, then lifted it and offered it to her. "You know what I like most about you, Angel?"

She reached for the glass, hoping he didn't notice that the question made her fingers tremble slightly. "I don't have any idea," she replied honestly.

"You don't take yourself too seriously," he said, then gestured for her to drink. "Go ahead."

She took the tiniest sip, surprised by the peppery, rich taste on her lips. "Oh...wow. That is not your twelve-dollar twist-off that I buy at the supermarket."

"No, it is not."

Before he sat on the other stool, he poured their glasses less than half full, but they were huge goblets, so it was plenty of wine. Then he scooted across from her and lifted his glass in a toast.

"To da Vinci's yellow blob?" she guessed, making him laugh again.

"I was going to toast to you, an endearing, humble, hilarious, and beautiful woman I am honored to bring to the inner sanctum, as you call it."

Heat rose to her cheeks. "You had me at endearing."

"You are, you know." He dinged her crystal rim with his and took a sip, locking eyes with her, then quickly looking down. "I don't...I'm not...Sorry to be bold, Angel."

"It's fine," she said softly. "We're adults. We can...flirt."

"Not my style, usually, but you definitely bring something out in me."

"As long as it's not a pink slip, we're good."

He laughed, but his smile faded.

"You're not really worried about your job, are you?" she asked.

Looking at the wine, he absently turned the glass, thinking for a few seconds before answering. "This position was definitely a stretch for me, and for the Biltmore."

"A stretch? You come from the MFA, for heaven's sake. You're extremely qualified."

"Maybe too much so, or at least qualified in another area of the *curatory* arts, if you will."

She thought about what Marjorie had said about the various "fiefdoms" within the umbrella company they just called "corporate," wondering again how he and his position might be caught up in that.

"Surely you have a champion in whoever hired you, right?"

"You're the daughter of a baseball fan, Angel. You must know that even champions strike out."

"But you have to swing," she reminded him, lifting her brows. "You can only hit the ones you swing at, my dad—and probably Babe Ruth or someone famous—used to say."

He lifted his glass. "To taking that swing with the *Magi*."

They toasted and she held his gaze again, very much hoping he didn't strike out. She liked him—as a boss, and a person.

When he put the glass down, he frowned as she heard a soft vibration. She thought it was her phone, glancing around for her bag.

"It's mine," he said, tapping his pocket. "And I definitely don't want to talk about my job—or yours—tonight. Tell me your hopes and dreams, Angel."

"Like what do I want to be when I grow up?" she joked.

"I get the feeling you're in the middle of being it," he said. "But yes."

She considered the question seriously. "I believe I want to be...let's see...an 'endearing, humble, hilarious, and beautiful woman.'"

He tapped her glass with his again. "Nailed it."

She laughed, dropping her head back as the wine and his heady compliments made her just a little dizzy.

He leaned in and braced his elbows on the table, ignoring another text, which was something she appreciated.

"You want to know something?" he asked after a moment. "I think it's fair to say I have more to learn from you than you have from me."

"To learn? About Biltmore?"

"About how to gracefully and successfully build a new life after the one you had falls apart. And about the Biltmore, especially the powers that be. Also, you might teach me a thing or two about what someone who doesn't have six degrees in art history is really looking for when they walk into a museum."

"Wow." She breathed the word, aware that she, too, had her elbows on the table and both of them were inching closer as if an invisible thread drew them together. "I guess I know more than I realized."

He didn't answer, just moved a centimeter closer, the electricity arcing between them.

"Angel," he said on a gruff whisper.

"Elliott," she sighed back.

"This is not in your job description. I don't want to—"

She closed the space. "Neither is drinking in the inner sanctum. I'm not afraid if you aren't."

"Afraid? That's not..." He exhaled as the vibration hummed again. "And someone doesn't want me to kiss you."

"That someone would not be me."

Smiling, he reached into his pocket. "Let me get rid of..." He froze, staring at the screen. Then he blinked and shook his head.

"Is something wrong?"

"Everything," he said in a stiff, stilted, strained voice. "Everything's wrong."

"What?"

He lowered the phone and leaned back, his broad shoulders sinking with him. "*The Adoration of the Magi* isn't coming tomorrow."

"Then when?"

"Never. Another museum swooped in, paid a fortune, and...took the exhibit."

"What?" She practically stood with shock. "They can't do that! It can't be legal! We'll fight this, we'll fly over there and get it, we'll—"

"We'll lose," he said softly. "It's the Louvre and they are tightly connected with the Uffizi..." He shook his head. "It's a cabal of museums that are much more powerful than...the Biltmore Estate."

She heard the soft, subtle note of disappointment. Because this museum would never be part of that world, she supposed.

"Oh, Elliott, what are we going to do?"

"I don't know, but"—he lifted his glass—"drink up, because I may not be getting another bonus bottle."

And she would not be getting that kiss.

# Chapter Fifteen

## Hannah

SILENCE.

Oh, the sound of achingly beautiful, utterly serene, and perfectly still...silence.

Hannah closed her classroom door after the last little darling hugged her goodbye for winter break, promising to be good for Santa Claus—the battle over who believed and who didn't finally fully their parents' problem—and now it was over until the next semester.

Usually, this was a joyous time of freedom for Hannah, topped only by the last day of school. But that goodbye was bittersweet. She loved these kids and always hated to hand them over to third grade. This break? Easy and much needed.

She was so ready to...

She swallowed a lump that always seemed to catch in her throat when she thought too much about her feelings these days. She still wasn't ready to celebrate.

Walking through the classroom, she fluttered a piece of tinsel dangling from a desk and smiled at the small mountain of gifts her students had lovingly placed under the artificial tree by the blackboard. She knew there were mugs and candies, hats and mittens, some notebooks, a bottle of perfume, and probably ten candles in that collection, many wrapped with the sloppy but loving hands of her students.

On a sigh, she dropped to the linoleum floor next to the tree, picking up one Santa-covered present with Layla Collins's careful writing on the paper.

*I love you, Ms. MacPherson! Merry Christmas!*

"I love you, too, Layla," she whispered, hating that tears stung her lids. What was wrong with her? She should be dancing with freedom and...freedom.

She had that in spades now. No kids, no lesson plans, no long recesses, no field trips...nobody.

"Stop it," she chided herself, pushing up because she wasn't in the mood to sit here and open all these presents right now. Better to take them home in a few bags and share them with Caro or the triplets, since no one needed that many candles.

Turning to look around the empty classroom, she spied a parka hanging over a desk in the back row.

Nick or Dan, of course. They both had been sitting back there while that last movie played—she'd run out of lessons and holiday game ideas. Walking toward it, she lifted the jacket, recognizing it as Nick Venema's.

How did he not notice he'd forgotten it when he went—

She heard the door click and turned with a smile,

fully expecting Mrs. Venema and her sometimes wayward but always good-hearted child.

But that's not who was standing there. For a moment, she couldn't breathe.

"Keith," she whispered, a little surprised at the way her stomach fluttered and tensed at the sight of him. Oh, dear. Was she that lonely?

Well, it was the first time she'd seen him since the breakup. He'd texted once—about something she'd left at his house—and didn't reply to her answer. But other than that? They hadn't spoken in well over a week, maybe ten days.

"Hey. I figured it would be quiet in here."

She glanced around, mostly because it was hard to look right at him. Keith looked wrecked. Like he'd been on a bender or a long journey or...had he been crying? His auburn waves were tousled, his reddish beard grown in.

"Yeah, it is. The old 'end of semester silence,'" she said, feeling awkward to be talking about that, but not sure what she should say. "I was just enjoying it."

"Sorry to bother you."

"You're...not." She knew she sounded hesitant. But why was he here? "Are you okay?"

"Oh, sure," he scoffed. "I'm just peachy."

That comment would normally be delivered with a sarcastic edge, but this time she heard nothing but pain in his voice. It made her stomach tighten even more.

"I know, it's...a hard time of year."

"No, Hannah," he said, taking a step into the classroom. "It's a hard time of *life*."

She swallowed and nodded, digging her fingers into the parka's fur collar. "I know. I'm..." She wasn't sorry, though, and she wouldn't say that. "I'm sure it is."

"I don't think you're sure of anything," he said, again with a lot of agony in every word.

"That's fair," she acknowledged. "This is certainly a time of...self-discovery."

He nodded and took a few more steps, his gaze leveled on her, his always a little ruddy complexion looking brighter than usual.

"What have you found?" he asked softly.

For a second, she thought he meant the jacket. Then she realized he was referring to self-discovery. And the question sounded deeply sincere.

As she considered how to answer, he came even closer, halfway down the center aisle between the desks. He looked so big in here, a room built for tiny people.

"Not too much," she finally said. "I had to get through the semester and then there's the holidays. I guess I'll discover myself in the new year."

"Why would you wait?"

She frowned, not following as she watched him take a few more steps, now about five feet from her.

"Why not discover who you are and what you want right now?"

"I don't know what you mean, Keith."

"I mean...I have," he said. "In fact, I've done nothing but think since you walked out that door."

Nodding, she clutched the jacket tighter, pressing it against her chest as she studied him. He looked like he'd done a lot of thinking...maybe some drinking, too, though he was perfectly sober right now.

Sober...and very serious.

"I'm sure you have," she said, searching his face, trying to figure out why he was here.

"Would you like to know what I discovered, Hannah?"

She nodded, less tense because he didn't seem angry or spiteful right now, but beaten and maybe nervous.

"Well, I discovered that life without Hannah Jean MacPherson is..."

She held her breath while he waited three or four heartbeats to finish. Somewhere in the back of her mind, she was surprised he knew her middle name, but she stayed silent while he visibly dug for the next word.

"Miserable," he finally said with a humorless laugh. "Also lonely, boring, pathetic, full of regret and sadness, and...yeah, miserable. Do I need to go on?"

Her heart shifted as his tone and expression softened with every word.

"Because I will," he said. "I'll go on for as long as I have to, Hannah, because I'm not leaving here until you come back to me."

She sucked in a breath, blinking at the declaration—she truly hadn't been expecting that.

She waited for a swoon...but nothing happened.

"And I know"—he held up his hand as if to stop her

response, even though she was silent—"things have to change. I get that and I'm...okay with that."

"Okay with...what?" she asked, still not sure what he was saying.

"With...you know. Change. And by change, I mean... the big M." He rolled his eyes, a mix of embarrassed and nervous.

"Do you mean marriage?" she asked, more confused than anything.

He couldn't even say it! That just made her certain she'd made the absolute right decision.

"Yes, Hannah. That's what I mean."

She let out an exhale and tried to wrap her head around this. Was this his new game? Was he saying he'd talk about getting married—or *the big M*—and hope that would satisfy her? Because—

"Hannah, I mean it," he said, coming closer to nearly close the space between them. "If that's the way to keep you in my life, then..."

"You have to want it, too, Keith. It's not *punishment*."

He gave a hollow laugh. "I know, I know. I'm just... not romantic and cheesy like that. It's not my style, Hannah."

"I know," she said, holding his gaze and seeing just how determined he was.

It wasn't his style, but at least he understood what she wanted. But now, would she—

"So here goes nuthin'," he said, so softly she wasn't sure she'd heard right.

Very slowly, he cleared his throat, reached into his pocket, and lowered himself to one knee.

Wait...*what*? What was he—

"Keith!"

"Hold up there, Hannah. I have to do this." He blinked, his eyes misty, and looked up at her, opening a black box to reveal a small, antique-looking sapphire ring. "Hannah Jean MacPherson, will you marry me?"

She felt her soul leave her body as she stared down at him in utter disbelief. And despair.

She'd waited and waited, longed and imagined, spent so many nights in tears, so many hours dreaming, so many years wanting nothing but this very moment.

And now? Now...

"Hannah? My knee hurts. It's my aunt's ring that belonged to my grandmother. Doesn't that count for anything?"

"It's...everything," she whispered. And nothing that she wanted.

How did she tell him that?

Trembling, she managed a shaky breath, trying to find the words.

"Is that a yes?" His whole face lit up and that was sweet. So sweet. But...

She didn't want to marry Keith Kelly and now, after years of begging, she was about to turn him down.

What was wrong with her?

She loved the man—she certainly used to. She'd ached to marry him—she'd thought it all the time. She knew him better than anyone and *she wasn't getting any younger*.

But that, she knew, was not a reason to say yes. There was only one answer, one way to end this, one simple word.

"No," she breathed. "I can't."

His whole face fell as he stared back in shock.

"*What?*" He barked the word, wincing as he pushed up. "You're saying no?"

"I'm saying...yes—"

"Oh, thank God—"

"Yes, I'm saying no." Oh, goodness, she was all over the place and shaking for real now. "I mean, I...I..."

"Hannah." He choked her name. "This is all you wanted. The ring. The proposal. The wedding. The whole deal."

No, no, *no*. "How can I explain it to you?"

"With your mouth. Now."

She shuddered at his tone of pure disgust. "Keith, I don't want the...the *trappings* of romance. I want love."

"And me proposing isn't...love?" He looked skyward and stabbed his hand in his hair, pulling it back in frustration. "Do you even know what you want, Hannah?"

Right then, she didn't. She knew that she didn't want someone who so totally and completely didn't get her.

There had to be more, right? It had to be better than...one gargantuan compromise, didn't it? He made marriage sound like a penalty or payment. That wasn't what she wanted.

He grunted and stuffed the ring box back into his

pocket, inching back. "I'm not gonna ask again," he said gruffly. "This was hard enough."

"That's just it, Keith. It shouldn't be hard. It should be beautiful and exciting and thrilling and—"

"Gotcha." He gave her a flat palm. "You were right the first time, Hannah. I should have just let you go. We're good. We're done. We're...done," he repeated, nodding as he backed away. "You have a merry Christmas and a good life, kid. It was a decent run."

With a tight smile, he turned and walked out, closing the door very quietly behind him.

She pressed her face into Nick Venema's jacket and cried.

"Hannah!" Noelle opened the front door wide, reaching for her, concern etched on her features. "Are you okay? Have you been crying?"

"I'm..." Her voice was rough, but then, she'd been driving all over town and through the mountains, thinking and replaying and, yes, sobbing. She'd ended up here at Noelle and Jace's ranch, knowing in her heart that she needed her friend. "Keith proposed."

"What?" She pulled her inside, lifting her left hand. "I don't see..." She looked at Hannah's face. "Oh, honey, you said no."

"I did."

Jace came up from behind her, curious to see who was at the door. "Hey, Hannah," he said. "You all right?"'

"She is not all right." Noelle wrapped an arm around her, pulling her closer. "She needs love and maybe wine and whatever she wants."

Jace's eyes flickered and he nodded. "Privacy," he said softly, then turned toward the den. "Hey, Cass. How 'bout we take Sprinkles for her walk? I need some air and—"

"Yay, Daddy! I'm coming!" The little girl shot out, then stopped. "Oh, hi, Aunt Hannah. Do you want to come with us?"

Hannah smiled, the sweet invitation tugging at her heart. "I'm going to stay here and talk to your...to Noelle."

"'Kay. Let me get my coat and boots."

She shot off toward the kitchen and Jace shifted his attention, and smile, to them. "Do you need anything, Hannah?" he asked. "Can I get you—"

"I'm fine, Jace. I promise. I just want to talk to Noelle."

"She's all yours." He put his arm around Noelle's shoulder and pressed a soft kiss on her hair. "Well, not literally. She's mine, thank God."

A few minutes later, with one more kiss on Noelle's cheek, Jace walked out with Cassie in the lead, chattering about her goat.

"What can I get you?" Noelle asked, guiding her toward the kitchen. "What would make you happy?"

"That." She pointed toward the door that just closed.

Noelle frowned, not following. "Sprinkles, the darling goat?"

"Jace, the darling husband," she replied on a sad sigh. "Noelle, he loves you so much you can feel it when you walk into the house."

"Oh, Hannah." She led her to the table. "It took me forty years to find that kind of love."

"Was it worth the wait?" Hannah asked.

"I'm not even going to answer that. Red or white? Or tea or coffee or hot chocolate, which is always on the menu here."

"Actually, tea sounds perfect."

"Done. Now, tell me everything."

Hannah relayed the whole proposal as well as she could remember it. She finished as Noelle brought two steaming mugs with dangling tea bags to the table and settled in across from her.

"You did the right thing," she said softly.

"How do you know? And please don't tell me no one ever really liked Keith, because I don't think I can stand to hear that now."

"We all liked Keith," she assured her. "We didn't like that he refused to commit to you and, for that reason, never really felt like he leaned into the whole clan, but he's been in your life a whole lot longer than we have."

"So, so long," Hannah said, blowing on the tea. "Eleven years. I cannot believe I gave him that much of my life."

"Don't regret it. You learned and grew and probably

had a lot of fun. But as the clock ticked, you knew what you wanted."

"And he just offered that, so why did I say no?"

Noelle looked at her with that same expression Hannah gave a second-grader who knew the answer to a question but wasn't sure if they should say it out loud.

"I don't really love him," she finally whispered.

"Only you know that."

"I don't love him the way I imagined a woman loves the man who's on one knee in front of her. But the thing is, Noelle, I would have said yes two weeks ago. What changed?"

"Will you throw hot tea at me if I say the hottie at the Christmas farm you were flirting with?"

"One exchange doesn't wipe away eleven years," Hannah replied. "I'm not that shallow." She made face. "Am I?"

"Of course not. But what one exchange can do is make you realize your value, and that there are good men out there—someone who would put you on that pedestal and take care of you and treat you like a queen."

"Someone who wouldn't make me an afterthought," she agreed.

Lifting her mug for a toast, Noelle nodded. "You deserve that love, Hannah."

She took a sip of the steaming tea, letting the peppermint flavor cover her tongue. "I still can't believe I said no."

"I can't believe he popped the question in your classroom."

Hannah rolled her eyes. "It's so Keith, you know? Quick and easy. But I feel...free."

"Of course you do. It's literally the first day of the rest of your life."

She smiled at the cliché. "It really is. I was hanging onto that last goodbye, feeling so blue that it happened the way it did, but now, it's truly over and I can..."

"Go see long-haired Paul Bunyan."

"Stop it."

"Well, you can give him a chance. He's interested."

She took another sip of tea, feeling a tad guilty when a little shiver of anticipation went through her.

"He is and...maybe I could be, too. Maybe." She swiped the topic away with one hand, definitely not ready to talk about another guy when she'd just turned down a marriage proposal. "How are you guys? What's new?"

"Oh, you know...Christmas."

There was something off in Noelle's voice—maybe it had been there the whole time, but Hannah was too wrapped up in herself to notice. A note of sadness or... something.

"Oh!" Hannah leaned back and suddenly realized what it was. "When I almost called you Cassie's mommy. I caught myself, but—"

"No, no, that's not it. Not exactly." She settled into the chair, looking as if she was considering letting out a confidence. "It does have to do with being a mommy, though."

Hannah gasped softly. "You're pregnant?"

"I'm not," Noelle quickly said. "And if I want to be—which I do—it seems I need a surgery to correct a less-than-perfect uterus."

"Really? What is it? Are you okay? Are you in pain? How did you find out?"

"No pain, no symptoms, just no pregnancy. Eve talked me into seeing a fertility specialist, who found the issue. The surgery isn't too complex, but if I don't have it, I'm not likely to conceive or, if I do, a miscarriage is a very high probability."

"Well, then you have the surgery," Hannah said with zero doubt.

But Noelle looked like she had plenty of doubt.

"I don't know. It's a risk, especially at my age, and I do have Cassie. Even though..." She gave a sad laugh. "She won't call me Mommy."

"It's just a word," Hannah said. "She knows you as Noelle and loves you as if you were her mother. Anyone can see that."

"I know," Noelle agreed. "She'll come around. And I love her and don't want to do anything to scare her or make her unhappy. Is surgery worth...that risk?"

"Of something happening to you?" Hannah asked.

"She's already lost one mother. That said, she wants a sibling, desperately." Noelle shook her head. "I don't know what to do."

"My dad would say to pray."

"Jace did. We were just talking about it this morning," she said. "We decided to table it until after the tree lighting, and make a decision by Christmas."

Hannah smiled. "What does he want you to do?"

"Whatever I want. It matters not to him, although...I kind of think he'd prefer I don't take the risk. We're very happy as we are, but...you know me. Always trying to climb the ladder to the next accomplishment and control Mother Nature *and* Father Time, even though neither one of them wants my assistance."

"Oh, dear," Hannah sighed. "Sometimes we're our own worst enemies, aren't we?"

"True that." Noelle pushed up and glanced outside. "They'll be home soon, and hungry. Will you stay for dinner?"

"I'd love to but my empty apartment calls me."

"Hannah! Stay with us. Cassie will make you laugh and I will make you happy and Jace will make all of us something amazing to eat."

Hannah looked up at her, ready to say no and go home, but suddenly, there was nowhere she'd rather be than with family. "Too good to pass up," she said.

"Unlike that marriage proposal you nixed," Noelle cracked, making Hannah's jaw drop. "What, too soon?"

Hannah laughed, feeling better already. "Not a minute too soon. And before they come back, can I ask you...do you really think I should go out with Brandon?"

Noelle gasped. "I have an idea! Bring him to the tree lighting! You can continue the kiss tradition."

"There's a tradition?" Hannah asked.

"Edna Covington kissed her husband there for the first time in 1962, and they got married, like, six months later."

"Oh, please, that's hardly a trad—"

"And I kissed Jace there for the first time in twenty-five years and we got married in less than six months." She gave a smug smile. "One more and it's officially a tradition."

Hannah laughed, but only to cover the fact that the very idea gave her chills. "I guess I could see if he wants to go."

Noelle grinned. "And just like that, she's back in the saddle. That didn't take long."

Shockingly, it did not. And Hannah knew why—she'd made the right decision with Keith. It hurt and it was sad, but it was definitely the right thing to do.

# Chapter Sixteen

## Noelle

As THE DAYS ticked closer to the tree lighting, Noelle had to force herself not to whip out her tablet and check off her to-do list.

But everything, she decided, was done. So was the Christmas shopping, wrapping, and baking. Mid-week, three days before the lighting, she went through the house in search of Jace, who said he had some paperwork to do.

She found him in the kitchen, tapping at his laptop, the late afternoon sun spilling into their cheery room. "How's the billing going?" she asked.

"Just...about...." He closed the computer and looked up at her. "Done for the year," he announced with a solid note of satisfaction. "Good feeling."

She nodded and looked around the perfectly clean house, which seemed...almost too clean. And she knew why. "I miss Cassie when she spends the night with your parents."

"Yeah, it's quiet without someone singing in her room or marching out of the mudroom."

Noelle smiled. "With her muddy boots still on."

"You don't mind that, do you?"

"I don't mind anything she does," Noelle admitted. "Even the muddy boots."

He nodded, pushing the chair to lean on its back legs. "You know, back in the day—pre-Noelle—I hated when Cassie would go do an overnighter with my parents like this. I needed it frequently, too, if I had to make a house call and didn't want to drag her along. In fact, there were times I didn't know what I'd do without them. Jenny's parents were up in Pennsylvania, so it all fell on my mom and dad."

"They adore her," Noelle said softly.

"They do and I think they're thrilled to get her on nights like this, so we should do it more often, no matter how much we miss her muddy feet and singing. That said..." His brow rose playfully. "We do get a quiet, romantic dinner together, then some fireplace gazing with our favorite nightcap, and..." He leaned in for a kiss, but she backed away, reaching for her vibrating phone.

"Hang on, I think that's the tree lighting committee group chat."

He rolled his eyes. "I created a monster."

"We're three days from the event," she said, tapping the screen. "And Tony Jessup has a report from the PD and fire department on—" She blinked at the words *major snowstorm coming.* "Oh, boy, we got trouble."

"What?"

She stood. "Let's turn on the Weather Channel. Apparently, there's a major storm set to hit on Friday."

He made a face. "I wonder if that's why so many of my patients have been acting weird. Horses sense when a storm's on the way."

She was already in the den, punching the remote. "This could impact the tree lighting."

"The event is Saturday night," he said. "I wouldn't worry too much."

That was like asking her not to breathe. When a commercial flashed on the Weather Channel, she checked her watch.

"Local news? It's almost five. Oh, man. Storms in New York could shut things down for days."

"It won't be anything like that," Jace assured her as he settled on the sofa. "A big storm here is mostly up in the mountains. Downtown will be fine, assuming the one snowplow is working."

She whipped around to stare at him. "One?"

"Maybe two or three. We're technically a southern state," he said, clicking through his phone, no doubt reading about the storm. "Snow is rare here except, like I said, up in higher elevations. We might get a good two or three inches here but it'll melt quickly. And in downtown? Honestly, not a problem. People will come to the event, I promise."

She hoped he was right. Perching on the end of the sofa, she clicked on the news, but they weren't talking about the weather yet.

"Still, I worry about things I can't control."

Chuckling, he pulled her back to snuggle closer. "And that, my dear, could be your middle name."

"I'm trying," she said, but it was hard where the tree lighting was concerned. "I know I don't have control. I listened at church last week. But..." She wrinkled her nose. "*I yam who I yam*, to quote my father, who was quoting Popeye. And right now, I *yam* facing the storm of the century on the weekend of my tree lighting."

He chuckled. "It's a small nor'easter. Not a huge deal."

"Oh, really?" She pointed the remote at the TV when the word "snowstorm" appeared in giant, frost-covered letters.

And with each word the announcer spoke, everything became more serious. All the news jumbled together in one big headline: Major storm...up to twelve inches of snow...severe weather warnings...possible power outages.

"Power outages?" She shot forward. "Exactly what I was worried about!"

"They'll have a generator."

"But will it work to light the tree?" she asked. "Not to mention flickering Edna's lights."

"The storm's hitting Friday night," he reminded her gently. "You'll have twenty-four hours to work out the kinks."

"Kinks don't always work out in twenty-four hours," she said, grabbing her phone. "We have three days to create a plan, and we're going to. I'm calling an emergency meeting."

"Now?"

"Yes. I'm going to ask everyone to come here, if they can, where I can set up a game plan and a war room—"

"A war room?" He choked the words.

"This could be a catastrophe, Jace. And my name will be all over it. We need to set up contingency plans, lay out the generator situation, and get everyone aware that things could go south."

He just smiled at her. "You're cute when you're in control."

"Except I'm not. The weather is, and I have got to make sure this goes off without a hitch."

He nodded, looking resigned to what was happening. "How about you invite them here for dessert and coffee after dinner? We have enough Christmas cookies to feed a small country. And it's more comfortable, less...war roomy."

*More Southern hospitality*, she thought, appreciating the idea right down to her soul. She leaned in and kissed him again. "Did I mention how much I love you anytime in the last five minutes?"

"No."

"I do and I will forever and ever." Another kiss, and then she started texting. "Jace, this event really, really matters to me."

"I see that."

"I want it to be perfect and no one, not even the God who controls the weather, can ruin it."

He slid her a warning look. "Careful, hon. He really is in control and might very well want to teach you a little lesson about that."

She huffed out a breath and thumbed her text, knowing he was probably right, but hoping that didn't mean...power outage. Because if Noelle hated anything, it was to be powerless.

WITH THE EXCEPTION of the first meeting at Noelle's gallery, the committee had only gotten together again through texts, one Zoom call, and the brief visit Noelle had made to Edna's home. Noelle had spoken to each of them individually, but she knew from experience that there was strength in the groupthink.

So she was delighted when they all agreed to come over—even Edna, who rode with Harry—to address the storm situation.

And as they arrived, Noelle was grateful for each of their skill sets on the project. Tony was the voice of reason, calm and wise. Harry knew every nuance about the tree delivery, placement, and wiring, and brought oodles of experience to the event. Joanna represented dozens of local retailers and small businesses that were setting up booths.

Edna was...Edna. She'd no doubt put a stop to every good, but different, idea even though she and Noelle had more or less worked out their differences.

After they chatted and settled in around the kitchen table, it became clear that the only other person who was quite as concerned as Noelle was Joanna.

"My people are freaked out," she shared with them after they stopped to listen to the latest weather report.

"Snow could kill foot traffic and that means they've spent a lot on their booths and won't get a return."

"There's no snow predicted for Saturday," Tony said. "We'll have the roads plowed and, if you like, Joanna, I can see if we can get some guys with shovels to clear paths to each booth in the adjacent park, if that's even necessary."

"That would be great," she said, making a note.

"And when does the tree get delivered?" Noelle asked Harry.

He made a face. "My son and I were going to bring it late Friday afternoon so the electrical team can set up on Saturday morning."

"Cutting it close, Harry," Noelle said.

"That's what we always do," Edna said, adding her usual two cents.

He acknowledged that with a nod. "I'll break with tradition this once and get it up a day early. I'll contact the electrical crew and, Tony, you'll have those generators standing by, just in case."

Tony made a face. "We have a limited number and they have to stay with first responders, the fire stations, and the police department. We are also committed to supplying backup to hospitals, if needed. They probably won't be, but I'm not confident we'll have the equipment for anything non-essential—"

Edna put her teacup down with force. "The tree lighting is essential."

He nodded in deference. "I mean essential to safety,

security, and saving lives, which is pretty much the main objective of police and fire."

She sniffed, probably realizing she couldn't win that argument. Neither could Noelle, but they wouldn't need generators if she had been allowed to order the battery-powered LED system she wanted. Too late for that now.

"Then without power, we can't have an event," she said, thinking aloud.

Edna flipped her hand like she could wash away that inconvenient truth. "There isn't going to be a power outage." When they all turned to her, she tipped her head. "I just know this."

No doubt her husband had texted from heaven. But Noelle just smiled at her while she mentally tried to figure out how they could secure generators between now and when the snowstorm hit.

Who would have generators she could borrow or buy?

They spent the better part of an hour making contingency plans for booth placement and the generators—if they could get them—and parking if plowing left snow blocking the lots.

Then she tapped her tablet screen and moved to the next item—the backup plan if all went south.

"Okay, then," she said. "Let's talk about an alternate date if this simply can't happen."

All eyes turned to her, and every one of them—including Jace, who was leaning against the counter, listening but quiet—looked surprised.

"Uh, you can't turn that ship," Harry said. "We don't have another tree and this one is fresh."

"The retailers can't arrange for all those booths to be installed on a moment's notice for a different date," Joanna added.

"The fire and police event calendars do not change, especially the week before Christmas," Tony chimed in. "There are permits, personnel, and problems. The date can't change again."

"You can just cross that idea off your list." Edna tapped her nail on Noelle's screen. "We've already moved it from the fourteenth to the twenty-first, which is not what my husband wanted. It won't budge."

And neither would they. Noelle tamped down the desire to stand and make an impassioned speech about why they had to have a full contingency plan.

But as she scanned the table, she caught the tiniest glimmer of a warning in Jace's eyes, even though he stayed in the background by the counter. Deciding to heed it, she nodded and closed her tablet.

"Then I say we're ready, come what may." The words tasted like sand in her mouth, but were well received.

When it was over, Noelle managed a smile and lots of warm goodbyes and promises to stay in constant contact as they got closer to the storm and tree lighting.

Closing the door with a final goodbye to Joanna, she turned with a sigh to her husband.

"Well, that was...about what I expected. And no generators! I have to figure out something. You have one, right?"

"Everyone has one, but they'll all want them if the power goes out."

"What should I do?" She heard her voice rise, but he smiled and walked toward her, arms outstretched.

"Listen to me, honey," he said, pulling her into his chest for a hug. "You're bringing an amazing set of skills and business acumen to this project and we're lucky you are."

"I feel a 'but' coming on..." she half-joked, not really welcoming a dressing down from him on her approach.

"*But* this is a snowstorm, so I think you have to, if you'll excuse the pun, let nature take its course. And as far as the event? Let the small town be the small town. Let them figure out the parking and the generators and the plowing, even if the answer is, 'We don't have that.' Let them do it the way it's always been done." He kissed her forehead. "That's the tradition."

She eased back, looking up at him, loving him as much in that moment as ever before. It wasn't a dressing down—it was solid advice.

"Let the small town be a small town," she repeated. "I like that."

He pulled her closer when the phone in her hand vibrated.

"Ignore." He kissed her. "Ignore." He kissed her again, a little longer, then murmured into her lips, "For the love of God and the time we have left tonight, ignore."

She wanted to but couldn't resist turning the phone she held over his shoulder so she could see the screen.

"Oh, you don't want to ignore this."

"You'd be wrong..." Another kiss, but she inched back and lifted her brows.

"It's your mom. Might be about Cassie."

"Oh." They broke apart. "Then get it," he said, making her smile as she tapped the screen and speaker button.

"Hi, Carol," Noelle said. "Everything okay?"

"We're fine, but someone..." She lowered her voice to a whisper. "Wants to come home."

"Oh, okay." That was a surprise—Cassie loved movie and popcorn night with her grandparents. And they'd planned to wrap presents and make even more cookies. Maybe she'd had one gingerbread man too many.

"Is she feeling okay?" Noelle asked, instantly concerned. "Not sick or anything?"

"Homesick," Carol said with a soft laugh, making Noelle and Jace share a look of disbelief. "She misses her mommy."

Noelle sucked in a breath as the words hit. "Did she... did she say that?"

"Well, not exactly," Carol said, making Noelle's heart slip a little. "But she said she wants to read her goat book with you tonight so she can really sleep well."

"Aww." Noelle bit her lip. "Of course. We'll come and get her now."

"She's packed her little bag already," Carol said with a smile in her voice. "She loves you so, Noelle."

She pressed her hand against her chest as the statement hit her heart, saying goodbye while holding Jace's smiling gaze.

"Well, what do you think of that?" she said. "She misses her...mommy."

He squeezed her in a quick hug. "I think that you should let nature take its course."

"And let small children be small children," she added with a laugh.

He kissed her one last time, lingering with a sigh of resignation that they wouldn't be alone tonight. "You're a quick study, Mrs. Fleming. C'mon. Grab your coat and let's get our daughter."

He turned to go get his jacket, so he didn't see the tears that welled up in Noelle's eyes. Tears of joy and hope and motherhood...in all its iterations.

# Chapter Seventeen

## Angie

"So, I guess the good news is none of you have to work this weekend and anyone who wants to put in for paid time off next week is free to do so." Elliott leaned back and scanned the faces of the curator staff around the table. "Merry Christmas...I guess."

No one laughed or even smiled, making Angie's heart break. She'd felt as shattered as Elliott Quinn looked when he called the meeting today with the sad and sorry news that *The Adoration of the Magi* would not be coming as a featured holiday art exhibit after all.

After the stunned reaction, the team only had a few questions, a couple of bitter comments directed toward the offending museum—which weren't too bitter, considering it *was* the *Louvre*—and some weak words of encouragement. Elliott fielded all of that with grace, honesty, and a bit of gallows humor.

When the meeting ended, the team rose, chatting softly with each other, a few wishing each other Merry Christmas as they filed out.

Angie stayed seated, very slowly closing a notebook

she hadn't needed, reluctant to join the parade of well-wishers out the door. Elliott put some papers in a folder, checked his phone, and finally, when they were alone, looked across the conference room table at her.

"Well, that went about as expected."

She gave him a sad smile. "You handled it well and I don't think anyone's mad about extra days off."

He stood slowly, picking up the file and phone, all the while holding her gaze. "I could feel your support, Angel. Thanks."

"Of course. I know you were cheated by the Louvre."

"You know and I know. My boss up in corporate?" He rounded the table and walked down to where she sat, pulling out the chair next to her and dropping into it. "He just thinks he made a big fat mistake hiring me."

She winced, inching back. "Sorry to hear that."

"Yeah, I think I'm the subject of more than a few meetings this holiday." He shrugged. "And a month ago, I wouldn't have been able to say this, since I came in with the small-mindedness of a big-city guy. But..." He added a slight emphasis. "I have found quite a few things to like in this town. One in particular that I like very much."

Her heart swooped around in her chest like a teenager's. "Yep. I get that," she said, trying to keep it light.

"Stupid me," he added.

"How so?"

"Falling for someone right as I'm about to get the royal boot out the door."

She searched his face, not hearing too much after the

"falling for" part. "Do you really think they'd fire you over this? It wasn't even remotely your fault."

"I don't know. Apparently, there's a meeting of the department heads tomorrow to finalize a number of staffing issues. My boss said to meet him at the downtown offices on Saturday morning for the decision, one way or another."

"Eeesh. And on a weekend, too. I'm sorry," she added. "And sad."

"Are you?"

She turned her hand, threading their fingers. "Hey, I don't bash into just anybody's car, you know."

Chuckling, he leaned a little closer. "Was it all part of your evil plan to steal my heart?"

"Did I?" she asked, the very idea making her head a little light.

"What do you think?"

"I don't know, Elliott. I can't remember the last time I stole...a heart."

He exhaled softly. "Consider mine whisked away by a thief in the night. So, since I'll know my fate on Saturday, why don't we go out that night? We can celebrate or cry in our beer. Or another bottle of good merlot."

"Saturday is the tree—"

Diana poked her head in and they both dropped their hands and backed away, probably looking guilty as sin. "Angie, there's someone here to see you."

"Me?" She stood, shaking off the intimate moment. "Who could—"

"It's me!" Noelle called from behind Diana, suddenly

appearing in the doorway, totally surprising Angie. "I kind of need an emergency favor. Are you busy?"

"She's all yours," Elliott said, standing quickly.

"Noelle, what are you doing here?" Angie asked.

"Begging." She turned to Diana. "Thank you for finding her." Then she walked in, her attention split between Elliott and Angie. "I'm sorry to interrupt. I can wait in your office if—"

"No, no, it's fine. We were just talking. Elliott Quinn, this is my sister, Noelle Fleming. Noelle, meet Elliott."

"Ohhh," they both let out the exclamation of recognition in perfect unison, then laughed.

"One of the triplets," he said.

"The new boss," she replied.

"It's like you already know each other," Angie quipped. "Yes and yes. Is everything okay?" she asked Noelle, since the in-person visit was rare and unexpected.

"I need generators," Noelle said. "And I need them bad. Did you know we're having a massive snowstorm tomorrow? The tree lighting is the day after and nothing will light if there's no power. Can I borrow generators?"

"Can she?" Angie asked Elliott.

"I have no idea, but if I wanted to find a generator and arrange to borrow it, I'd ask you," he said on a laugh. "And if you need my permission to take them off-site, you have it." He winked at her. "Not much to lose if I get in trouble, eh?"

She gave a dry laugh at that. "I actually do know where to get them, if we have extras. There's an equipment manager on the estate and if anyone at the Biltmore will have generators, it's Bucky. I had to use them when we lost power during a big lightning storm last summer."

"I cannot thank you enough for this," Noelle said. "I will pay or do anything."

"Not necessary," Elliott assured her, eyeing Noelle as if he were looking for similarities to Angie and, of course, they were there. "You're Angel's sister and that's all I need to know. I'll leave you to it, ladies. And..." He looked at Angie. "I'll text you about Saturday."

"Okay, great." She felt a soft flush when he left, but more because of the curious way her sister was looking at her than the personal exchange.

"Did I, uh, walk in on something...*Angel*?" Noelle asked, lifting a brow.

The flush deepened, but she added a soft laugh because, after all, this was Noelle. "Maybe almost. And yes, we're going out on Saturday."

"I hope by 'going out' you mean bringing generators to the tree lighting." She made a face. "Sorry to be single-minded."

"It's fine. It's you." Sighing, she reached for her phone to place the call to the equipment manager, who would definitely be the keeper of the generators. "Elliott's probably leaving anyway."

"What? Why? Didn't he just get here?"

"It's a really long story, but..." She tapped her contacts and found the manager's name. "Hang on. Let me find out what's possible."

Angie had the conversation with Bucky, who

promised to call her back in ten minutes, so while they waited, Angie walked back to her office with Noelle.

There, with the door closed, she told her sister the whole story of the *Magi* being yanked by the Louvre.

"That's truly preposterous," Noelle said. "And also, sadly normal. Especially with the big guys like the Met and Louvre. They love nothing more than to throw their weight around."

"So should he lose his job over it?"

She flinched and shook her head. "Gah, no. Man, I don't miss corporate life anymore. It's so...capricious. Who knows what politics are going on in the background or who wants their own person in the spot?"

Angie nodded, knowing there was plenty of politics. "Don't they realize that lives—and budding romances— are at stake?"

"You like him." It wasn't a question, and Angie appreciated that. Noelle knew her as well as anyone, just like Eve did.

"A lot," Angie admitted, and it felt good to say so. "But my timing is bad and our geography could be highly undesirable. There's one museum in Asheville."

"Plenty of art galleries, though."

"He's a curator," Angie said. "And I was really enjoying watching him start to find the beauty in this place."

"Shouldn't be hard," Noelle said. "There's beauty everywhere." She leaned over the desk and grinned. "Especially in this office."

"Stop." Her cell buzzed and Bucky's name flashed.

"Save your flirtatious energy for the equipment manager, who might need to be sweet-talked into generators." She tapped the phone and put it on speaker. "Talk to me, Bucky."

"I can part with two of them," he said without preamble. "But you have to pick them up on Saturday at two and have them back by Sunday morning."

Noelle nodded enthusiastically. "I'll get Jace's truck. Yes, please."

"Done and done, Bucky," Angie said. "We'll be there on Saturday at two." She hung up and gave Noelle a victorious look. "I'll help you because I know the guy."

"I love you," Noelle said, reaching across the desk. "You know I mean that. I wish I could help you. Wish I could find a job for your new boyfriend."

"He's not..." She just waved it off. "You want to help? Call in a favor at the Met and get a replacement for *The Adoration of the Magi*. Surely they can part with a Rembrandt or two."

Noelle snorted. "The Met? I'd have to sell my first-born and..." Her voice faded out for a second, making Angie look closer when she didn't finish.

"Well, you're not giving up Cassie for love or money."

Noelle just stared at her.

"Cassie?" Angie said. "You know, your daughter?"

Noelle nodded, clearly distracted. "I do. She had to come home early from a grandma sleepover because she missed me."

"Aww." Angie beamed. "I love that you have her, Noelle."

"I love that I do, too." She stood and grabbed her bag. "I also love that you got me two generators and I swear, if I could pull a famous painting out of thin air for you, I would."

"I understand that you can't."

She blew a kiss and went to the door, opening it, then turning and looking at Angie for a long moment.

"I'm waiting for the parting 'Angel' shot," Angie joked.

"No, no. I just...never mind. Thanks again, Ang. You da best." One more blown kiss and Noelle was gone, leaving a faint trail of her beautiful perfume and a smile on Angie's face.

Then she remembered she had a date with Elliott on Saturday night and that smile grew bigger.

## Chapter Eighteen

*Hannah*

HANNAH WOKE on Friday morning with one thing on her mind—a Christmas tree. She didn't want to go one more day without one.

Okay, maybe the *purveyor* of Christmas trees was the real thing on her mind. But whatever the underlying motivation, she hated that she'd passed on the tree in her little home.

December twentieth wasn't too late, was it?

Not if she happened to know...the right people. And, oh, he was *right*, wasn't he?

It took until three in the afternoon for her to find the nerve to drive up the winding road to the tree farm for the third time that season. No field trip or family outing this time.

Just Hannah and, she hoped, Brandon.

For the past few days, she'd thought about him a lot. Yes, it was a little soon to consider a new relationship and, yes, the idea terrified her.

But Hannah was tired of her life being dictated by fear, tired of waiting for her life to improve, tired of being on the outside looking in at all the love and happiness around her and not having some of her own.

She had to make a choice and take action—even if it meant rejection.

Something told her Brandon Fletcher wasn't going to reject her. He looked at her with warmth and interest, found every excuse to casually take her hand or touch her shoulder, and he'd asked her to go ice skating with him.

That was not a man who was about to rebuff her interest.

Gripping the steering wheel as the first fat flakes of snow started to fall, she powered through the last few curves and rounded the bend near the top of the mountain.

She'd heard some talk of a storm, but hadn't paid too much attention. However, as she pulled into the large lot and looked around, she suddenly realized she might be the only one who hadn't paid attention.

The tree farm was absolutely empty. There were no cars, no kids, no...Brandon.

Climbing out of her car, she pulled on her parka and looked around, surprised and deeply disappointed.

She walked up to the sales shack, aching to see the little hot chocolate stand or hear the laughter of excited families loading up their firs and pines. Her gaze fell on a hand-painted sign that said, "Closed for Storm! Come Back Before Christmas!"

*Closed?* She didn't want to come back. She was here *now*. Looking around, she sighed, spying a curl of smoke from the main house on the eastern perimeter of the property.

That's where Brandon's parents lived, she recalled, and he...

She turned and faced the opposite direction, remembering the secret pond where he wanted to skate with her. Should she try to find that cozy cabin tucked into the woods?

*But when you're ready, I'll be here. Skates are hanging beside the cabin door and if I'm not cutting down trees, I'm inside with a fire and a good book.*

His invitation echoed in her head, nudging her forward.

Pulling gloves from her pocket, she squinted in the direction where she'd walked with Brandon.

Could she find her way back to that pond and cabin? She'd have to go on foot, since there was no way to drive, but she sure didn't want to get lost on the side of the mountain when nightfall was only a few hours away.

That would not be good. But was that enough to make her turn around and give up? That would just be giving into fear and paralysis, and where had that gotten Hannah in life?

Alone.

On a deep sigh, she took a few steps toward that side of the property, trying to remember the route. Down that hill, along a path, around a curve, and down a bit of a slope...there was a man. A man she liked a lot.

Zipping the parka all the way up and slipping into

the gloves, she made sure she had her phone and her keys, then took off, blinking when a snowflake hit her face.

As she started down the hill, she felt a smile pull and grow with each step. This was what she wanted from life —to be audacious and bold and take a—

"Oh!" She slid on an ice patch, nearly losing her balance.

—risk.

"Dang it, Hannah," she said out loud, her words caught in the chilly breeze. "Don't break a leg on your way to audaciousness."

Righting herself and slowing to a careful trudge, she reached the bottom of the first slope, then turned left, following the snowy path until she turned...right? Which way was that lake? Why hadn't she paid closer attention when she'd walked here with Brandon?

Because she'd been flirting and laughing and feeling things. Now, she could only feel cold feet and wet snow.

Squeezing her eyes shut, she remembered the walk with Brandon and...yes, right. They'd definitely gone right. Heading that way, she steadied her breathing and lifted her face to the fading sun, feeling the cold flutter of snowflakes as they fell on her cheeks and eyelashes.

It felt good to take a chance. Good to pursue this... romance. Because, face it, that's what she was doing.

She slowed her step as she came to the steep drop where she'd held his hand, certain she was in the right place. Well, kind of certain.

Without Brandon to lean on, she crouched down and

essentially rode on her bottom and back over the snow-covered dirt path, easily making it without a mishap.

She rested there for a second, feeling oddly victorious, then looked around again. She just had to go... oh, boy.

This did not look anything like she remembered. Was that grouping of pine trees there when Brandon brought her? Wasn't there another hill?

She walked some more, longer than she remembered, so she stopped, turned and...grunted in frustration, her booted feet moving slowly from cold and uncertainty.

"I'm lost," she muttered, hating the feeling of her heart climbing up in her throat. "I went out to pursue a man, conquer my fears, and...now I'm going to die in a snowstorm, lost in the mountains. Great. Just great."

Tears stung, mixing with the cold flakes. She reached into her pocket and pulled out her phone, but she didn't have a single bar.

Tamping down panic, she continued back in the direction she'd come. With each step, she got a little more turned around.

"Okay, okay. Think." She tried her phone again—no luck—then took a deep breath, wiped a tear she didn't want to shed, and relied completely on her instincts to head...somewhere.

Her foot slipped again, this time sliding right out from under her. She careened on ice and snow, slid down the slope, arms flailing as a shriek escaped her throat.

She landed in a soft bank of snow, inches from the

trunk of a pine tree. Several pine trees, actually, which were...

Wait a second! She pushed up and peeked over the rise of the embankment that stopped her fall and let out a quiet hoot of victory.

There was the small cabin tucked into the woods. An icy pond reflected the gunmetal-gray sky and snowflakes fell over...a skater.

One man in the center of the ice, gliding like he was literally flying, wearing a sweater and jeans, brown locks fluttering. He held a hockey stick, flipping it left and right, pushing a tiny black puck that was completely in his control.

For a split second, she couldn't breathe. There were too many emotions—too much relief, an overdose of adrenaline, the blinding elation that she'd beat the elements and fear. Most of all, she ached to go be with that man. The feeling was so strong, she could taste it.

She did it! She did it! She didn't get lost, she didn't crumble or melt or fall—well, not too hard—and she'd found him.

Brushing back some hair that had fallen in her face, she made her way to the cabin, glancing at him as she walked. He had no idea she was there. No idea, she imagined, that anything in the world existed but that ice, that puck, and his personal strength and grace.

She reached the cabin and spied about five pairs of skates hanging on hooks. She picked up a white pair that looked close to her size, and dropped onto the bench to put them on, not at all surprised that her whole body was unstable after the battle with the mountain.

Tying the laces, she stood, wobbly at first, but it was easy to see the skate-friendly path that led straight to the pond from here. Taking a deep breath of freezing air, she started toward him, just about at the edge of the ice when he turned and sliced the ice to bring himself to a complete stop.

"Excuse me, but..." His voice trailed off as he glided closer, near enough that she could see his frown transform into a smile. "Hannah?"

"Hey."

"What are you doing here?"

"I came for a tree"—and you, she added mentally—"but I think I'll stay for a skate."

He zipped straight to her, tossing the hockey stick as he reached her and extending both hands. "I can't believe this."

She took his hands and held tight, gazing at him, lost again. Only this time, she knew exactly how to find her way.

Still zinging with adrenaline, high from the adventure, and aching to be close to him, she slid across the small space that separated them and wrapped her arms around him.

"Believe it," she whispered. "Let's skate."

"Can you?"

"Apparently," she said with a smile, "I can do anything."

She could, actually, skate fairly well, but nothing like Brandon.

An hour or so later, after playing one-on-one hockey, which he let her win, and zipping around the pond holding hands, Hannah was completely breathless. They only stopped when so much snow had fallen, they couldn't skate.

"Not bad, girl," he joked, giving her head a playful rub as they walked back to the cabin. "And I can't believe you found your way here."

On a skating break, she'd told him about her adventure.

"I'm pretty proud of myself," she said. "Not something I'd normally do."

"Ah, the comfort zone. Always my place on the rink of life, too."

She looked up at him, confused by the comment. "Is there a 'comfort zone' in a hockey game?"

"Not officially, but there should be." He looked around, taking in the amount of snow. "I guess I can try to get you down the mountain in my truck, but you can't drive a car now, even four-wheel drive. They'll plow in the morning but not tonight."

She drew back and looked around. "I'm stuck here?" Her voice rose as the realization hit.

"It'll be fine," he promised her. "You can have my room and all the space you need. I can make us dinner, a fire, and I have games and movies. Whatever you like. But please, don't try to drive home in this. It wouldn't be safe."

She checked the steady snowfall and nodded. "Sure. I can stay." After all, it was a day of taking risks.

"Had enough? I shouldn't have told you about my highlight reel." Brandon held up the remote and put the TV on pause. "I don't have to relive my glory days."

"But it's so fun to see Number 75 whizzing down the ice. Finish this game."

He rolled his eyes and hit Play. "Okay, but I'd rather play Scrabble again."

"A little bit more." She nudged him, wondering, not for the first time, if she'd ever sat on a sofa with Keith and watched a hockey game and not realized she'd been watching "Fletch" play for the Pittsburgh Penguins.

Suddenly, the screen went blank, the room went dark, and there was nothing but silence.

"Lost power," he said, sounding resigned as he stood and walked to the fireplace. "Anyway, I made the goal."

"Do you think you'll miss playing?" she asked.

He hoisted some split firewood from the pile next to the hearth and tossed it onto the grate, causing a crackling spray of sparks and more flames.

"I was ready to get off the ice," he said after a minute. "I've always known this place, this farm, was my future and I'm okay with that. I just..."

She waited, inching forward. "You just what?"

He held up a hand. "Don't want to freak you out."

"Freak me out? I am alone in a cabin with you, stuck in a house with no power. I think if I was going to be freaked out, it would have happened sometime between our delicious sandwiches, the Scrabble game where I kicked your butt with a *bazooka*—the word, not the actual thing—and the highlight reel."

He smiled. "Fair enough but I would have won if you hadn't stolen that triple-word score from me. I had *quilted!*"

She laughed, the echoes of their first few inside jokes already making her feel so comfortable with him. "Tell me. Nothing will freak me out," she assured him.

Returning the poker to the stand, he wiped his hands on his jeans and sat down next to her. Not too close, but near enough that she could see a shadow in his blue eyes as he brushed back a lock of his hair and thought about what he had to say.

"I really want to be a tree farmer."

"*Oookay.* Why would that freak me out?"

"Because most girls—the ones I've met and liked over the past ten or twelve years, at least—aren't very impressed by that." He gave a self-deprecating laugh. "They are impressed by the NHL, however, and the bright lights of pro sports fame."

She thought about the young woman who'd gotten engaged on TV and imagined that gorgeous creature seeking those bright lights.

"I've been serious with two really great women," he continued. "Neither one of them could abide the idea that I'd be taking over my family's tree farm, living a fairly rustic life in the mountains, and depending on what I've saved to build a future." He angled his head and lifted both brows. "Tree farming is not the most lucrative business, but I can always teach the local boys how to play hockey."

She took a slow breath, trying not to say what she was thinking—that the life he just described sounded like a dream to her. That she'd jump on the tree farm band-wagon so fast, she might topple the thing over. That he'd just articulated her...fantasy.

"With all due respect to those women," she said, "who I'm sure were lovely and nice, they've never been to Copper Creek or the Blue Ridge Mountains or they'd know what they're missing."

"Actually, they were both here. Met my parents, saw the farm, and..." He chuckled softly at a memory. "My first ex—a New York runway model and Instagram influencer—ran kicking and screaming. No real surprise there."

"And the other?" she asked.

"She was a little more open to the idea of living here —as a vacation home when we wanted to do 'rustic.' She assumed we'd live in my five-bedroom McMansion outside of Pittsburgh. She owned a very successful PR firm up there, so there was no way she'd consider being a tree farmer's wife."

"Oh, that's a shame."

He shrugged. "Better to find out before you're married, right? Sorry, but what can I say? My heart is here, on this land, in this business, and that isn't gonna change."

And *her* heart basically folded in half. If she thought he was cute before, he just became...perfect.

Too perfect? Too good to be true? Too soon to even think these things?

She felt his gaze on her, searching her face, waiting for her response.

"Brandon, I'm a second-grade teacher at Copper Creek Elementary who grew up on this mountain," she said, choosing her words carefully. "I totally understand having your heart here and not in a five-bedroom McMansion."

He blew out a breath, his eyes as warm as the fire. "Yeah, Hannah. You get it."

For three, four, maybe five thudding heartbeats, they just looked at each other in the firelight, silent and barely breathing. Was it her imagination that electricity hummed even though there was a power outage? Was she dreaming that a connection was being formed during that long look?

"Well," he said, suddenly a tad awkward as he slapped his thighs. "It could get very cold tonight. I have more blankets, but I'm going to recommend we sleep here in front of the fire to stay warm. I can take the floor and this baby"—he patted the worn leather sofa—"is next-level comfy. It's all yours."

She nodded slowly, reining in her emotions and just how much she wanted to take his hand, to kiss him, to tell him...she'd *love* to be a tree farmer's wife.

"That sounds good," she said, forcing a casual smile to cover the confession that she'd surely regret.

"And I want to call my parents and check on them," he said, surprising her a little but underscoring what she already knew—he was caring, kind, and considerate.

"I'll text my family, too," she said. "Assuming I have a cell signal now."

He disappeared into the other part of the cabin—presumably where his room was—then came out a few minutes later, laden with three more blankets and some clothes on the top.

"They're fine," he reported. "All tucked in and under blankets. I grabbed some sweatpants and a jersey, and some wool socks." He gestured toward the clothes. "Feel free to change so you're comfortable and warm."

"That was thoughtful," she said, taking the clothes but looking at him, thinking and wondering...did he even *have* a flaw? Of course he did. All men did. All *people* did.

But how long would it take to find it, assuming she was given a chance to look? Or was Hannah just setting herself up for another colossal disappointment that would hurt even more than the one she'd just endured?

He stilled his movements after a second and eyed her. "You okay?"

"I...I was just..." She shook her head, giving an uncomfortable laugh. "Never mind." She pushed up. "I'll go change."

Holding the clothes tight to her chest, she slipped away into his undersized—and already freezing—bathroom and pulled the roomy sweatpants and a giant Penguins jersey over her clothes. Fuzzy socks on top of her own and she was...not exactly dressed for a date. But she was warm.

When she came out, she found the coffee table dragged to one side and two makeshift beds. One was on the sofa with a crisp white bed pillow and at least three fluffy blankets, and the other on the floor with one very old quilt and a throw pillow she'd seen on a chair.

"Your phone's buzzing," he said. "Might be someone from your family."

"Many someones," she said when she picked it up and skimmed the texts.

"Everybody okay?" he asked.

"My dad said the power's out down there, too," she said. "Noelle is totally freaking out, though."

"That's your cousin? I met her the other night, right?"

"Her aunt is married to my dad, so we have no idea what that makes us, but yes, you met her."

"Why is she freaking out?"

"She's in charge of the tree lighting in town and without power? Nothing lights."

"Oh, my dad mentioned the new committee chair," he said, nodding. "Now I get the connection—she's married to Jace Fleming, right?"

"Yep." She lowered herself to the sofa, sliding under the many blankets he'd provided. "Maybe your dad told you that Noelle wanted to light the tree with battery-powered LED lights, but at least one person on the committee wouldn't let her. Now she's scaring up generators and praying."

"He did tell me, since I'll be providing the tree solo next year. Yeah, old Edna likes things done according to tradition." He turned to the fire and then got another log. "She better pray hard and get lots of generators. We got her a huge tree this year."

Hannah winced. "Poor Noelle. If the event is a disaster, she'll take it personally. Plus, there's that...silly tradition."

"About the old lady's husband's ghost, who shows up when the lights flicker at the bottom?"

"You know that?" Hannah laughed.

"Well, we provide the tree every year, so yeah, my dad told me."

"There's actually a very sweet story that goes with that," Hannah said. "Apparently, that's where Edna, the lady, and her husband had their first kiss, just when the lights came on. He called it their last first kiss."

That made him smile. "Cute."

"It gets better. Noelle and Jace had theirs at the tree, too, and both those couples were married six months later."

"Huh. Now that, I never heard," he said. "Sounds like a little Asheville Christmas magic."

"Not this year, because there are no lights if there's no power."

"I might try to scare up another generator, if we can spare it."

"Thank you. I'll tell her." She texted another note to

the group chat and did her best to assuage Noelle with news of a possible generator loan.

"You really want to turn your phone off to save the battery," he suggested, finishing with the fire and folding to the floor with his one thin blanket.

She did, snuggling deeper into her nest. "I don't think the division of warmth was fair," she said, fluttering the top covering. "Please take this?"

"And stay awake all night listening to your teeth chattering? Not a chance."

She laughed softly, the echo of her earlier thoughts coming back as she studied his silhouette against the orange flickering flames.

He stared into the fire, quiet for a moment, the light catching the waves that brushed the collar of his sweatshirt.

What is he thinking about, she wondered. What really made him tick? Was he interested or just a player who knew that pretending to be "small town" would be all it took to get them under the blankets together?

He turned and caught her looking at him, his brow lifted in curiosity. "You look...uncertain."

Oh, she sure was. Uncertain and a little terrified.

"I was just wondering..." She took a breath, trying to figure out how to ask all those questions, but she chickened out. "Why don't you have a Christmas tree? Too much like work?"

He looked a little dubious, as if he didn't for one second believe that's what she was thinking about.

"No, I was going to get one, but...I don't know." He

lifted a shoulder and glanced at the overstuffed bookshelf and well-worn furniture. "Decorating a Christmas tree alone? Hanging a star and some tinsel strands? No presents underneath? It's just kind of sad and pathetic, don't you think?"

She laughed softly. "Exactly why I don't have one. But I decided I wanted one after all, which is why I came up here today."

"Really? And here I thought you....I honestly thought you came to see me."

"Well, I did," she admitted. "Under the guise of getting a tree."

"You didn't need a guise," he assured her, moving closer to the fire and rubbing his arms. "And I'll find you a beauty tomorrow."

"You're cold," she said. "Please take this blanket."

"No, it's fine. I've spent the better part of my life on ice, so a little cold doesn't bother me."

She stared at him, still struggling.

"Honestly," he said, misreading her expression.

"It's not that, it's..." She wrapped the blankets around her tighter, digging for the courage to be candid and raw. She could do this. She had to. "I'm just trying to figure out if you're for real."

"Me? Real?"

"You're...a little too good to be true."

He looked surprised by that, his lips lifting into a smile that curved the scar she was so used to, it had become familiar. "I'm not too good, Hannah. But I am true. You'll never find anyone truer."

She let out the softest whimper, suddenly aching just to hold his hand and be near him. That was all, just...to be close to him.

Without a word, she clung to her blankets and very, very slowly slid off the sofa, easing herself to the floor.

"Are you giving up the comfy couch?"

"I'm not giving up anything." She reached behind her for the big pillow, laying it next to his little throw pillow. Then she spread out the three blankets over the one he had. "I'm offering...warmth."

Holding her gaze, he exhaled and very easily slid under all the covers next to her. "And I'm accepting it. Thank you."

Wordlessly, they lined up next to each other, not pressed together but close enough that the temperature instantly increased under the blankets. She curled up on her side, facing the fire, and he stayed behind her, respectfully not so much as putting a hand on her shoulder.

But she could feel his breath and the power of him, secure and safe.

They stayed like that for a long time, the only sound the fire crackling in the silent cabin.

As she closed her eyes and felt her whole body relax and start to drift to sleep, she heard the blankets move and felt him lean closer.

"Hannah?"

"Hmm?"

He lifted up a little, his mouth close to her ear when he whispered, "Why don't we have our first kiss at the tree lighting and see if that folklore is all it's cracked up to be."

She inhaled softly, and the breath caught in her throat. Very slowly, she turned, so close she could have kissed him right then and there. But neither one of them moved. Instead, they just looked into each other's eyes in the firelight and smiled.

"You sure you want to test the fates like that?" she asked softly.

"I've never been more sure of anything."

"Yeah. I'd like that," she whispered the understatement of the century.

"Goodnight, Hannah. Sleep well."

She turned back to the fire and closed her eyes on a sigh.

Was he too good to be true? Guess she'd find out tomorrow.

But tonight, for the first time in a long time, she felt nothing but the protective warmth of a man...who might be exactly what she'd been waiting for.

# Chapter Nineteen

## *Angie*

"The Biltmore Estate is *closed*." Even through the phone, Angie could hear the low-key panic in Noelle's voice.

"Not really surprised," Angie said, sipping water as she stared out at the snow-covered Blue Ridge Mountains from the sunroom. "No one has power, including my inoperable coffee maker."

Noelle sighed with audible frustration. "I need those generators but there's no information about when the estate will open. Do you know?"

"Probably when full power comes back," she said. "But weren't we going to pick those generators up this afternoon? It's early."

"Do you think there will be a generator available for me at two o'clock?" Noelle asked. "Your buddy Bucky will have his pockets lined by desperate people by then or—"

"Or the Biltmore will need them," Angie finished with a much more plausible possibility. "Look, as soon as the roads are cleared, I'll head over there and twist some arms. Hopefully, I'll know the guard on duty because I don't have an all-access pass."

"How about your bearded boyfriend?"

Angie snorted. "He's not...never mind. Yes, he has the pass but today's not good. He's supposed to meet with his boss this morning, although it's anyone's guess if that's happening. I suppose they could do a call, but I don't know."

"Please, Ang, I need help. I need generators if I have —excuse the pun—a snowball's chance of lighting that tree tonight. There's no way to reschedule now since my committee simply didn't put into place a real contingency plan."

In the distance, Angie heard the rumble of a noisy engine, and that meant good news.

"They're plowing Creekside Road," she said. "Meet me at the Biltmore?"

"I'm in town dealing with a bunch of stuff like vendors who are flipping out, volunteers who are nowhere to be found, carolers who want to quit. But I'll get there as soon as I can. Please promise Bucky anything —free art, publicity, a kiss on the lips, or cold hard cash. I need those generators."

Angie chuckled, because when Noelle wanted control it was both beautiful and a little terrifying, but she wanted to help her sister.

She checked on Brooke, who was in a teenage coma and just wanted to sleep, and texted Elliott to see if he could get her on the property. Once the plows went the other direction and she knew it was clear, she took off for the Biltmore Estate.

The forty-minute drive took an hour and a half with many of the stoplights not working and a surprising amount of traffic moving at a snail's pace.

But in that time, Elliott didn't call or return her text, which kind of made Angie's stomach burn with stress. Not only did she think that meant the meeting with his boss didn't go well, she worried that she couldn't get onto the property. Would her staff badge be enough?

She doubted it, not if the entire estate was without power and they'd closed the offices and all tours.

As Angie pulled up behind a few cars in line at the main entrance, she let out a noisy grunt when she saw a guard behind the desk was someone she definitely did not know.

The first car finally pulled out to make a U-turn and leave. As the line moved forward, her phone rang with a call from Elliott.

"Oh, thank goodness," she said, tapping the speaker button. "I need you."

He gave a soft laugh. "Now that's the greeting I want to hear today."

"I mean...for getting on the property," she replied. "I promised my sister some generators, remember?"

"Ah, I do remember and I wanted to help you." His voice sounded somber and she winced, waiting for the bad news that he couldn't get her onto the property. "So, yeah. I have my pass. Are you at the main gate? I'll come down for you."

She wanted to ask so many more questions but the car in front of her was also doing the U-Turn of Death and she didn't want to face the guard without Elliott. She followed suit, and pulled into a small space near the street to wait for him.

While she did, she texted an update to Noelle, who said she was on her way and optimistically driving Jace's truck, even though he had to go on a vet call that morning. After that, Angie sat for a moment and studied the snow-laden trees and visible grounds of the Biltmore Estate.

She'd worked at this beautiful place for a year now and had experienced all four seasons—each utterly different and glorious. She loved it here, she thought with a sudden punch of emotion. If she were facing the possibility of leaving—as Elliott might be—it would break her heart.

And if he left? That would kind of break her heart, too, she admitted to herself. She liked spending time with him, liked the attraction and electricity, the humor and the intelligence, the sheer loveliness of the way he respected her skills and showed true interest in her.

Without a doubt, she could see herself getting involved with him and—

A tap on her passenger window startled her and she whipped around, expecting the guard to tell her not to park here. But it was Elliott, wearing an expectant expression and dangling a badge from a lanyard, looking just as sharp and attractive as he had in her imagination.

She flipped the lock and gestured for him to come in.

"Get in here and bring your cute...all-access pass," she quipped when he opened the door.

But the chuckle seemed a little forced and the normal twinkle was definitely missing from those ever-changing eyes as he climbed in.

"Everything okay?" she asked.

He let out a slow and noisy breath. "Let's get to the generators," he replied. "I already cleared it with the guard, so take the right lane and she'll lift the gate. And she'll let Noelle in, too."

"You are made of awesome," she murmured, driving toward the gate and shooting him a glance every few seconds. In the small space of the vehicle, she could practically taste his stress.

"Why do I think it did not go well with your boss?"

"Because it did not go well," he said sullenly.

"Oh, Elliott." Without thinking, she reached a hand toward his and he took it, giving her a squeeze.

"I'd say it's okay, but it's not," he told her. "Do you know where you're going? Wait, dumb question. You know this property better than George Vanderbilt himself did."

"Kinda. I'm going to the equipment shed, which is... whoa." She slowed the SUV at a snowy road. "Going to be a challenge to get there, but we will. Tell me what happened, please."

Still holding her hand, he let his head fall back and closed his eyes. "I have until Monday to 'solve the problem' of a feature piece of art—one that must be on the order of *The Adoration of the Magi*—or I can pack my bags and print my resume."

"No! Why wouldn't they let you stay through the holidays? That's brutal."

"Yeah. Well, whatever. That's not the worst of it."

She rolled over crunchy snow and peered through the trees in the direction of the equipment shed, happy to see the small road that led to it had been shoveled, if not plowed.

She needed both hands to grip the wheel, but managed to slide a look at him when he was silent a beat too long. "What could be worse?"

He looked out the window, facing away from her.

"Elliott?"

"They want to cut the department...significantly."

She gasped softly. "Fire people?"

He turned and stared ahead, eyes narrowed as she realized exactly what that meant for her. Last hired, the least amount of experience, and no impressive credentials? She was toast.

"Why?" she asked.

"Reorg. Budget. New year, new approach. The usual."

But nothing about getting fired from her dream job was *usual*.

She groaned as she pulled up to the shed, her frustration divided between this ghastly news and the sight of four generators just loaded onto a flatbed and about to leave.

"I hope that wasn't the last four," she muttered,

driving into what she hoped was a parking lot, but snow covered any lines.

"I'm sorry, Angel," he said. "I really feel like this is all my fault for ignoring the family home and trying to turn it into an art museum."

She studied him for a moment, exhaling softly. "I know you do, but I don't blame you. It isn't your fault—or the department's—that the Louvre flexed and stole the *Magi* from us. Firing you for that is ridiculous and down-sizing is stupid."

"But it's happening."

"Is it? We have until Monday. I'm not giving up yet. I've been up against worse things in my life and won."

"You have?"

She swallowed, slipping back in time. "Last year, we were this close to losing the cabin." She made a centimeter of space between her finger and thumb. "Everyone was ready to hand the place over to an inter-loper. But...something happened. A miracle? Divine intervention? A big, fat surprise? Yes to all. We believed and had faith, so that's what I have right now." She smiled. "It's Christmas. Isn't there always a miracle?"

He looked right into her eyes, inches away, the connection powerful.

"And you need to know that I am going to follow the instructions Marjorie left in your file."

She cocked her head, not following. "What did they say?"

He inched closer. "She wrote, 'Don't let this one go.'"

"Oh." Angie thought of her coffee with Marjorie and

how she'd said, quite clearly, that she would tell her replacement not to let her go. She'd meant it.

"What if you don't have a choice?" she asked.

"I have a choice. I'll make the list. Your job is safe and..." He took her hand and brought it to his lips. "I don't want to let you go. Not from here..." He tipped his head toward the estate. "And not from here." He pressed their joined hands against his chest. "Because you, Angel, are the real Christmas miracle."

She shivered and sighed. "Oh, Elliott. That's sweet, but we need an *actual* miracle—"

Noelle banged on the hood of the SUV, making them separate and look at her wild-eyed sister.

"—and we might have to waste it on a generator," she murmured as they took off their seatbelts and climbed out.

Bucky wasn't there. No one had heard from him and the only person working was a part-time intern from last summer who lived within walking distance of the estate. He was overwhelmed with the requests from various buildings for generators and snow removal equipment, so Angie's verbal agreement from Bucky was worthless.

After making an impassioned plea, flashing Elliott's all-access pass, and promising the intern a job in an art gallery that he didn't want, they were told to wait.

So the three of them climbed into Angie's SUV to stay warm.

Elliott was quiet. Noelle was texting constantly. And Angie just tried not to think about the fact that she might get fired on Monday.

"Hey, I know him." Elliott leaned forward and pointed toward a man walking into the shed.

"Really?" Angie squinted at the older man with white hair sticking out from underneath a ballcap. "I don't."

"He helped move some furniture in my office when I first got here. He's a Red Sox fan and we had a good talk." He opened the passenger door. "Hang tight, ladies. I'm going to talk to him."

The minute he got out, Noelle put her phone down and leaned forward. "I know why I'm a ball of stress, but why is it so tense in this vehicle? I could cut it with the proverbial knife."

"Because"—Angie turned around—"he's getting fired over the *Magi* issue and they want to downsize the curators. Goodbye to my job and..." She rolled her eyes. "That dumb little romance I was thinking about having."

"You are kidding me!" Noelle slapped the seat. "Not fair!"

"No kidding."

"Can't you get something to replace it?" Noelle asked.

"A 'household name' piece of art by Monday?" Angie shook her head. "I don't think that's the answer. But there has to be something we can do, some way to change their minds."

"I think..." Noelle looked down at her phone. "Oh, wait a second." She read, texted, read, and texted some more, focused on the device and the mountain of challenges she was facing for tonight.

Understanding Noelle had her own issues, Angie turned back around to look at the shed and watch one more generator go out the door, swallowing frustration at the whole situation.

Elliott jogged out of the shed, looking a little more hopeful than when he went in, pulling the door open and dipping his head into the car.

"Can you guys wait here for ten or fifteen minutes? We might have a solution."

"Of course," Angie said. "What is it?"

"A long shot." He grinned at her. "And you were right. We might be using our only miracle this Christmas. But..." He looked back at Noelle.

"I would be so grateful there really are no words," she said.

"Then hang tight." He winked at Angie and headed back into the shed. A minute later, she saw him walk outside and disappear around the back.

It took way more than ten minutes. During the half hour he was gone, Noelle got out of the SUV to take a call, pacing and breathing out cold air as she chatted on the phone.

Angie recognized when her sister was deep in "work mode." Last year when they'd spent a month at the cabin, the two of them shared a room and Noelle was a relentless workaholic in her role as an art dealer for Sotheby's. She never met a problem she didn't want to solve, and it sounded like she had plenty of them today.

Clearly, she approached the tree lighting business with the same dedication and determination, talking to... whoever she was talking to.

It left Angie with way too much time to spin through a million different possibilities and come up with...a pink slip.

She'd always known the arrival of a new boss could mean her demise, but she didn't know he'd be taking her heart with him. Not that she was in love with the man, but she could be. Now she wouldn't have him or the Biltmore, but at least she'd had the best year of her life.

She had Brooke, the cabin, and the divorce from Craig was behind her. She had experience and knew she loved working—maybe she'd take the job at Noelle's art gallery.

Aunt Bitsy always said God has a plan. But what if she hated His plan?

She spotted Elliott and the guy in a ballcap, navigating the snowy hill toward the shed. He gave her a thumbs-up and then called to Noelle, who quickly finished her call.

Angie climbed out and let her heart lift with the sense that he had indeed produced a miracle for her family, and she adored him for that.

Five minutes later, the two men loaded two generators—the last two on the property—onto the back of Jace's truck. Noelle was giddy with joy, and threw her arms around Elliott and thanked him profusely.

"I owe you a gigantic favor," she said, leaning back and looking into his eyes. "I *will* repay you."

"Not necessary," he said, giving her shoulder a warm, brotherly pat. "I'm happy to help."

She blew kisses to both of them, then pointed Elliott. "He's a keeper, Angie. See you there!"

Angie turned to Elliott, beaming at him. "You are a miracle worker!"

He put both his hands on her cheeks, his fingers cold and surprisingly rough on her skin. "I like 'keeper' better."

Her smile faded. "But if we don't come up with one more miracle for the *Magi* problem, then I can't keep you."

Looking into her eyes, a smile lifted behind his close-cropped beard. "That begs the question. Do you want to?"

"Very much," she answered without hesitation.

His eyes shuttered with what looked like bone-deep satisfaction. "I have no idea how much time we have left together, but I don't want to spend one minute of it on that problem. Why don't we—"

"Thanks again, Mr. Quinn!" Ballcap Guy hustled by, folding the straps they'd used to hoist the generators.

"We should be thanking you," Angie said.

"Oh, he already did." The man reached into his pocket and pulled out a small acrylic box. "I've been coveting this thing since the day I saw it in his office. My brother's gonna go nuts when I give him this." He tipped his cap—a Boston Red Sox hat. "Merry Christmas!"

As he disappeared inside, Angie tried—and failed—to close her dropped jaw.

Elliott did it for her, with one tip of his finger on her chin. "He really wanted it and I've enjoyed it long enough. His brother's sick and...it was an easy decision."

"But...but...you bartered for the generators with your beloved *Yaz-autographed baseball?*"

He wrapped his arm around her shoulders and leaned over to place a kiss on her hair. "Sometimes you need a Christmas miracle, sometimes you *are* the Christmas miracle. Now, where were we?"

"On what we're going to do today," she said. "What do you want to do if not solve our career-ending *Magi* problem?"

"I don't really care, as long as it's with you," he said. "I think your sister will need help, so why don't we go into town, do what we can to help her set up, walk around in the snow, hold hands with goofy smiles on our faces, and have a romantic dinner before the generators light up the night?"

She let out a soft laugh. "That sounds perfect."

Almost as perfect as he was.

# Chapter Twenty

## Noelle

"You got that, Cass?" Noelle asked as the two of them pushed up from the frozen ground behind the tree. "All you have to do, according to our wonderful electrician known as Daddy, is flip that switch a minute or two after the whole tree lights. Go ahead, try it."

Cassie, small enough that she could fit under the lowest branches, reached for the switch. "Like this?"

Immediately, the bottom three rows of lights on the tree came on.

"Now flick it back and forth a few times."

Cassie did, making the lights flash.

"Perfect!" Noelle exclaimed, helping Cassie to her feet.

"I love this!" Cassie's face was bright from the cold and excitement. "I get to be the ghost of Mr. Covington."

"Shhh. No one can know," Noelle said. "I'll give you the signal and you slide under and do your thing."

"It's really nice of you to do this, Miss Noelle," Cassie added, taking her hand as they walked around the massive tree. "I like making sure that old lady isn't sad."

"That's sweet, honey. And speaking of, I see that *old lady*." Noelle whispered the last two words. "She's over there with Joanna and Tony and it looks like they need me. Go stay with Daddy over by that last booth."

"'Kay. When do all the people get here?"

Good question. Noelle looked around the four-way intersection in the heart of town, down the roads, and to the park that had plenty of vendor booths, ready to sell candy and hot chocolate and homemade ornaments...but very, very few people.

Considering the festivities started in about an hour and the tree lighting was in two? Not good. By now, the place should be swarming with tourists and locals, easily a thousand or more.

They were lucky if there were twenty-five people, not counting the vendors—and there weren't many of them.

"Soon, I hope," she said. "But there's still a power outage, and most people are staying tucked in by their fires, I'm sorry to say." She gently nudged Cassie toward Jace as Tony Jessup waved her over again, looking serious enough that Noelle braced for a problem.

There'd been a mountain of them today, but she approached Tony, Edna, and Joanna with a smile.

"Hey, team," she called. "It's just about go time."

No one answered, but shared looks that said...there was definitely a problem. How much worse could it get than sparse crowds and low lights?

"You better tell her," Joanna said to Tony.

Noelle did not like the sound of that. "Tell me what?"

"The carolers backed out," Edna said. "And Harry's stuck at the tree farm."

Which was why she didn't get that last promised generator, she assumed. But the carolers? That wasn't *such* bad news. "Okay," she said brightly. "We have the tree and everyone can—"

"And we need to take your generators," Tony interjected softly.

"Excuse me?" She couldn't have heard that correctly. "Take my...*why*?"

Tony stepped forward. "We have multiple emergency situations that the fire department is handling," he said. "Mountain Vistas Assisted Living is begging for additional generators, as their main backup failed."

"Oh." She put her hand over her lips. "That's not good."

"And there's a list of local residents on oxygen and many of them are in need as well. The department just put out a call for volunteers to offer up their generators, and I was on my way to ask you if you'd agree to give up yours when I saw these guys."

"You don't have to ask," Noelle said, pushing away disappointment at the very thought of freezing old folks or patients on oxygen.

No one was going to *die* so she could keep control and power. "I'll get my husband to help you."

"Some of the booth vendors brought flashlights and are using battery-powered LEDs," Joanna said, stepping away. "But plenty of them needed the second generator, so I'll go break the bad news."

Noelle was about to follow Tony when she caught sight of Edna turning away as if she didn't want anyone to see her face. No doubt she was embarrassed for fighting the suggestion that they use LEDs, too, and expected a snide, "I told you so," from Noelle.

But Cassie's little voice echoed in her head...*I like making sure that old lady isn't sad.*

Out of the mouths of babes, right?

"Edna," Noelle said, reaching for her. "I know this isn't what you wanted."

"It's fine," she said, blinking tears. "I'd like to handle the disappointment as well as you are."

"Trust me, I'm breaking on the inside," she said, holding Edna's mitten-covered hand. "He'll still be here," she added. "I know he's watching down remembering that last first kiss."

The older woman looked up at her, all the sharpness gone from her expression. "It's not really him," she said softly. "I know that."

"But it's the idea of him," Noelle suggested.

She nodded. "This silly tradition gave me a connection to him," she whispered. "It was like I didn't really have to say goodbye. But it's been years now and I *do* have to say goodbye. It's just so difficult when you love someone that much."

Without thinking, Noelle wrapped the much smaller woman in a hug, adding a squeeze. "He was lucky to have a wife like you. And you never know—maybe the power will come back on in the next two hours." She inched back and added, "If it does, Gil will get all the credit."

Edna laughed and wiped a tear. "You go figure out how to break the news that there's no tree lighting tonight. I'm going somewhere warm to get a cup of hot coffee. Oh, by the way, we're not missing anything with those carolers." She leaned in and whispered, "They're always off-key."

"Good to know," she said on a laugh.

"And, Noelle." She reached up and surprised Noelle with a mitteny pat on the cheek. "You've done a fine job on Gil's event and I appreciate how you tried to keep up all the traditions. I hope you'll do it again next year."

"Of course I will," Noelle promised, giving her another hug before heading over to where Tony and Jace were disconnecting the generators.

A few feet away, she spotted Hannah leaning over and chatting with a very animated Cassie, no doubt getting a complete rundown on what was happening. Or *not* happening, as the case may be.

How had this gone so far south? Why couldn't Noelle *fix* any of this? Every time she solved a problem, a bigger one took over.

"You look like a woman on the hairy edge of tears." Bitsy suddenly appeared next to her, a loving arm already around Noelle's shoulders.

"This is not going as planned," Noelle said with a bittersweet laugh as they hugged.

"How many times do I have to tell you that these are God's plans, not yours?"

"Apparently many." Noelle bit her lip and looked around at the meager crowds, the unlit tree, and the miserable faces of the vendors as they got the news about the electricity. "But maybe it's in His plan to get the power back in the next..." She glanced at her watch. "Less than two hours now."

"It might be, but it might not be," Bitsy replied. "Whatever happens, He should be glorified."

With her whole event crumbling, Noelle didn't really want to get into a theological discussion with her passionately Christian aunt. But frustration nipped at her.

"Wouldn't He be more glorified by a lit tree, some noisy but off-key carolers, and the joy of Christmas all around?"

"Hey, you guys." Hannah came closer, holding Cassie's hand, the two of them sharing a somewhat conspiratorial smile. "Mind if I take Cassie for a little bit of a secret mission? Just to my school."

Noelle cocked her head, not sure why they'd go back to Hannah's elementary school right now.

"She has an elf costume," Cassie added quickly. "You know I wanted to wear one tonight."

"But this whole thing is about to be over," Noelle said.

"Maybe not," Cassie said with undaunted and precious optimism.

She was about to argue but Cassie's eyes were twinkling. If an elf costume would make her happy, why not?

"Okay. Stay in touch with me." She gave Cassie a kiss and hugged Hannah, whispering, "Why are you doing this?"

Her friend leaned back and looked at Noelle, giving

her a chance to see her curls had been tamed and she had a little more makeup on than usual.

"Not important. But don't let Brandon Fletcher leave if—when—he shows up."

Noelle was about to tell her that Brandon's father wasn't even here yet, but Cassie yanked Hannah's arm, practically dancing on her boots to get that elf costume.

With a wave, they were off...just like Noelle's generators and her crowds and her high, high hopes.

Bitsy put an arm back around her and squeezed. "Sometimes God teaches you a lesson about who is really in control."

Noelle just looked around at the dimly lit disaster with no carolers, no heat lamps, no festive lighting, no piped-in songs, and as the clock neared eight, no buildup to the big moment.

"Lesson learned, Lord," she said on a sigh. "Loud and clear."

AS DARKNESS DESCENDED, a few more people—a scant few—showed up for the skimpy festival. Lit only by phones, flashlights, a few vendor booths that had LED decorations, and a bright full moon, Noelle did her best to socialize and connect with people.

After all, that was the original reason she'd signed up for this thing.

Eve and David and their kids arrived, all hyped for

the lighting that wasn't. Then Caro and Nate appeared with their two. Angie and Elliott joined them, with Brooke, the three of them howling with laughter like they were having the best imaginable time.

At least someone was having fun.

When Tony gave her the word that Duke Energy said it would most likely not restore the power until morning, Noelle had to make a decision.

Leaning into Jace, who'd stayed close to her, she whispered, "I guess I can't put it off anymore," she said morosely. "Even with people's flashlights and phones, it's really dark now and way past the scheduled time to light. I wanted to wait for Cassie and Hannah to get back, though."

"Hannah just texted me," he said, glancing at his phone. "They're almost here...with a surprise. Any idea what it is?"

"I hope it's a generator but I think it's an elf."

"Oh! There they are." He squinted into the darkness over her shoulder. "Cassie's the elf, but what are they carrying?"

She spun around to see Cassie and Hannah trudging toward them, each hauling a plastic bin.

"I told Aunt Hannah all my ideas!" Cassie called as they rushed to meet each other, dropping her bin and straightening her green elf hat. "And guess what she had at school?"

She popped open one of the containers...which was full of long, thin plastic glow sticks.

"We keep them in storage at school," Hannah told them, glancing around the event.

"I told you we could use them!" Cassie exclaimed. "If we give one to everyone here, they can make a circle necklace but instead of wearing them, they throw them on the tree!" She flung out her hand to demonstrate. "And they can't throw one unless they make a wish. And...and..." It was like you could see the wheels turning in her little head. "If they hook a branch, their wish comes true. It's a *new* tradition!"

Noelle and Jace shared a look of true disbelief.

"Well, I guess a tradition has to start somewhere," Noelle said, reaching to lift her little girl in the air. "Cassie, you are one in a million, you know that?"

She dropped her head back as Noelle spun her, giggling, but then grew serious and scrambled down. "We gotta pass out glow sticks! Help me, Aunt Hannah!"

Noelle turned to Hannah, who was not paying any attention, but looking everywhere in the small crowd.

"I haven't seen him," Noelle said, taking a not-too-wild guess who she was searching for. "But I heard Harry was still at the farm, so it's possible they got snowed in up on the mountain."

"No, no." Hannah shook her head. "The plows came before I left him this morning—"

"*Excuse* me?"

"Nothing like that, Noelle. I got snowed in at the tree farm and...and we planned to meet and...never mind." She shook her head. "It's not important."

But she sure looked like it was important.

"Maybe he heard the whole thing was being canceled for lack of light and power," Noelle suggested.

She waved a glow stick. "Not anymore, thanks to your daughter. Come on, let's pass the torches, so to speak."

"I'll help," Jace offered. "Noelle, you should go up to the stage and tell these folks to start tossing and wishing. It's a Cassie Christmas this year."

Laughing at that, Noelle made her way to the small platform at one side of the tree. She climbed up and looked out at the thin crowd as they waved their glow sticks, the mood lifting with every stick as they figured out how to bend, crack, and create a little light.

"Okay, hey, everyone!" she called. Without a microphone, it wasn't easy, but Uncle Sonny whistled for her and Eve's boys yelled for all those gathered around to listen.

There couldn't have been more than forty or fifty people, but they settled to listen to her, a few spotlighting her with their flashlights.

"We need Asheville to provide the light this year! So, make your glow stick into a circle..." She showed them how to connect the ends, having made many glow stick necklaces with Cassie. "And toss it on the tree! Make a wish and if you hook a branch, your wish will come true!"

She heard Cassie's cheer, the loudest of all for the newest Asheville Christmas tradition.

But no one came forward.

"Come on! Like this!" Noelle took her glow stick, turned to the tree, and made a wish. A simple, secret wish that she fervently hoped would come true. Why not? She had nothing to lose and so very much to gain.

Then she flung it as Cassie had directed. It caught on a branch, the only light on twenty feet of darkness.

"Make your wish and help us light the Asheville tree!" she called out.

No one moved until Eve nudged her boys, who looked sheepish and not interested in going up to the front of the crowd and throwing a girls' necklace at the tree. Well, not all of them. Little Sawyer was already twirling his circle around his finger like a gunslinger, eyeing the top of the tree.

"I bet I can get mine to the top!" he announced.

That got a cheer as he scrambled forward and Noelle could have kissed the child. "Don't forget to make a wish," she said.

"I wish I don't get laughed at when I miss," he joked, really winding up for a toss. "Three...two...one...here goes!"

He chucked the multicolored circle high in the air, snagging a branch about two feet from the top. There was more applause, and another little guy rushed forward.

"I can beat that," he called, whipping his stick, but it landed under Sawyer's.

"I got this!" James yelled out, followed by Bradley, then Josh, then at least six more boys and girls she didn't know, all vying for the top.

Before long, the dads—and a few moms—were in on the game, every single one of them chucking their glow sticks—and coming back for second, third, and fourth tries. As they tossed, they wished.

Cassie came to Noelle's side to watch, her whole face lit as bright as any Christmas tree as her ideas came to life.

"I wish for a car!" a teenage girl yelled.

"Wish again!" her dad countered from the crowd, getting a huge laugh.

"I wish for a puppy!" said a little boy barely old enough to get his glow stick halfway up the tree.

A few wanted PlayStations, one young woman asked for world peace, but a hush fell when Edna Covington came closer. She stood at the base of the tree for a moment, holding her glow stick, her eyes misty.

Enough people knew the folklore that nearly everyone gathered stayed still and quiet, waiting for the octogenarian to say something about Gil, the event's founder, that would no doubt leave no eye dry.

But she turned to Cassie and held out her glow stick. "Your mother told me you have a beautiful voice, so I wish that you would sing."

Cassie's mouth opened to a sweet little O. "Really?"

"And hang that for me. No other wish, just a hello to someone special."

Cassie nodded and held the glow stick close, with reverence. Silently, she walked to the lowest branch and hung it right where the flickering lights were supposed to be. Then she climbed up on the stage, fixed her elf hat, and opened her mouth.

"We wish you a merry Christmas, we wish you a merry Christmas..."

Instantly, the crowd joined in, singing *a cappella*, tossing colorful rings, and somehow changing the world from darkness to light.

Jace came closer, his expression as emotionally wiped out as Noelle's heart.

"This is absolutely the best tree lighting ever," he whispered to her. "You did it."

"I gave up control," she said on a laugh. "And look what happened!"

A couple in their thirties came forward and asked Cassie if they could sing, and she gave them the platform.

The small crowd, all bundled in parkas and scarves, formed a semicircle in front of them, and suddenly the man's deep voice rang out with the words, "Silent night, holy night. All is calm, all is bright..."

Behind her, Jace wrapped his arms around Noelle and nestled her into his chest while they stood transfixed by the notes and words.

"Someone's calling you," Jace whispered, reaching into her jacket pocket.

"Anyone I want to talk to is right here," she said.

But he slid the phone out of her pocket and read the screen. "Janice Margolis?"

She gasped and spun around. "No! I'll take that." She seized the phone and scrambled out of the crowd, her heart hammering with hope.

A few feet away from the singing, she put a finger

over one ear and, smashing the phone to the other, she answered with one question. "Did you get it?"

"Yes!" the woman said. "On Monday!"

"Hallelujah!" She practically danced as she disconnected the call, scanning the crowd frantically to find Angie and Elliott, the two of them standing much like Jace and Noelle had been.

She made her way to them, just as yet another singer climbed up and started singing "Rockin' Around the Christmas Tree" and the whole thing turned into a holiday talent show.

"Hey, you two," she called, waving and working her way closer to her sister and her new man. "I have news for you."

Angie and Elliott met her halfway. "You did it!" Angie exclaimed. "And even after they took your generators!"

"Sorry about that," Noelle said. "But they went to a good cause and the fire department promised to get them back to the Biltmore tomorrow morning. And..." She bit her lip and nearly screamed with excitement as she looked at Elliott. "I told you I'd repay you."

"It's not necess—"

"One of my best friends works at the Museum of Modern Art in New York," she interjected, unable to wait another minute.

"Oh?" His brow lifted. "Got me an interview, did you?"

"So much better." She reached out and took each of their hands in hers. "I got you *Starry, Starry Night* by

Vincent van Gogh from Monday until the first week in January."

For a moment, they both just stared at her, the only sound the raucous singing behind them.

"Did you hear me?" she asked.

Angie let out a shriek, turning to Elliott who threw his arms around her. They jumped a few inches in the air and then he planted a beauty right on Angie's lips.

"I guess you heard me," Noelle joked. "And are doing your best to keep that kissing tradition alive."

They broke the lip-lock then both of them smashed Noelle in a hug.

Laughing, Noelle asked Elliott, "Will that save your job?"

"Are you kidding? I'll probably get a promotion! *Starry, Starry Night?* How did you do that?"

"She owed me a favor and I passed it along to you. Merry Christmas to my new favorite couple."

"I can't believe this!" Angie exclaimed, hugging her so hard Noelle could barely breathe. "You are a national treasure, Noelle Chambers Fleming!"

"I'm not, but that painting is."

Brooke came closer to find out what the excitement was, then Bitsy and Sonny, then Caro and her crew, along with David and the boys and before long, a tight circle of family had gathered for a spontaneous celebration that exceeded every one of Noelle's highest hopes.

As they hugged and laughed and shared their joy, Bitsy sidled next to Noelle with that classic Aunt Elizabeth "I told you so" look on her face.

"I know, I know," Noelle said. "His ways, His plans, His miracles."

Bitsy just smiled. "And now, sweet girl, you've learned the lesson."

Laughing, she turned to Jace, who had an utterly exhausted elf holding his hand.

Had she really learned the lesson, though? Was she going to force her own miracle, or let go of control?

Well, she'd made her wish. Would it come true?

As she put her hand on Cassie's back—her little savior of the night—and looked into the eyes of the man she'd love until the day she died, Noelle already knew her wish had come true. She'd just have to find the right time to tell Jace her decision.

# Chapter Twenty-one

## Hannah

"Go HOME," Hannah prodded Noelle, who was moving through the motions of cleaning up like a zombie.

"I can't. Jace's parents took Cassie home and he's going to help me with the last of it." She nodded to the glow stick-littered ground. "He's worried people with dogs will walk here tomorrow and he's convinced the glow sticks might have poison in them."

"They are a little sus." Hannah looked at the many sticks, now dark and officially trash, left behind. "And everywhere. Hey, I brought the poison, I'll pick them up. I don't mind. I need to...process. And by process, I mean lick some serious wounds."

"He never showed?" she asked softly.

Hannah shook her head. "I should have known he was too good to be true."

"No, no. I'm sure he has a good excuse."

"Please." Hannah rolled her eyes. "I'm fine, Noelle. We had one night, not even a date, since I basically got stuck at his house. I shouldn't even be thinking about another relationship so soon after breaking up with Keith and Brandon knows that and..." She wrested the trash bag from Noelle and snagged one of her gloves. "I have my phone light and you can finish up over there with the vendors."

Noelle sighed in resignation. "Okay, thanks a ton. The sooner we get out, the better. I am ready to collapse."

"Then collapse in the arms of your husband," Hannah said. "At least you have one."

"Hannah!"

"Kidding," she said, giving Noelle a playful jab. "Now off with you before they make you sign up for next year."

"Too late," Noelle cracked, giving her the other glove. "I'm right over there in the park with Jace and Joanna. We'll walk you to your car when we're done." She leaned in and gave Hannah a hug. "Don't be sad."

"Eh. One guy isn't going to make me sad," she said, digging for brightness when she felt as fizzled as one of the dead glow sticks.

When Noelle headed back to the vendors breaking down in the park, Hannah went to work around the base of the tree, which was sadly faded to nothing but a few glimmering sticks. The many that had "missed" littered the ground, so she bent over to scoop up a pile of wishes that would never come true.

How was that for poetic justice?

"Well, look who's picking up the trash now that she's thrown hers out."

Startled, Hannah shot up and blinked in shock at the

sight of Keith. He looked a little ruddy, rough, and very unhappy.

"You scared me," she said, exhaling sharply.

"Everything scares you, Hannah. That's your problem, you know that?"

She blinked and drew back. Was he seriously going to pick a fight now? "I'm busy, Keith. You should go."

But he didn't move, his eyes narrow and just red enough to make her hope he hadn't been drinking.

"I'm right and you know it. You're afraid of everything and that's why we didn't make it."

"It is?" she scoffed. "I think we both know why we didn't make it. If someone was afraid of something, it was you."

"Hey, I offered."

Too little, too late, she thought, but she swallowed the comment because this wasn't the time or the place. They were done.

But he stared at her, looking like he had a lot to say and didn't know which mean comment to pull up first.

"Just go, okay? Leave me alone."

He looked around, side to side. "You think it's safe out here?"

There weren't any people near them, and it was so dark that it was hard to see the vendors packing up booths in the park.

"I'm perfectly safe. Please. Go."

When he didn't move, she bent over again, hoping he'd just walk away while she did her work here. And then—

"I don't wanna give up."

She looked up, aware that he'd come a few steps closer and actually loomed over her.

"It's too late."

"Why?" he demanded. "We had a breakup. That happens. Let's get back together. We'll start from scratch, back to square one. Dating and...all that stuff. Then we'll get married. We can still have kids, Hannah. We can—"

"No." She ground out the word, standing straight again. "I don't want that with you."

"Well, if not me, then who's going to want you?"

She gasped softly, the breath trapped in her throat at the insult, which was salt on her already ragged heart. "Keith, please let me—"

"I'm serious, Hannah. You're deep in your thirties. You're a small-town schoolteacher who could probably lose a few. You're not exactly an Instagram model, you know."

"No, Keith." She squeezed the plastic bag, her palms sweating in the rubber gloves. "I don't know. Please, by all means, continue the list of my many, many flaws. I'm not pretty? I'm not smart? I'm not young or important or sexy—"

"You are every one of those things."

They both whipped around at the voice, preceded by the sight of a tall man with soft brown hair brushing the collar of a Pittsburgh Penguins parka.

For a moment, she couldn't speak.

"And a lot more," Brandon added, his blue gaze locked on her, his silky locks moving as he rounded the tree and walked closer. "Pretty? You're stinkin' gorgeous. Smart? You beat me at Scrabble. You're young enough to navigate a mountain, fit enough to push a puck down the ice without falling. And, if you ask me, a teacher is the single most noble profession in the world."

"Well, nobody asked you, pal." Keith puffed up at the sight of the other man.

Hannah, on the other hand, darn near melted.

"I'm so sorry I'm late," Brandon said to her, closing the space and reaching for her. "Blame the deer and her fawns who got trapped on the big lake and the ice cracked. The entire fire department was up to its eyeballs with the power outage, and all that warning you about the phone battery? Mine was the one that died. I'm sorry, Hannah."

He pulled her into a hug, strong and real enough to take her breath away. And long enough to bring Keith one step closer.

"Who the hell are you?" he demanded.

With his arm still around a speechless Hannah, Brandon extended his other hand. "Brandon Fletcher."

Keith stared at him in abject shock, his gaze dropping to the Penguins logo, then back to the other man's face.

"No way," he muttered. "There is no—"

"You must be Hannah's ex," Brandon said, dropping the hand Keith refused to shake.

"Fletch?" Keith's voice rose as he visibly realized who he was talking to. "The right-wing defenseman Fletch?"

Brandon gave a quick laugh and looked down at Hannah. "Someday they'll say, 'You're the tree farm

Fletch,'" he joked, adding a squeeze. "With the awesome teacher on his arm."

She finally managed to breathe. "Are you for real?" she whispered, and never meant a question more.

Keith came closer, his expression changing from wonder to fury. "What are you doing with her?" he demanded. "She's my girlfriend."

"Keith—"

Keith swiped away whatever Hannah was about to say. "I swear to God, man, if you don't let her go..."

Brandon sliced Keith with a look. "Probably not a good idea to pick a fight with a hockey player. We're kind of experts on the subject."

Keith inhaled so hard, his nostrils flared. "You can't... you can't...have her."

"And you can't say who has me and who doesn't," Hannah said, her voice steady and strong. "We're finished, Keith. I've moved on and you should, too."

"You heard the lady," Brandon said, standing stone still except for the arm he tightened ever so slightly around her shoulders. "Please don't make this rough."

Keith's shoulders dropped just enough that Hannah saw the very second the fight left him. He sighed, gave her a sad look, then closed his eyes.

"Have a good life, Hannah," he muttered, taking a step backwards before turning and disappearing into the darkness.

They waited and watched him leave, then Hannah looked up at Brandon, nearly letting out a whimper of relief and happiness.

They didn't say a word, just got a little lost in each other's eyes. Then he put his hand on her cheek, his fingers cold but tender.

"Hannah," he whispered, the word sounding as beautiful as a warm breeze.

"I have to ask again," she said. "Are you for real?"

He just laughed and wrapped his arm tighter. "I am, and so was the deer and the phone with no battery. I'm so sorry."

"Don't you dare apologize. You just defended my honor."

"Meant every word," he said, his gaze moving over her face like he was trying to memorize every feature. "And I told you I'd be here for the tree lighting and that... kiss tradition you told me about."

"It's not really a tradition, and there was no real lighting."

"But there still could be a kiss," he said, moving a tiny bit closer, his lips hovering over hers, his eyes open and holding her gaze. For one moment, one time-suspended nanosecond of anticipation, the world disappeared.

"Your last first kiss, Hannah." He whispered the words against her lips and she let her eyes close and her body soften while their lips touched with a warm spark of—

Blinding bright light. A crackle of electricity. A distant shout and then a cheer from someone in the park.

Breaking apart, they looked up at the tree, bathed in thousands of white lights, as bright as the sun, twinkling and breathtakingly beautiful.

Speechless, they turned back to each other with disbelieving laughs.

"And the tradition continues," he said, coming closer for another kiss. This one lasted so long, she had to get up on her toes and cling to his shoulders to keep from tipping over with dizzy delight.

People started gathering from the booths, cheering and taking pictures of the tree. With one more light kiss, he stepped to the side just as the bottom three rows of lights started to flicker.

"Look! Brandon, look! It must be real."

"So real." He pressed his lips to her ear to whisper, "Tradition says six months. I say we go for it."

She turned her head, looked into his eyes, and officially fell in love right on the snowy streets of Asheville, keeping the city's greatest tradition alive.

# Chapter Twenty-two

## Noelle

"SORRY I'M LATE!" Angie called as she blew in with the blustery wind to Noelle's house on Christmas Eve afternoon. "But I brought wine! Really, really good wine!"

She came into the kitchen where Noelle and Eve were just setting up the afternoon snacks for the sisters' newest tradition—Birthday Triplet Lunch.

Noelle had made it up a few days earlier, and was so happy her sisters agreed to add one more thing to their busy December calendars. But their December 25$^{th}$ birthdays would get lost in the huge family Christmas gathering. So, now that they all lived in the same town for the first time in many, many years, Noelle wanted one afternoon just for the Chambers triplets to toast another trip around the sun.

Plus, since she was born right before midnight, it was technically Eve's birthday, and she acknowledged that by wearing the plastic tiara Cassie had lent her before she and Jace headed out for a few hours.

"Ooh, that is good," Eve said, giving Angie an air kiss

that nearly knocked off her crown as she checked out the wine label. "How'd you score this?"

"Brace yourselves," she said, rounding the counter to kiss Noelle. "I mean *really* brace yourselves."

"You stole it?" Noelle guessed.

"You won it in a company raffle?" Eve suggested.

"Oh, I know." Noelle snapped her fingers. "You got it as a bonus for having the most successful outside art exhibit in the history of the Biltmore. I'll take that," she joked, grabbing the bottle.

Angie settled on a barstool and popped an olive from Noelle's charcuterie. "Not in a million years will you guess how I got that bottle."

"Tell!" Eve demanded.

"You, my sisters, are looking at the Biltmore Estate's newest Staff Curator, which is a promotion from my former position of Associate Staff Curator."

Eve gasped. "Angie! That's fantastic."

"I know. It pays to kiss the boss," she joked.

"That is not why you got that promotion," Noelle said, knowing her sister's strong capabilities on the job.

"In a sense it is, but I'm okay with that," Angie explained. "Elliott went into corporate and fought for me to not only get the promotion but to be given my own little newly created department—the Heritage and Legacy Archives Division."

"Ooh, fancy," Eve laughed.

"And important," Noelle said.

"It's both," Angie told them. "And it means that nothing—not a candlestick, armoire, or dining room chair

—in the 'home' of the Vanderbilts or their staff can be touched, changed, featured, or placed anywhere without my approval and my staff of one. An intern, but still."

Noelle and Eve both reached out to high-five her, shouting their congrats and hugging her.

"And it *is* due to *Starry, Starry Night*," she added, looking warmly at Noelle. "The exhibit is such a hit that all my department has done is field inquiries from other outside companies and top-level museums. It's elevated us and I'm so grateful."

Noelle waved off the gratitude. "Happy to help. Should I open this baby?" She lifted the bottle and looked at Angie.

"Bring it tomorrow for family Christmas," Angie said. "I'm too old to day drink."

Eve gave a thumbs-up. "Happy to hear. It's water for me, since we have to stay up until midnight putting the last of the gifts out and David has to set up the ping-pong table we've got hidden in a neighbor's garage. I'll drink tomorrow."

Noelle happily agreed and reached for a chilled bottle of Pellegrino. "Sounds good. But let's move into the den. Jace made us a fire and the tree is all lit."

A minute later, they were settled together, happily snacking and toasting their bubbly water in wine glasses.

"But I have more news," Angie said, her smile as bright as the tree behind her. "Elliott is moving to a new job."

"What? No!" Noelle nearly choked. "How? Why?"

Angie held up her hand. "It's all good. He's going to

corporate to head a museum division, which means he's ten minutes from the estate."

"And no longer your boss," Eve said. "Which I guess is good and bad."

"Good because now we don't have the uncomfortable situation of working together and being involved. Better because this is what he wanted in the first place and he's thrilled with this job. But best of all?" She gave in to a huge smile and a shiver of delight. "Marjorie wants to come back!"

"Really?" they asked in unison.

"She hates working at the Getty and her son and his family have decided to relocate to North Carolina! So I get my favorite boss back and do not have to keep my romance a secret."

"Romance, huh?" Noelle asked, sharing a look with Eve. "We knew it."

Angie laughed. "I'm so happy, you guys. Best birthday ever."

"It really has been a good holiday," Eve said, leaning back. "I feel like we're really honoring so many of the Asheville traditions that were important to Mom and Dad, and still making new ones, like this."

"It has been a season of traditions," Noelle said. "I was darn near suffocated by them at the tree lighting, but it all turned out so well. And Hannah still isn't down from Cloud Nine. She's spending Christmas Eve with Brandon's family and he's coming to the cabin tomorrow for our family celebration."

"Love is in the air!" Eve exclaimed with a happy clap.

They chatted for a while about that new romance, reliving the drama of the tree lighting, and toasting to Jackie taking her first steps the day before.

Finally, Angie turned to Noelle and narrowed her eyes, leaving no doubt what question she was about to ask.

"Yes," Noelle preempted her. "I have made a decision. And I'm telling Jace tonight."

"Which means you won't tell us first?" Eve asked.

She looked from one to the other, considering if she should. She'd told these two women of every major decision in her life first before anyone. But now she was married and Jace deserved to know before anyone else.

"I can't," she said. "I simply have to tell Jace and hope he's happy with my decision."

"Are *you* happy with it?" Angie asked.

"Very much so," Noelle said.

"Whatever you decide," Eve said, "we are here one hundred percent, through thick and thin, no matter what."

Angie leaned closer. "Can I ask when you decided?"

"At the tree lighting, actually," she said. "I wished for clarity, and in an instant, I got it." She lifted her glass and held it up to her sisters. "To the year ahead, Chambers triplets. To clarity, love, family, and each other."

They clinked and laughed and celebrated forty-one years of their sisterhood and lives.

Noelle sat back, covered in peace and anticipation of the life ahead.

It was officially Christmas and past midnight when Jace finally finished assembly on the purple light-up electric scooter that would be waiting for Cassie when she woke up tomorrow morning.

"It's a beauty," Noelle said as she placed the last of the gifts under the tree. "Just a bow and we can call it."

"That was a bear," he said, leaning back to look at his handiwork.

"David's doing a ping-pong table singlehandedly," she reminded him.

"Oh, the boys are going to love that."

"We all are," she said, patting the sofa next to her. "Pour the sherry and stoke that fire, my dear husband. It's our time. And it's officially my birthday."

"Happy Birthday, Noelle." He smiled at her. "You get more beautiful every year and I can say that as a man who knew you at twelve."

"We do go way back, buddy, don't we?"

"Way." He went to the fire to add a log and bring it to life.

While she waited, she took a minute to drink in the gifts, all wrapped in ribbons and bows, plus the tree, the fire, and the man she loved.

"This is why I didn't day drink with my sisters," she said, accepting the glass he offered when he poured them both a sherry. "I knew I wanted this with you."

He tapped her crystal with his. "To our first married Christmas, Noelle. May we have many more just as happy, but with less scooters to assemble."

She smiled and took a sip.

"Unless there are," he said quickly. "Which is fine, too."

She slid him a look, silent for a beat.

Without drinking, he set the glass down, his gaze on her. "You decided."

"How is it you can read my mind?"

"Because I know you and love you." He studied her for a long moment, waiting. "Well?"

"When I was at the tree lighting," she said slowly, "I was battling with all that new tradition-old tradition stuff. It dawned on me that what was weighing on my heart was just another battle with tradition."

"How so?"

"The expectation of having my own baby in order to feel...complete. And that's just...crazy." She took a breath and looked at him. "Because this family is as complete as it could be and if I did anything to risk what we have, it wouldn't be right."

He inched back, his gaze on her, his expression unreadable. "You're not having the surgery."

Without saying a word, she took his hand in both of hers and held it tight, her heart kicking up for some reason.

"I'm not," she said. "And that means I'm not having a baby."

Looking up at him, she expected a flash of disappointment, but he just stared at her and let her continue.

"I don't need to mess with God's plans or tempt fate or...or take a risk just to appease an arbitrary goal," she said, meaning every word. "I'm already a mother to the most amazing child I could dream of. And, I hope you'll agree, but I'd like to just keep the status quo."

"Oh, honey!" His voice cracked as he put his arms around her. "You have no idea how much I wanted to hear you say that."

"You did? Why didn't you tell me you felt that way?"

"Because it was your decision, not mine, Noelle. Your body, your dream, your decision. But I'm really, really happy with the three of us." He kissed her lightly. "I have never been happier."

She slumped against him, shocked at how relieved and satisfied she was with her decision. "I love you," she whispered.

"And I love you." He added a kiss on her hair. "And if you—"

"Shh." She sat up.

"What's wrong?" he asked.

"Did you hear that?"

They sat still for a second. "I don't—"

Noelle shot to her feet. "Cassie's crying."

"What? I don't hear a thing."

But she was out of the room and down the hall in a flash, drawn to the soft sniffles that meant her little girl wasn't happy. On Christmas Eve? What could be the matter with her?

"Cassie?" She stepped into the dark room. "You okay, baby?"

She sniffed.

"What's wrong, Cass?"

"Nothing," she said, her voice thick.

But Noelle knew better. She walked to the bed and sat on the edge, using the soft light from the hall to find her way. There, she brushed back some of Cassie's pale waves, and felt tears on her cheeks.

"Honey, why are you crying?"

"I didn't get my wish."

"You don't know that." She reached down and wrapped her hands under Cassie's arms and eased her up so her nose didn't get stuffy. "But you will tomorrow morning. You're just excited because it's the night before Christmas."

"I didn't put this on my list but I wished for it when I threw my glow stick at the tree lighting."

Guess it had been a big night for both of them. But then she remembered something Cassie wanted very much...and wasn't going to get. "Honey, I know you want a baby brother or sister, but Daddy and I love our family just as it is. You're going to be our only child and we are so happy about that."

She looked up. "That's not what I wished for."

"Then...what?"

She let out a shuddering sigh. "I wished my mommy would—"

Noelle's heart stopped.

"—send me a secret message. Ever since you told me

about that man flashing the lights, I was hoping for something like that."

"And I also took you under the tree to show you how to do it," she said softly. "There was no secret message." She stroked her hair and rooted around for the right words. "Your mommy is always watching over you. You don't need to get signs from above."

"But I need her to tell me it's okay."

"What's okay?"

She blinked at tears and wiped her little cheek. "To call you my mommy now."

Is that what was stopping her? Poor baby, suffering so.

"Honey, I am your mommy now. And she will be your mommy forever. You have two of us now."

"But I want to call you...that."

Noelle felt her own tears well. "It doesn't matter what you call me, Cass. I'm here to dry these tears, to listen to you sing, to help you learn how to do life, whatever you need from a mommy. You can call me anything you want."

She looked up, a sad desperation in her eyes. "I want to call you Mommy."

Noelle swallowed against a lump in her throat. "I want that, too, angel." She pulled her closer for a hug, kissing her hair. "But if you can't or it feels funny, I understand. I love you very, very much."

Cassie squeezed her. "I just wanted her to, you know, flash a light or leave a feather or give me something I would know was from her. I needed her to tell me that it was okay."

"Oh, darling. Sometimes you have to make these hard decisions by yourself," she said, all too familiar with the process. "Sometimes you have to weigh all the feelings, what feels right and what feels wrong, and think about the people you love who are involved, and then...give it to God. He'll guide you. Close your eyes and say a prayer and God will tell you exactly what to do and when to do it."

He certainly had worked that way for her this past week.

Sighing sleepily, Cassie slid back down to her pillow. "'Kay."

"And when you're ready, Cass, you can call me anything at all. Except Sprinkles. That's taken."

That made her giggle as she snuggled down, satisfied.

"You ready for sleep?" she asked, stroking her hair.

Cassie nodded and turned on her side, her favorite sleeping position.

Noelle leaned over and placed a soft kiss on her cheek. "Good night, my darling daughter. You say that prayer now."

"I will," she answered on a shuddering sigh of exhaustion.

Noelle stood, smiled down at her, and walked slowly to the door. Jace was in the hall, listening.

"I love you, Cass," she called.

"I love you, too...Mommy."

Her little voice floated from the bed, making Noelle

freeze at the word. She pressed her hands to her lips, tears springing.

Trying not to sob, she stepped outside and slid into Jace's waiting arms.

"Merry Christmas and Happy Birthday," he whispered in her ear.

Oh, yes, it was certainly merry and happy. And, like the future, so very bright.

Want to read more from Hope Holloway and Cecelia Scott? Great news! These authors have another family saga series chock full of sweet romance, light drama, the occasional mystery, and lots of emotion. And the entire series are all available in digital, paperback, audio and Kindle Unlimited!

# The Destin Diaries

Seven summers. Two families. One beach house. And a diary that holds all the secrets.

*A brand new heartwarming family saga co-written by bestselling women's fiction authors Hope Holloway and Cecelia Scott.*

The Summer We Met (Book 1)
The Summer We Danced (Book 2)
The Summer We Made Promises (Book 3)
The Summer We Kept Secrets (Book 4)
The Summer We Let Go (Book 5)
The Summer We Celebrated (Book 6)
The Summer We Sailed Away (Book 7)

# About the Authors

**Hope Holloway** is the author of charming, heartwarming women's fiction featuring unforgettable families and friends, and the emotional challenges they conquer. After more than twenty years in marketing, she launched a new career as an author of beach reads and feel-good fiction. A mother of two adult children, Hope and her husband of thirty years live in Florida. She spends her non-writing time walking the beach with her two rescue dogs, who beg her to include animals in every book. Visit her website at www.hopeholloway.com.

**Cecelia Scott** is an author of light, bright women's fiction that explores family dynamics, heartfelt romance, and the emotional challenges that women face at all ages and stages of life. Her debut series, *Sweeney House*, is set on the shores of Cocoa Beach, where she lived for more than twenty years. Her books capture the salt, sand, and spectacular skies of the area and reflect her firm belief that life deserves a happy ending, with enough drama and surprises to keep it interesting. Cece currently resides in Florida with her husband and beloved kitty. Visit her website at www.ceceliascott.com.